Foreign Body

Foreign Body

A Comic Novel
by Roderick Mann

Futura

A Futura Book

Copyright © 1973 Roderick Mann

First published in Great Britain in 1973
by Cassell Ltd

This edition published in 1987
by Futura Publications, a Division
of Macdonald & Co (Publishers) Ltd
London & Sydney

ISBN 0 7088 3398 5

Typeset by Leaper & Gard Ltd., Bristol, England
Printed and bound in Great Britain by
Hazell, Watson & Viney Ltd.
Aylesbury, Bucks

Futura Publications
A Division of
Macdonald & Co (Publishers) Ltd
Greater London House
Hampstead Road
London NW1 7QX

A BPCC plc Company

1

He's bored, I thought, I'm just not interesting enough.
He'd much rather have a pretty girl lying here, droning
on about her sex problems.

He'd been spoiled, that was the trouble; all those
years spent listening to stories about Latvian dwarfs,
hunchback gardeners, fathers wearing mothers' knick-
ers and boys garroting the family cat. He just wasn't
interested in my story.

I shifted position on the leather couch and looked
across at him. He was sitting at his desk, looking at me
intently. I smiled. He didn't smile back.

'It's certainly an odd story,' he said.

'I know that.'

'Hard to believe, actually.'

'I suppose it is.'

'You were never found out?'

'No; never.'

'How long did all this go on?'

'Oh, months.'

'Extraordinary,' he said.

He scribbled something on the pad in front of him.
Nothing to do with anything I'd said, I was convinced.
Probably a reminder to have the Rolls serviced.

'I'm not quite clear why you've come to me,' he said.

'Sir Laurence Wainscott-Evans recommended you.'

'Did he?' he said. 'Did he indeed?'

'He seemed to think you were the best in your field.'

'That was nice of him.'

I looked at the ceiling again, wondering how many
other tormented characters had lain on this same
couch, searching for comfort.

'I hoped you might be able to help me,' I said.

7

'I'm a psychiatrist,' he said. 'Not God.'

'Is there nothing I can do?'

'You could sell your story to the Sunday papers,' he said lightly. 'That would get it off your chest.'

'It isn't on my chest,' I said. 'It's on my conscience.'

'Frankly I think you're making too much of it,' he said. 'We don't know for certain that you caused this woman's death. She might have died anyway. People do, you know.'

'She'd be alive today if it hadn't been for me,' I said.

'That goes for a lot of people,' he said. 'Motorists kill hundreds every day. So do bomber pilots. So do doctors. Larry Wainscott-Evans has knocked off more healthy patients than anyone in this street.'

'That doesn't make me feel any better,' I said.

'Pity,' he said. 'I rather hoped it might.'

He got to his feet, elegant in his black jacket and striped trousers, and went over to the window.

'There are roughly 3,600 million people on this planet,' he said. 'You do realize you're not the only one with a problem?'

'I'm the only one with this particular problem,' I said.

'Perhaps,' he said.

He turned.

'Are you married?'

'Yes.'

'English girl?'

'That's right.'

'Does she know?'

'No,' I said. 'She doesn't know.'

'You've never wanted to tell her?'

'Many times,' I said. 'There are reasons why I can't.'

'That must make things difficult?'

'It does.'

'Mmmm.'

He returned to his desk.

'Nice girl, is she?'

8

'Very.'

'No racial problems? You being an Indian, I mean?'

'None at all.'

'Can't be easy, being an Indian in Britain?'

'It's easier than being an Indian in India,' I said.

'Ah,' he said, thoughtfully. 'Yes. I expect it is.'

He scribbled something else on the pad.

'How did you meet your wife, may I ask?'

'I picked her up in the street.'

'Interesting,' he said. 'Better than a formal introduction, I shouldn't wonder.'

'You misunderstand,' I said. 'She'd been run over.'

'Run over?'

'Yes,' I said. 'That's how it all began ...'

2

I had this job at a small hotel in Calcutta. The Deedar. The outside was scabrous and the inside beggared description. It couldn't have been decorated since Clive of India went home, taking his loot with him. But I was glad of the work, and the chance to put a few rupees between myself and the thousands sleeping out every night on the pavements.

My job was night-clerk. From six at night until six in the morning, with one night off each week, I was in sole charge of the rickety reception desk and the unshaven, myopic old ruin who sloshed about in carpet slippers and posed as our night-porter. He had a limited command of English and carried around a reference which he would proudly show to everyone. It was from an English couple living in Calcutta and it read: 'Hassan was in our employ for only three months. Any employer who gets Hassan to work for him will be very lucky indeed.'

I had to allocate rooms and decide which people should be made to pay the 5 rupees in advance. During the entire time I was at the Deedar I only once allowed a man to check in without paying, and they found him hanging from the bedroom door next morning.

I had been fooled, you see, by the fact that he came in alone. Most of the men came in with women, for it was that kind of hotel. Night after night I would sit behind my desk, perched on a cane stool, listening to the sounds of the Deedar. And Phil the Fluter's Ball had nothing on the Deedar Hotel on a hot summer's night.

A great many Westerners, I have discovered, look upon Indians as a rather spiritual race. A few hours at the Deedar would have changed their opinion. All night long the shrieks and cries went on, mixed with the steady thump of fornication upon the ramshackle beds.

The sight of so many couples coming and going sometimes roused me to such a state of excitement that I could not stop trembling. On these occasions, if there was nobody about, I would creep up to the first floor lavatory, from a crack in whose side-window there was a view straight into Room 6.

What I saw there would usually reduce me to a gibbering pulp within minutes, for I always put the prettiest girls into that room. It was always some time before I could resume my duties, shaking and restless, at the desk.

But I went, whenever I could.

It wasn't a bad life, as bad lives go. The work was not hard, and I had my room and board and a handful of rupees each week. Twice a day, down in the basement, Hassan, myself and the crone who cleaned the rooms would sit at a dirty brown table while the cook, an unsightly ruffian, doled out food from a great black vat which everyone swore had once been used in a British Army canteen. If this were so it should, of course, have been dubbed unclean and polluted, having once been used by outcasts.

I ate there regularly for the first few months. And, if I were the last to leave, I would sneak odd bits of food to give to the stray dog I had befriended and which used to wander in from the streets to keep me company.

One night, however, the dog disappeared and next day the meat was particularly gristly. I knew without asking what had happened. The ruffian cook had thrust its pitiful carcase into the pot. 'You shouldn't be so fussy,' Hassan admonished. 'Dog is a treat compared with some of the muck he puts into that pot.' He was probably right, but after that I ate my meals at a shabby café around the corner.

Most mornings, before going to my room to sleep, I would saunter through the town, stepping carefully over the still sleeping masses on the pavements, brushing past the beggars clustered outside the Grand Hotel, and make my way to the Maidan where, at week-ends, polo was still played much as it had been in the days of the British Raj.

I had grown up believing in Britain. Only by imitating Britain and things British did India seem to have a chance of attaining a better life — such things, for instance, as one toilet per village, though not necessarily with water.

Britain, to us, represented all that was wise and powerful. An uncle of mine who worked as a punkah-wallah in Delhi would return to our village from time to time bearing tales of town halls built like Renaissance palaces and railway stations designed like Gothic cathedrals. Listening to him, we would marvel at the taste and wealth of the British. When I finally saw these places I was shocked. How could they have allowed such monstrosities to be put up? Years afterwards, when I got to London and saw what the British had done to their own towns, I realized that they might be forgiven for what they had done to ours.

The village where I was born was remote; so remote, indeed, that, as in three-fourths of India's 600,000 villages, most of us grew up without ever seeing a white man. The wonders of his Thunder Box and his Cockle's Pills meant nothing to us. He was as remote to me, as a boy, as the Great White Father himself across the seas.

Life in our village was exceedingly grim. The place consisted of about a hundred mud huts, one or two of them with shaky verandas in front and all of them with tiny wooden stockades at the rear for the cattle.

We had two bullocks and one cow, which father affectionately called Mother, and it was my ugly sister's contention that he paid more attention to these three beasts than he did to us. Which, of course, was understandable; they were his living.

There were six of us in our hut. My smelly grandmother, my mother and father, my elder brother Ranjit, my ugly sister Deepali and myself. We lived mostly on rice, chapattis and dhal, with curried vegetables on special days. The special day we were all waiting for was when father finally unloaded Deepali. In India a girl is not supposed to marry until she is fifteen or so, but father was convinced that a girl was old enough by the time she was twelve. In the old days, he would say, most of them were off and running at ten. And it was true. My smelly grandmother got married when she was eight.

Father had already been to the local marriage broker to discuss Deepali, and been told that if he brought along her horoscope the broker would attempt to find a young man of the same sub-caste whose horoscope was harmonious. After that meeting two sets of parents had come along to inspect Deepali who stood there in her best sari while they walked around her.

On both occasions, having inspected her at some length, the parents shook their heads and wandered off without even asking how large a dowry father could come up with. Deepali, it seemed, was just too ugly, what with her pock marks and thick lips. In the old days there used to be a saying that the two ugliest things in

India were the water-buffalo and the British private soldier. They hadn't seen my sister.

Even now, looking back on it, I can hardly believe the awfulness of the life we lived there. Every morning father would go off to bathe his feet in the village pond, brushing his few remaining teeth with a green twig picked up en route. Then, still wet, he would set out with his bullocks to work in the dust-covered fields around our village.

At night-fall he would return, eat the meal mother had prepared over a fire of dried cowdung, bathe his feet once again and spend the rest of the evening with the other farmers talking to the village head-man. The head-man had a radio and knew what was going on in the world. Or as much as All India Radio knew.

My father earned very little, and what he did get he kept in a small tin box which none of us was allowed to touch. It also contained a small amount of gold which he had inherited from his father. When father died custom decreed that we use part of these savings to buy pots of clear butter and perhaps some herbs and slivers of sandalwood to sprinkle on his funeral pyre. He was happy in the knowledge that he had two sons to light the fire. This, at least, removed some of the stigma of having an ugly, unmarriageable daughter.

My brother Ranjit and I would go to school every day in the neighbouring village. I was a good student. I had already mastered English, and was an avid reader of anything I could get my hands on. An English missionary had passed our way, years before, lingering just long enough to fertilize two of the village girls and bestow upon the head-man — along with a Bible — a copy of *Newnes' Family Doctor: A Complete Guide to India's Railways*; Part 3 of Frank Harris's *My Life and Loves* and *Murray's Guide to India, 1920.*

All five books I quickly read. What's more, thanks to a remarkably retentive memory, I was able to quote from them at will.

After school we could spend the rest of the day as we pleased. Most of us used to go down to the village pond where we would sit and watch the village girls coming down to fill their copper jugs with water.

Most of them were married, for few survived as single girls into their late 'teens. Those who did were a source of permanent wonder to me. Other boys in the village would boast of their conquests of these girls. 'You can't imagine what it's like,' they'd say. Too well I could imagine what it was like. And did, night after night, tossing and turning in my bed. But I firmly resisted the temptation to help myself, for even in India we had been brought up to believe that such activity brought on blindness, paralysis and an early death. And one or two passages in *Newnes' Family Doctor* added strength to this conviction. There it was, under 'Youth and Sex': 'Very few boys escape the worst danger into which it is possible for a lad to fall — the artificial stimulation of the reproductive organs. Who can doubt that many lives are thus prematurely shortened and many constitutions prematurely enfeebled ...'

Convinced that I was doomed should I as much as touch myself I resorted to frenzied physical activity. Night after night I would go racing across the darkened countryside, dodging the boulders and huge banyan trees, trying to wear myself out so that I could drop, exhausted, upon my string bed and think no more of girls.

It never worked.

3

Six months after starting work at the Deedar, disaster struck.

I was becoming more and more neurotic. The sight of our customers coming downstairs with contented looks on their faces was beginning to unnerve me. Sometimes they would tip me, with a sly smile, or give me a knowing wink on the way out, and I would stand there trembling, gazing after them as they walked briskly into the street.

Was there no justice? Why should I, healthy and fit, have to stand by and watch others enjoying themselves? But how did you meet girls? And, having met them, how did you know they were that kind? On the few occasions that I had risked a flirtatious look at some girl, all I had got back was a blank stare. Yet I was not unattractive; I didn't chew betel and I washed a lot. Why should the land of Kama Sutra so determinedly withhold its pleasures from me?

One night, around eight o'clock, a man checked into the hotel with a girl. She was quite astonishingly pretty, her face devoid of pock-marks, her skin the colour of coffee-cream. She was wearing a pale-blue sari, edged with gold and the white bodice over which it was draped outlined quite clearly the most perfectly curved breasts. I couldn't stop staring at her and, as the man signed in and counted out the rupees, she gave me the sweetest and shyest of smiles.

Oh, intoxication! Oh, joy! I had never seen anyone even remotely like her; a girl as out of place in that den of thud and wallop as a pig in a synagogue.

For several minutes after they had gone up to Room 6 I sat there on the cane stool, my mind racing. Then, unable to contain myself, I crept up to the first-floor lavatory. And there, putting my eye to the crack in the window, I beheld a sight such as I had never seen before.

The man was sitting on the edge of the bed while the girl, my vision of beauty, crouched before him.

Merciful heaven: there had been nothing of this in *Murray's Guide to India, 1920.* I had heard talk of such things happening, but to actually see it. A tight knot formed in my stomach. It all seemed awful and terrible and wildly exciting. Surely, I thought, they must both be struck down by a thunderbolt.

But no.

At length it was over, and they both got up. I sat there for a long time, quaking. Then, realizing that the man was making for the door, I raced downstairs to the desk.

'I have to go out for something,' the man said. 'My wife does not wish to be disturbed.'

His wife? What kind of an idiot did he take me for? What wife would turn in a performance like that?

'Leave everything to me, sir,' I muttered, pocketing the rupee which he slid across the desk.

Had I not been in such a state of anguish I would have left it at that. But I was beyond sane reasoning. The thought of the girl lying naked on the bed in Room 6 numbed my mind. The minutes went by, and I knew I could restrain myself no longer. Creeping upstairs, I stood for a moment outside her door, and then burst in.

She was lying on the bed, her breasts cupped in her hands, smiling to herself. When she saw me she shot upright.

'What do you want? What are you doing here?'

Torn between panic and passion, I stood rooted to the floor, my mind taking in every detail of her nakedness. Then, squeaking with lust, I leaped.

'No,' she said. 'He's coming back ...'

As she spoke the door opened and the man stood there, a bottle of beer in his hand. He took two strides forward as I pulled myself off the girl and then hit me a stunning blow. And I passed out.

I was sacked next morning. The owner, an officious little man, came round in person and roused me from my bed.

'I want you out of here today,' he snapped. 'And next time you try that game, don't pick on a policeman's girl.'

16

A policeman's girl! Wouldn't you know it!

Thus did I join the ranks of those who loaf the streets by day and sleep on the pavements at night. I had fifteen rupees in my pocket, saved from my wages. Twelve of these I put aside in case of real emergency; the remainder I allotted for food.

I knew I had to get another job quickly. I also knew it would not be easy. Calcutta was bulging at the seams with out-of-work men, impoverished and bedraggled, moving aimlessly from one place to the next.

I tried the jute mills, without success. I tried some of the big offices, but they were not interested. I tried the railways, clutching my *Complete Guide* under my arm, but they had nothing to offer a chap whose only experience was in running a second-class brothel. I tried the Great Market, hoping there might be a porter's job going, but there were hundreds there before me.

Then, towards the end of the third week, hanging about the shipping offices like a scavenger dog, fate held out a titbit. A man who had been to the Deedar from time to time spotted me. He was a typical clerk, grade 12 and greasy. But he had a desk. And an office.

'What are you doing here?' he asked, mopping his forehead with a filthy handkerchief. 'Planning to stow away?'

'I lost my job,' I said.

'Lost your job, eh?' He sat back, locking his pudgy fingers together, looking at me with interest. 'And what are you going to do now?'

'I don't know,' I said. 'Anything, I suppose.'

'Anything,' he said, sharply. 'That's no good. You must be specific. How old are you?'

'Twenty-three,' I said.

'Twenty-three.' He repeated it with distaste. He began leafing through a large black file on his desk. There seemed to be hundreds of names on it. 'You understand,' he said, without looking up, 'there are certain things I can do, as an official, and certain things

I cannot.'

'Of course.'

'Can you read?'

'I can. And speak English.'

'Excellent. Excellent.'

What kind of job could he have in mind for me, I wondered. Some executive post perhaps?

He stopped, his finger on the file.

'By the way, how did you get your job at the Deedar?'

'By chance. One of the boys from our village had the post. He decided to move to Delhi the day I arrived here, and recommended me for the job.'

'Did money exchange hands?'

'I gave him twenty rupees.'

'Hmmm. And how much have you now?'

'About twelve.'

'Twelve!' He thrust the file aside.

'It's no good,' he said. 'There's nothing. You've come at a bad time.'

'Oh, no ...'

'Listen.' He leaned forward. 'I have a thousand people on my books for every job that comes up. Did you know that? One thousand.'

'So I have no chance?'

He shook his head.

'It's difficult, with only twelve rupees.'

'If I had more, could you get me a job?'

'It's possible,' he said.

He leafed through the file again.

'There's a job as a deck-hand on the *Cathay*, sailing next week.'

'A deck-hand!'

'Hundreds are after it,' he said, severely. 'It sails for England, you see.'

'I don't understand.'

He leered, showing a row of betel-stained teeth.

'If one has the right connections, young man, one

18

does not come back.'

'The right connections?'

'The right papers, that sort of thing.'

'But where does one get such papers?'

He sighed, slamming the file shut again.

'There are ways,' he said. 'Now, if you'll excuse me ...'

But I was excited. England! The dream!

'How much would such papers cost?' I said.

'A thousand rupees,' he said.

'And the job itself? The job on the *Cathay*?'

'About two hundred.'

Twelve hundred rupees. And I had twelve. While he sat there looking at me. I took out my handkerchief, untied the knot in it, and counted out my fortune: a five-rupee note, six ones and some silver.

Oh great Lord Shiva, I prayed: give me insight now.

And, suddenly, there it was. Insight.

'Listen,' I said. 'Can you hold the job for me? For just two days.'

A flicker of interest showed in his black eyes.

'You think you can raise the money?'

'I'm going to try,' I said.

'I will wait,' he said. 'One wants to help.'

I thanked him and went out into the streets, brushing past the pedlars with their razor-blades and American pens, and walking on towards the big shops with their brass trays and white shawls and carved statues. The streets seemed noisier than usual and from a restaurant nearby the pungent odour of curry made my stomach churn with hunger. But my mind was racing. Twelve hundred rupees ... twelve hundred rupees ... twelve hundred rupees ...

'Hey, you want a woman?' A beggar boy sidled up.

'No. Go away.'

In my village father would be coming in from the fields and mother would be cooking the evening meal. I found my thoughts turning towards them; dear, sweet, simple people, not at all like the villains I had met in Calcutta.

As dusk was falling I went to the railway station and spent my remaining money on a ticket home. When the train arrived at the crowded station I had to fight to gain even a foothold on the outside of the last car. I would have to hang on all the way, it was clear, but it would be worth it. I wanted to see my beloved parents once more; to say nothing of my beloved grandmother, my beloved brother and my beloved sister.

There was something else. I wanted to rifle my father's beloved tin-box.

Ram Das, being of sound mind but thieving disposition, was on his way.

4

London was not at all as I had imagined it. For one thing, it had not occurred to me that there would be so many Indians about. I had supposed, rather naïvely, that I would be rather unique; there would be me and the Indian High Commissioner and perhaps a handful of others. Yet here I was, up to my armpits in Asians.

Then again, people did not seem to be too friendly. It took me the best part of two days to find a room in which to stay. Most of the places I tried wouldn't even let me through the door. The grim-faced gorgons in charge took one look at me and shook their heads. At first I couldn't understand it. Had word preceded me? Did they know already that I was a thief, that I had robbed my poor old father of his life's savings? Then, as the refusals mounted up, the truth sank in. I was being turned away because of my colour.

Just as I was becoming desperate, I fell in with a seedy-looking Indian lavatory attendant named I.Q. Patel. We found ourselves sitting at the same table in a ratty little café in Brixton, and, on learning of my problem, he told me there was an empty room in a house nearby where he had lodgings.

'It's nothing marvellous,' he warned. 'And they don't allow more than three to a room. But it's better than the streets.'

He took me there when we had finished our meal. There was a sign in the hallway reading: 'No Women', and this depressed me immediately. No women what? No women wanted? Surely not! No women in sight? Much more likely. Well, the hell with that. I wanted a sign reading 'Yes, Women'. Dozens and dozens of them, foaming and frothing and giggling and squealing.

But I took the room. And paid a month's rent in advance — £8. It was a narrow passageway of a room, with a small iron bed and peeling wallpaper and a squat, ugly window overlooking a courtyard full of huge lorries. These started up, according to Patel, between three and four in the morning, which accounted for the fact that the room was vacant so often.

The house was like an ice-box and that night I got into bed fully clothed. And, sitting there shivering, I made a list of the advantages and disadvantages of my situation.

Under Advantages I wrote: my own room; my own key; next door to lavatory. Under Disadvantages I wrote: cockroaches in room; the same key fits all doors; next door to lavatory. It came out about even.

But I refused to be depressed. I was in London. The dream had come true. And, casting my eyes about my room, I was sure that, with a little thought, it could be made quite habitable; a place others would envy. I might even give tea-parties from time to time. People would talk about them. 'Ram's tea-parties,' they'd say. 'You must get invited.' But I'd be very particular.

The next thing was to get a job. And once again I.Q. Patel came to my aid.

'With your qualifications,' he said, 'there are only

three things you can do; work in the public lavatories, sweep the streets or join London Transport.'

Since he worked in the public lavatories himself he did not recommend them except to students of human nature. And as for sweeping the streets, it could be cold work, especially in the winter.

That left London Transport. So I applied. And three weeks later, much to my surprise, I found myself a fully-fledged bus conductor, lurching about on the swaying decks of a Number 3.

It was hard going.

We Hindus believe that reincarnation continues until the highest caste, Brahmin, is reached. This happens only after the soul has returned many times and suffered much. And it was clear, after only a few weeks on the buses that I, Ram Das, had a long way to go.

Talk about suffering. Only those who have tried to control an enraged crowd of Londoners struggling to get aboard a packed bus at six o'clock on a rainy night know what it really means. If that sort of stampede occurred in prison they'd turn the fire hoses on them.

Many times, creeping into my little room, bruised and battered, I found myself looking back, almost with affection, to the Deedar. And that magical view of Room 6.

For the sign in the hall downstairs summed up my life exactly. No Women. No Women was what it said and No Women was what I got. London swung for others, perhaps, but for me it stood stock still.

All the way over on the *Cathay* my imagination had run riot. I was en route for the home of Drake and Cromwell and Wellington. I was going — assuming my papers got me through — to live among the race whose history stretched from Crécy to Dunkirk. That was exciting enough, but there was more, much more. London, everyone said, was the wildest town in the world. You couldn't go wrong. A copy of *Esquire* taken from the tourist lounge, convinced me of it: 'London is today, without question, the filthiest city in the world. At every turn, in districts like Soho, one is offered girls or boys, or I daresay goats, if one happened to be interested ...'

Great dollops of dhal. Goats! Even in India we didn't go that far. Well, perhaps in some of the remoter districts, but nobody made a habit of it. What a place London must be! Carnaby Street and Chelsea and the Regent's Palace and Train Robbers. Where did the debauchery start, I wondered. At the dockside? Would I see them at it even as I disembarked, rocking the packing cases with their passion? I knew, I just knew, that within a matter of weeks I would be drinking champagne from some naked girl's slipper.

How different was the reality.

Instead of Ram, the handsome young Indian on his first visit to London, so attractive and appealing after all those pasty-faced whites, sought after far and wide for his dusky charm and throbbing virility, it was Ram the bus-conductor, cowering for safety beneath the stairs of his bus as militant girls thrust past him, heading for home and beans-on-toast and randy boy-friends. And he not daring even to say Hello, lest they start screaming rape and get him lynched from one of his own bus's handstraps.

Then I met Norah Plumb.

5

She boarded the bus late one Friday night just as we were leaving Brixton, and went straight up to the top deck.

There was no one else up there, so I waited a while before following her up. It had been a busy night, and my feet were hurting.

When I rolled out her ticket she sat back, her coat

open, looking at me with frank, friendly eyes. She wasn't exactly pretty, but she was definitely sexy, and she had an enormous bust.

'You look tired,' she said.

I nodded, leaning against the back of one of the seats. 'We've been busy.'

'When do you finish?'

'After this. We're on the last run now.'

'Then what do you do?'

'I go home.'

She giggled. 'To India?'

'Of course not,' I said. 'I live in Brixton.'

'All right,' she said. 'I was only making a joke.'

She kept looking at me, her lips slightly parted. She really was rather attractive, despite the acne around her chin. And with that huge bust she looked sort of squelchy; I had the feeling that mounting her would be like clambering over a mound of blancmange.

'What about you?' I asked. 'Where do you live?'

'Up the road,' she said. 'Gipsy Hill. I go dancing Friday nights down your way. At the Palais.'

'Oh, yes.' I had never heard of the Palais, but it sounded rather splendid.

I inclined my head towards her shoulder bag, which bore the initials N.P.

'What's that mean?' I said, feeling bold. 'Not permitted?'

'Now then,' she said. 'None of that. If you must know it stands for Norah Plumb. That's my name.'

'Mine's Ram Das.'

'Ram what?'

'Ram Das,' I repeated.

She was sitting sideways on the seat, and her short skirt had ridden up, exposing a huge area of thigh. She made no attempt to pull it down.

'Where are you from?' she asked.

'Calcutta,' I said.

'An uncle of mine was there once,' she said. 'He said

24

everybody slept on the streets.'

'Not everybody,' I said. 'But a lot of people.'

'Sounds horrible,' she said. 'No wonder you all want to come here.'

By this time her skirt was almost round her waist and I could see her pants, which were white and faintly transparent.

'You know what,' she said invitingly. 'You ought to come dancing one night. It's loads of fun.'

'Perhaps I will,' I said.

Just then a crowd of people got on the bus, stumbling noisily up the stairs. Norah Plumb pulled herself upright and straightened her coat. We got busy again at that point, and I didn't get another chance to talk to her. But when she got off, a few stops later, she gave me the friendliest of smiles.

'See you,' she said.

'I hope so,' I said, fervently.

6

'I hope so ...'

What a stupid, fatuous remark. What a crass piece of bovine witlessness. She'd been asking for it; begging for it. She'd even paused by the Used Tickets container to give me more time. And I'd done nothing.

Restlessly I turned on my side, unable to sleep. What a useless race I belonged to; what a lot of passive, aimless sheep we were. Non-people. Born to fail. The British were right to fire us out of cannons. We deserved no better.

Around midnight there was a knock on the door and Patel came in.

'I saw your light,' he said. 'You're awake late.'

'I can't sleep,' I said.

He came over and sat on the edge of the bed. 'What is it? A woman?'

I nodded.

'White?'

'Yes.'

His eyes took on a glitter.

'Is she pretty?'

'She's quite pretty.'

'How old?'

'I don't know. About twenty, I suppose.'

He frowned.

'That's too old,' he said. 'They're no good when they're that old. You have to get them earlier; around fifteen. Fifteen is the ideal age. Where did you meet her?'

'On the bus.'

'On the bus? She's a prostitute?'

'Of course not.'

He sat there, looking at me carefully. I might have been something on a slab that he'd been called in to identify.

'I have a curious feeling about you,' he said. 'And I am seldom wrong. I used to be a medium, you know.'

'A medium what?'

He shook his head.

'My boy, your ignorance is truly overwhelming. A medium is a person who makes contact with the dead. We Indians are supposed to be particularly good at it.'

'Why is that?'

'I haven't the faintest idea,' he said. 'But there it is. Anyway, as I say, I worked as a medium for a while. And four times out of five, much to my surprise, I got things fairly right.'

'You really received messages from the dead?'

He clucked irritably.

'Don't be ridiculous. Of course not. Though, I must admit, sometimes I did feel vibrations from certain people. No; all you've got to do is waffle on about how

26

people must watch out for their health and talk a great deal about Jack and Harry and Pat.'

'Why is that?'

'Because it seems there are Jacks and Harrys and Pats in almost every family.'

He grinned.

'Really, it is astonishing how gullible some people are. Wouldn't you suppose, were it possible for the dead to make contact with us, that they would come through with something a little more intriguing than "Tell Uncle Arthur to watch out for his back"? Wouldn't you think they'd say: "I've met Him, and, my goodness, He's huge" — or something like that? Anything other than the trivia that's spieled out. But that's what people seem to want.'

'I'm surprised you gave it up, if you were so good at it.'

'I used to find it difficult not to laugh,' Patel said. 'Anyway, lavatory work is less of a strain.'

There was a strange intensity in his gaze as he looked at me; it seemed to bore straight through me.

'I can tell you this,' he said. 'You are going to be a success. I don't know how, or where, but you will do well. I see that quite clearly. So you must prepare yourself for it.'

I was becoming interested. I sat up in bed, propping a pillow behind my back.

'How do I do that?'

'For a start,' he said, 'you must acquire some polish. You are a nice-looking fellow, for an Indian, but you lack polish. So you must read books and learn about things. If you work at it there's no knowing how far you could go.'

'What sort of books?'

'All sorts of books,' he said firmly. 'Have you ever read a book?'

'I've read five,' I said. 'And memorized them.'

'That's a clever trick,' he said.

'I have a photographic memory,' I said. 'I can picture

27

a whole page in my mind at will.'

'Then you have a head start,' he said. 'You must go to the public library and read everything you can get your hands on. You must learn how to behave with people. That way you will be ready when opportunity knocks.'

'Like tonight.'

He frowned.

'I don't follow.'

'Opportunity knocked tonight,' I said, bitterly. 'And I did nothing.'

'Listen,' Patel said sharply. 'I'm not talking about that. I'm talking about real opportunity — the gate to fame, riches and success. Not picking up some lump on the bus.'

'She wasn't some lump on the bus,' I said, defensively. 'She was a very nice girl.'

'She probably just fancied a bit of black for a change,' Patel said.

'A bit of black what?'

He got to his feet.

'Really,' he said. As he shuffled out, he called over his shoulder: 'Remember what I've said. I feel strongly about you. There are vibrations.'

After he'd gone I lay back on the bed and tried to compose myself for sleep. But it was no use; my mind was in turmoil. Around four in the morning the lorries started up, with much crashing of gears and shouting. I abandoned all hope of sleep and, getting up, began polishing my brown sandals. 'There's no knowing how far you could go,' he'd said. By my sister's sopping sari, suppose that were true; suppose he had seen into my future? As dawn began creeping over S.W.2 I was still polishing my sandals; polishing, and thinking ...

7

I.Q. Patel was an unlikely character to find in a third-rate boarding house in Brixton. For one thing, he had been to Calcutta University; for another, he had some money.

He could, he was at pains to point out, move to more cheerful quarters any time he chose. But he was used to the house in Brixton. He had been there a long time. And, on occasion, he was permitted to sleep with the landlady — 'and that's no small thing at my age'.

A casual inspection of the landlady when I first arrived had already convinced me that Patel was getting no bargain, even if he was seventy. She was a gross hag with a lantern-like jaw and a disgusting habit of sucking in her cheeks when she talked. She looked rather like a failed prostitute. But Patel was content. And it was free. And, come to that, he wasn't such a catch, either, with his sloping forehead and lined, leathery face and head which always appeared to be about to sink into his neck.

Still, he did have marvellous eyes. There was no doubt about that. They were coal-black and curiously compelling, the sort of eyes they put on the cover of books about hypnotism. They were the only things his wife had ever liked about him, he claimed. He hadn't liked anything about her and had dumped her, years before, in Calcutta. He had no idea what had become of her. 'I've got more important things on my mind' he would say.

Each morning at seven he set out for London Airport and his job in the lavatories. He liked it there, he explained; it was a splendid place in which to study human behaviour for the book he planned to write one day. There was another reason, he admitted one night; it was the best job he could get.

He made a good living out of it, he said, largely from tips. 'The trick is to run water in the handbasin and, if they don't use it, stand by the door and shame them.'

Patel had a great deal of style. There was no doubt about it. When we were out together, if he were asked about his job, he would draw himself to his full five feet four and say 'London Airport — Domestic Services', and make it sound for all the world as if he were in charge of BEA's air traffic control.

Two days after our talk on the bed, I began a crash reading course under his guidance. He was a surprisingly well-read man himself, and drew up a list of books he thought I might enjoy. Within a matter of days I had got through them all. Starting with appetizers like *Alice in Wonderland* I progressed rapidly to Well's *Outline of History*.

'Holy cow, you read quickly,' Patel said one night, coming in to find that I had just got through *The Pickwick Papers* in a couple of hours. But it was easy for me. I could scan a page in a matter of seconds and remember it, word for word, next day.

I began haunting the library the way a junkie haunts the chemists. I had to have books, and almost anything would do. Each night I raced back to my room the way a lover flies to his mistress. I tried to make it a rule to get at least six hours' sleep a night, but I seldom managed this. Long after the rest of the house was asleep I would still be propped up in my little bed, sucking up information like a vacuum cleaner. It was as if some secret spring within myself had been released, and a great hunger let loose. Ambition, they say, is a fuse that has no bang. Well, Patel had ignited that fuse, and for the first time in my life I saw a future.

It stayed cold, so it was no effort to remain indoors. Night after night, after a makeshift meal of beans or eggs at my rickety table, Patel and I would sit talking into the early hours. He seemed to know so much. And, like a sponge, I absorbed it all — whether it was the poems of Catullus or the sexuality of older women. Every topic we touched upon he illumined in an extraordinarily personal way.

'Why are you taking so much trouble over me?' I asked him one night.

'Because, my friend, one day you will repay me tenfold,' he replied.

I began reshaping my life in other ways. I learned the names of pop musicians. I acquired a few witty remarks. I began adding to my wardrobe. Together with Patel, who insisted I take some time off from my studies, I went to see films. And I took up dancing. Twice a week, at a small studio in Brixton, a woman with breasts like watermelons taught me the rudiments of some popular dances.

By the time spring arrived I was beginning to feel free from my past. India, and my life there, seemed to belong to a different world. And looking at myself in the small washbasin mirror one morning I was almost pleased. My skin looked better; I was no longer poorly dressed; my hair, black as boot-polish, shone with brilliantine. I no longer looked like a down-at-heel bus-conductor; I was beginning to look my True Self.

Buoyed up by this discovery, late one Friday night I went in search of Norah Plumb.

8

The Palais was hot and noisy and smelled of armpits. The band, mounted on a rostrum at one end, was going full-blast while on the dance-floor people cavorted about like dervishes. None of them seemed to be doing the dances I had learned.

31

Ranged along one side of the hall were girls of different shapes and sizes, standing about, chattering and laughing while at the end of the room, away from the band, a group of boys surveyed them critically. From time to time one of the youths would detach himself from the group and, going over to some girl, haul her on to the floor without so much as a word.

When I caught sight of Norah Plumb she was standing talking to another girl outside the Ladies. My first impulse was to rush straight up and ask her to dance, but I resisted it. For one thing I didn't want to make a fool of myself on the floor with some strange dance and, for another, she might be on her way to the Ladies.

I stood around for a while, trying to look as if I were waiting for someone. When she finally emerged from the toilet, I moved sideways until I bumped into her.

'Sorry,' I said. I turned to face her. 'Well, hello, fancy seeing you again.'

She frowned.

'Who are you?'

Morale took a quick dive.

'From the bus. Remember?'

The look of doubt slowly disappeared.

'Oh, of course. You look different out of uniform. I wouldn't have recognised you. Have you packed it in, then, on the buses?'

'No.'

'I never saw you again.'

'I've been working days, mostly, and studying at night.'

'Studying?' She waved at someone behind us. 'Whatever for?'

'I don't want to stay on the buses for the rest of my life,' I said.

'I don't blame you,' she said.

The music had changed to something I thought I recognized.

'Well we can't just stand here outside the Ladies,' I

said. 'Would you like to dance?'

'All right.'

We moved together on to the floor, and straight away she began swaying her body exotically to the rhythm of the music. The woman who'd taught me to dance hadn't done this and it made the going difficult.

Finally Norah said:

'You haven't been dancing long, have you?'

'I'm sorry,' I said.

'It doesn't matter,' she said. 'Anyway, would you mind if we stopped? I'm feeling awfully thirsty. I'd love a coffee.'

'All right.'

We left the floor and went over to the small buffet-bar and ordered two coffees. She looked down at my feet.

'Part of your trouble is those sandals,' she said. 'You can't dance properly in sandals.'

'I always wear sandals,' I said.

'Shoes are better,' she said. 'Shoes are much better.'

'I'll remember that next time.'

We stood there for a moment, listening to the music. There was a mirror behind the counter, and in it I could see some youths looking at Norah and leering. I didn't blame them; she looked very good indeed in her green blouse and trousers. Oh for a girl like her, I thought, in that grim abode of No Women. My life would change overnight.

'Are you married?' she asked.

I shook my head.

'Of course not.'

'No of course not about it,' she said. 'A lot of you Indians are married and just don't let on. Always after a bit on the side.'

'A bit on the side?'

'You know — sex.'

'Oh.'

'I was nearly married once,' she said, gazing into her cup. 'I was desperate to get away from home and there

33

was this man, very big and very well-developed, who lived up West. I had a mad crush on him. I like big fellows —' seeing my look she softened the blow a little — 'at least I did then. We talked about getting married. He used to come round home when my parents were out — they go down the social club two or three times a week — and, well, he was very passionate. The trouble was our dog used to sit outside the bedroom door and whine if we didn't let him in and if we did he'd just sit there, watching us. Eventually this man got fed up with it. "I can't" he'd say. "Not with that bloody dog looking on all the time. It's indecent." But there was nothing I could do about it. I couldn't lock the dog up or anything. He'd have whined so much we'd have had the neighbours complaining. Anyway, as I say, the man got fed up and that was the end of that.'

'Couldn't you have gone to his place?'

'No,' she said. 'They didn't allow girls there.'

No Women, I thought. No Women anywhere. We were doomed.

'And guess what?' she said. 'The bloody dog died a month after this man left me.'

'That was bad luck.'

'I never could stand it,' she said. 'A horrid dog it was. Horrid.'

'You don't look old enough to have been in love,' I said.

'I'm twenty-four,' she said. 'How old are you?'

'Twenty-three.'

'Oh, you're kidding?'

'No, really.'

'I'm baby-snatching,' she said. 'Fancy; you being younger than me —' she broke off, as the band launched into another number. 'Don't you just love this?' she said. 'I've got Sinatra's recording of it.'

'You haven't told me what you do,' I said.

'Me? I work at the dry cleaners up the road from here.'

'That must be interesting?'

'It's not,' she said. 'It's a bore. And the smell. The smell drives you potty.'

'What? The smell of the clothes?'

'No; the smell of the stuff they use to clean them. Awful, it is. I'd like to get out, and maybe I will. A man came into the shop the other day, some agent fellow, and said I ought to be a model, looking the way I do. He said I reminded him of a young Hedy Lamarr, whoever she is.'

'Isn't it difficult, being a model?'

'Of course it's difficult,' she said. 'You've got to look different; have that little something extra. But this agent man said I've got that. A young Hedy Lamarr, he said. Mum thinks so, too. She's always saying I ought to be a model.' She giggled. 'Can't you just see me, driving round in expensive sports cars, eating at all the posh places.'

'It would suit you,' I said, without much enthusiasm.

'A girl's got to be ambitious,' she said. 'Like you. You don't want to be a bus-conductor all your life, and you're right. Well, I don't want just to get married and be stuck in the suburbs like my mother, thank you very much. Who needs it?' She finished her coffee. 'Anything's better than that. So a girl's got to seize her opportunities. I've got this friend. She's twenty-four, same age as me, and going out with this old man. He's rich, of course, and takes her to lots of nice places, but he's over sixty; even older than my dad. 'What are you going out with an old geezer like that for?' I asked, when she started seeing him. And guess what she said: "Norah, love, nobody with his kind of money is ever old." And she's right.'

She put down her cup.

'Listen,' she said abruptly. 'I've got to go. I promised to go home with my friend Judy — that's the girl over there.' She pointed across the room to where a mousy-looking girl was gesticulating wildly. 'But I've got an idea. Why don't you come over Sunday if you've nothing better to do? You can have a meal with us.'

I had intended to spend the weekend with Patel, who wanted to discuss Bertrand Russell's *History of Western Philosophy*. But the prospect of a meal with Norah drove the plan from my mind.

'You mean it?' I asked.

'Of course I mean it.' She took a piece of paper from her handbag and scribbled an address on it.

'Here you are,' she said. 'Come about seven. Mum and Dad usually go to the Social around eight, so it won't be too much of an ordeal.' She smiled. 'There's something else,' she added. 'There's no bloody dog to worry about now.'

9

Norah Plumb lived in a shabby-looking two-storey house halfway up a steep hill, with waste ground in front and an endless, sprawling vista of ugly grey roofs behind. Dismal wasn't the word for the street; it was desperate. Hope had long since fled, abandoning the area to dustbins and decay.

When she opened the front door, I handed her the posy of freesias I had bought.

'For your mother,' I said.

'Well,' she said, pleased. 'That was thoughtful.'

Holding the flowers in her hand she led the way along a dark hall, past an open cellar door which let out a smell of gas and wet socks, and into the back parlour. It was a small room with hideous floral wallpaper and dark-brown furniture and green pitted lino on the floor.

Her father, an angry-looking man with a curiously flat face, as though he had been backed into by a lorry, was sitting in front of the fire, reading the paper. Her mother, a thin-lipped woman with ballbearings for eyes, was watching television.

'Well,' Norah said, brandishing the freesias. 'Here he is. This is Ram.'

They both looked up at the same time. And they both registered the same series of emotions: surprise, disbelief, fury.

'How do you do?' I said.

Neither of them spoke. They just sat there, looking at me. They looked at each other. Then, without a word, they got up and walked out. I turned to Norah.

'Did I say something?' I asked.

She shook her head. There was a look of bewilderment on her face. She was just about to say something, when there was a bellow from the next room.

'Norah!'

Something had gone wrong.

'Listen,' I said. 'If it makes things difficult for you ...'

'No. Wait a minute.'

She went into the next room.

I stood there in the parlour, looking down at my brown sandals. Evidently I was not welcome at the house of Plumb. Very well, then. I would go. But that would mean abandoning Norah. And Norah was the first girl who'd ever shown the slightest interest in me.

Then the door opened, and she came back, looking pale.

'I'm sorry, Ram,' she said, in a subdued voice. 'I didn't know they'd be like that.'

'It's all right,' I said. 'Really, I was just on my way ...'

'Oh, no.' She put a hand on my arm. 'Please don't do that. They've said you can stay for supper. They're going out later, anyway, to the Social. Please, Ram,' — her pressure on my arm increased — 'stay for my sake.'

Her eyes were beginning to moisten.

'All right,' I said, forcing a smile. 'I'll stay.'

Nobody spoke at all during the first half of the meal.

It was roast beef, a dish which, as a Hindu, I am not allowed to eat. I pushed the loathsome meat aside and made do with the mashed potatoes and runner-beans.

Finally, just when I was beginning to think I should make a run for it, Norah made a faltering attempt to start some conversation.

'Mum and Dad are looking for a bungalow, Ram, on account of mum's legs being bad and all these stairs.'

'Oh, really,' I said. 'That's interesting.' Seizing my chance, I added: 'That's a Hindu word, you know, bungalow.'

Her father's knife and fork dropped on his plate with a clatter.

'What do you mean — a Hindu word?' he asked menacingly. 'Bungalow's English; everyone knows that.'

His face had gone curiously mottled.

'I mean no disrespect sir,' I said. 'But bungalow comes from the Hindi. The British Army brought it back to Britain, along with words like shampoo and cot and loot and char ...'

'Will you listen to him?' Plumb snarled, glaring at his wife. 'Will you listen to all this cock?' He wheeled on me. 'Those are English words, see. All of them. Char means tea. Cup of char — haven't you ever heard of that? What the hell are you trying to pull?'

'I'm not trying to pull anything,' I said, concentrating on the last of the mashed potato. 'I just thought you might be interested.'

'Interested.' He gave a loud snort, and thrust his plate aside. 'You see,' he said to his wife, 'we should never have left India. It was a big mistake. We should have stayed on to civilize these black bastards.'

'Dad ...' Norah began.

'You shut up,' her mother snapped. 'Listen to your father. You might learn something.'

'Look at the things they did,' Plumb went on. 'Look at the Black Hole of Calcutta ...'

'Ram's from Calcutta,' Norah said, grasping at anything.

'Oh he is, is he?' Plumb leaned across the table. 'I expect it was some of your bloody ancestors who bunged our chaps down that hole and left them to die.'

'It was our country,' I said, deciding I'd had enough. 'It wasn't yours. Look at what your soldiers did. Blowing our people out of cannons; hanging them up in chains ...'

'Best thing for them,' Plumb said. 'You're not even civilized, you lot. There was a story in the papers only the other day about a Hindu family who hadn't washed for weeks — for weeks! — and you know why? Because their son had died and was being held in the mortuary, awaiting cremation. They said they couldn't wash until he'd gone.'

'Our religion forbids it ...' I began.

'Your religion forbids it,' he sneered. 'Some religion! Just a bloody good excuse not to wash.'

By the tiger Sher Khan, he was a bastard, this Plumb. I found my gaze straying out of the window to the waste-land beyond. Anyone standing there with a high-powered rifle could have picked him off quite easily. Just one squeeze of the trigger and that horrible head would be splattered all over the table, mixed in with the horseradish sauce. I wondered how difficult it was to get such a rifle ...

Thrusting the fantasy aside, I glanced at Norah, who looked as if she were about to faint. She gave me a small half-smile. And at that moment I made up my mind. I would revenge myself on the Plumbs in the way that would hurt them most. Forget the high-powered rifle. Instead I would have their daughter. I would ravish her with my beastly blackness. I would ...

The thought was broken by Plumb shoving back his chair and wiping his mouth with the back of his hand.

'I've had enough,' he said. 'Come on, Em.'

'What about the washing-up?' his wife said, her eyeballs bulging out of their sockets.

'*She* can do it,' Plumb said savagely, glaring at Norah. 'And *he* can bloody well help her.'

Mrs Plumb looked from her husband to Norah to me. For a moment she seemed undecided. Then, making a clicking noise in her throat, she followed her husband out of the room. A moment later the front door shut with a loud crash.

Once they had gone we sat for a moment, looking at each other. Then Norah began to cry.

'What a horrid evening,' she said. 'What a horrid, horrid evening.'

'It's all right,' I said. 'Really.'

'You'll never want to see me again,' she said.

'Yes I will. Honestly. I think you're a marvellous girl. You can't help how your parents behave.'

'Oh, Ram.'

'Now stop crying,' I said. 'We'll try to forget what's happened.'

She snuffled into her handkerchief for a while, and then we did the washing-up together. When we were finished she hung the dish-cloth on a hook and stood looking at me, as if trying to make up her mind.

Finally, she came over and kissed me full on the lips.

'That's for being so understanding,' she said. She brightened. 'Now, what about a cup of tea?'

I laughed: 'You mean a cup of char?'

'That's right,' she said. 'Let's have a nice cup of char.'

We had our tea, and then sat in front of the fire in the parlour.

'Is it really true?' she asked. 'What you said about those words?'

'Of course it's true,' I said. 'The British took home lots of words from India: pundit, jungle, veranda, buggy, dungarees — they're all from the Hindi.'

'That's fascinating,' Norah said.

'Not to your father,' I said.

40

'Oh him,' she said. 'He's an ignorant pig. He doesn't know anything.'

She came and sat on the floor by my chair and clasped my leg.

'Tell me more about India,' she said.

'It's a big country,' I said. 'More than half-a-million villages. Some big towns, like Calcutta, where I worked. It's very poor.

'Which is why so many of you come over here?'

'That's right.'

Her hand, which had been clutching my left leg around the ankle, strayed upwards towards my thigh.

'I'm glad you did,' she said.

'So am I,' I said.

Her hand slid further up.

'Have you ever seen a white girl?' she asked softly.

'Of course. Lots of them.'

'I don't mean that. I mean *seen*.'

She squeezed the inside of my thigh.

'Well, not really,' I said, suddenly excited.

She got to her feet.

'Now's your chance,' she said.

'What do you mean?'

'You'll see,' she said.

Taking my hand she led the way upstairs to a small, chilly back bedroom. In one corner there was a tatty curtain, behind which dresses bulged in profusion. In the other was a small, unpainted dressing-table. Along the wall opposite the window was a narrow bed.

I stood there for a moment, my heart bounding about, while she closed the door. Then, very gently, she manoeuvred me to the edge of the bed, and pushed me down.

'Sit there,' she said.

She began to unzip the back of her dress. I couldn't see much, because it was dark in the room, but I could see enough. And the thought of her partly-dressed body so close to me started a throbbing in my groin like a

41

frog's throat.

Ganesa, god of success, had not deserted me. This was it. In a freezing back-bedroom in Gipsy Hill, manhood was coming to Ram Das.

'What about your parents?' I asked, anxiously.

'There's no need to whisper,' she said with a giggle. 'They've gone to the Social. They won't be back for hours.'

In the faint light from the window, I could see her standing there in her bra and panties, looking like a small, plump ghost.

Then she moved towards me and kissed me full on the mouth, her hair tickling the sides of my face.

'Anyone would think you weren't interested,' she said, banteringly.

With a jolt I came out of my stunned state and began fumbling with my sandals. She helped me off with my jacket, and then my shirt and tie. 'Now these,' she said, huskily, unzipping my trousers and sliding them down my legs. She kept touching me, and the smell of her was everywhere. In a minute, I thought, I'll lose control entirely. But at last it was done and I was sitting there in my underpants, excitement mounting.

'Relax,' she said, pushing me down on the bed and removing my pants. Then she began stripping off her own underclothes, like a boxer preparing for action.

I reached out to pull her down to me, but she resisted.

'No,' she said. 'Wait.'

Moistening her lips with her tongue, she began moving her mouth about my body, at the same time exploring me with her fingers. It was as if a colony of spiders was holding a rally on top of me.

Suddenly she let out a gasp.

'Listen.'

Then I heard it too; the sound of the front door shutting and footsteps in the hall.

'Quick,' she said. 'For God's sake.' She began dressing hurriedly, pulling her dress over her naked body. 'Zip me,' she hissed.

Stumbling about, I zipped her up. Then I heard footsteps on the stairs. Ganesa, I groaned; don't do this to me. Don't make me have to face the bastard naked.

'Norah.'

'Yes, dad.'

'You in bed?'

'Yes, dad.'

'Well come on down. We want to talk to you.'

'All right.' Her voice almost broke. 'Give me a minute.'

I had my trousers on by this time, and was scrabbling around looking for my sandals.

She knelt beside me.

'Listen,' she panted. 'I'll go down to the back parlour and shut the door so they won't hear you on the stairs. But for heaven's sake be careful. And watch how you open the front door. They may have put it on the chain. Leave it open when you go, anyway; I'll close it later. All right?'

'All right,' I groaned.

She looked at me steadily, breathing hard, brushing her hair back with her fingers.

'I'm sorry,' she said. 'I'll make it up to you, I promise.'

When she'd gone I stood at the top of the stairs, my heart thumping. Then, as soon as the parlour door had shut, I made my way down to the hall. I felt quite ill, and when I reached the front door I had to lean against the wall for a moment. From the parlour I could hear the sound of voices, but I didn't stop to listen.

Once outside, I stood still for a moment, breathing in the cool night air. Then, half-running, half-walking, I made my way down the hill towards the bus stop. By the light of a street lamp I paused for a moment to take stock of myself. I was a mess. My shirt, the new white one I had bought specially for the occasion, was crumpled and marked. My black jacket was covered in hairs. My trousers were terribly creased. Still, I'd got away. That was the thing. The bastard Plumb had been outwitted. And what had Norah said? 'I'll make it up to you.' Too right she would; too absolutely right she would.

10

'It isn't easy, getting laid,' Patel said. 'Quite a problem, in fact. That's why I stay here. The hag downstairs isn't much to look at but she's handy. And, anyway, I never look at her.'

We were in his room, drinking tea, discussing my encounter with the Plumbs.

'Others don't seem to have much difficulty,' I said, despondently.

'Don't you believe it,' Patel said. 'It's the same for all of us. Anyway, the one you want is never the one you get. That's why so many of us wind up as monks, monsters or masturbators.'

He poured himself another cup, heaping sugar into it from a glass jar on the table.

'More tea for you?'

'No thanks,' I said.

'I can't live without tea,' he said.

He drank noisily for a while, deep in thought.

'Sometimes,' he said, 'I think there is no answer. You know what they say? Why own a cow when you can get all the milk you want from the dairy? Well, that's all very well in theory, but what happens when the dairy is closed, or your milk turns sour in the bottle, or you miss your regular delivery? No' — he shook his head — 'it's not that simple.'

'So what's your advice?'

'I have no advice,' Patel said, firmly. 'Except to

remind you that you'd save yourself a lot of trouble and money by practising Brahmacharya.'

'Thanks,' I said. 'That's very helpful.'

Brahmacharya was sexual abstinence. Gandhi had long advocated it, insisting that intercourse should be for procreation only. He was not successful.

Patel chuckled.

'I didn't think you'd go for that,' he said.

He added more sugar to his tea, stirring energetically.

'I thought up a plan once,' he said. 'I'm sure I could have made a fortune from it, if I'd ever put it into practice.'

'How did it work?'

'It was very simple,' he said. 'Think of the number of men and women who, when travelling, wind up in a hotel room alone. The social shackles are temporarily removed, they are away from family responsibilities, and they are feeling sexy. What could be more enjoyable than getting laid? But there is always the same problem — finding a suitable partner.'

He leaned forward, his eyes glittering.

'Now,' he said, 'with my plan anyone likely to find himself in this position would belong to an organization called InterPoke. It would issue cards, as the American Express and the Diners' Club do, and when the subscriber checked into his hotel he would present the card. The receptionist, who would be an InterPoke operator, and paid by them, would then get him together with a female InterPoke subscriber staying in the same hotel. Possibly, even, at a nearby hotel.' He sat back. 'What do you think of it?' he asked.

'It's a fabulous idea,' I said.

'It *is* good, isn't it?' he said, with a faint show of pride. 'Just think of the thrill of that knock on the door. What will she be like? Blonde, brunette or red-head? And how will she perform?' He sighed, conjuring up visions.

45

'Why didn't you do anything with it?'

'What the hell *could* I do with it?' he demanded. 'Who do you take an idea like that to? I thought of putting it up to *Playboy* at one time, but in the end I did nothing.'

Talking about sex had turned my thoughts once more to Norah. Patel noticed this.

'Now,' he said, 'enough of that.' He finished his tea. 'You must get your mind off this girl, if you are to be able to concentrate on your reading and studies. How can you think of wasting your time with this lump when there are such great things in store for you?'

'I can't be sure of that,' I said.

'I can,' he said, sharply. 'Remember what I said? I have this feeling about you. Anyone who can sop up information the way you do is bound to prosper. I've never seen anything like it.'

'But what good will it do me?'

'Stop talking like a child,' he said. 'What sort of a stupid question is that? It will get you out of this dump, for a start. It will forge a new life for you. But you must begin to concentrate again.'

Patel was right. I knew it. Ever since the débâcle in Norah's bedroom I had not been able to get her out of my thoughts. I would wake in the early hours of the morning, hot and headachy, remembering the touch of her lips on my body. Then, unable to sleep again, I would get up and clean my sandals and watch the dawn coming up over the grey roofs.

I wondered what had happened to her after I had fled. Had they given her a bad time? Had she decided that it just wasn't worth it, and put me out of her thoughts? And, if she had, would I ever get back into them?

Sometimes, I had visions of her caressing someone else, some horrid, hirsute ape, and the pounding in my head would become so intense I would begin to feel quite sick. Another man, enjoying those fruits which had been so cruelly denied me. It didn't bear thinking about. But I couldn't stop thinking about it. So obsessed did I become by the thought of this happening that my work began to suffer and I was reprimanded twice in one week by inspectors.

Even more serious, perhaps, was the fact that I had given up reading. I would try, night after night, but the pages would simply blur before my eyes. Patel, who knew my capacity for absorption, came home one evening to find me ploughing away at the same book he had given me weeks earlier.

'This is ridiculous,' he said.

There was only one thing to be done. I had to go in search of Norah — there couldn't be that many dry-cleaners in Brixton — and, having found her, get her out of my system.

Patel, with some misgivings, agreed to this.

'But remember,' he said. 'One week, and that's it. Then for heaven's sake let's get back to work.'

11

I couldn't find her, although I looked everywhere. I stood at the bottom of her road, hoping to catch her as she went home; I searched the dry-cleaners; I haunted the Palais. All to no avail.

Then, just when I was beginning to give up hope, she got on the bus late one Friday night. It was raining hard, and there was no-one else on board. I was hunched beneath the stairs, sunk in gloom.

'Well,' she said. 'Fancy seeing you again.'

My heart almost leaped out of my uniform. For one thing, she looked very good indeed despite her wet clothes and umbrella. For another, she was so obviously pleased to see me. Judging by the condition of her coat she had been waiting in the rain for some time. Perhaps she had even let an earlier bus go by in the hope of finding me?

'Norah,' I said.

'Kiss me,' she said, standing there with the water dripping from her umbrella.

'I can't,' I said, flustered. 'Not here.'

'All right,' she said, firmly. 'Then come upstairs.'

'Wait.'

I peered out along the dark road ahead, getting a faceful of rain. There was nobody in sight.

'You go first,' I said.

She gave me a long look and began to climb the stairs, her umbrella clattering against the side of the bus. I followed her with my eyes. Ankles, knees, thighs; the route to paradise.

When I went up she was sitting at the back, leaning against the window. She had taken off her coat, which was lying on another seat.

'Here,' she said, patting the place beside her.

I sat down and she took my face in her hands and kissed me. She felt very cold, but there was no mistaking the passion in her.

'I've missed you,' she said. 'I've thought about you every night. I didn't know how to reach you. I hoped you'd try to find me.'

'I did,' I said. 'I went to all the dry-cleaners; everywhere ...'

She kissed me again. This time with her lips parted.

'Don't do that,' I said. 'You'll send me crazy.' I pushed her away. 'Tell me what happened with your father?'

'He was just awful,' she said. 'He told me I was never to see you again. I said I'd leave home rather than agree to that.'

'What did he say?'

'Good riddance,' she said. 'That's what he said. Good riddance.'

'What will you do?'

'I'm going to try to find a room somewhere,' she said. 'I haven't had a chance yet, but I will. Maybe this week-end. I should be able to find somewhere quite easily. I give Mum four quid a week for food, you see, so I'll have that towards the rent.'

She moved closer.

'What have you been doing?' she asked.

'Thinking about you,' I said. 'It's been awful. I thought you'd decided I was just too much trouble.'

'Too much trouble?' She shook her head. 'You wouldn't have thought that if you knew what you did to me that night.' She laughed, softly.

So my fears had been groundless. She wanted me. She would get a room somewhere, and we would meet there. I would come to her, and we would have something to eat, and then we would make love. Sometimes I would take her flowers and other little surprises. Maybe at weekends we would stay in bed all day ...

'Remember what I said to you that night?' she asked.

'About what?'

'When dad came home and we had to get dressed in a hurry. Remember me saying I'd make it up to you?'

'I remember.'

'Well now's your chance,' she said.

Great bowls of hot curry. She wanted it there on the bus. Thundering along the darkened road, with rain beating down on the roof. What a prospect. Lust on London Transport, with people perhaps observing us from their bedroom windows as they closed the curtains: 'My dear, did you see what I saw ...?' But we'd be gone, before they looked again, and anyway they'd never believe it. Not on a bus. Not in Croxted Road.

'Kiss me, Ram,' she said.

Feeling suddenly triumphant, I thrust her down along the seat, so that her legs dangled over the edge. But as I bent over her I became acutely aware of the metal ticket machine pressing into my stomach. I pulled myself up and tugged at it.

'Don't stop,' she moaned.

Stop? I couldn't even start, not with that damn machine stuck between us. Angrily I tugged at it, trying to move it to one side. Just as determinedly, in front of me it stayed. Then, as I sweated and pulled, there was an unnerving sound of money spilling on to the floor and the entire contents of my leather money pouch cascaded out.

'Please, Ram,' she groaned.

She reached out a hand and pulled me to her, at the same time raising her legs on either side of me. As she did this her left shoe caught in the handle of the ticket machine and a whole spew of tickets reeled out.

Suffering swamis!

But the worst was yet to come. The bus came to a sudden, lurching stop and I heard shouts and laughter from below. I knew immediately what it was; that rough bunch from one of the South London clubs was getting on. Two of our conductors had already wound up with broken noses due to them.

Panic-stricken I heaved myself up while Norah grabbed for her coat. Oh, my father's cow; what an absolutely terrible disaster. It was just as I thought; I was doomed. I would end up an old man, bent and quavering, reading filthy magazines in the park; the oldest virgin in the history of the world. People would pay money to come and see me.

As the first of the youths came pounding up the stairs I scrabbled about on the floor by Norah's feet, picking up coins. Then there was a crush of legs around me and a lot of shouting and cursing, and just before the first blows fell I heard a shout from Norah. Then there was nothing; just black, empty nothing.

12

The hospital ward in which I awoke was full of old men, all moaning and wheezing and coughing. I looked around, bewildered. It was early morning. The nurses, many of whom appeared to be Indian, were bustling about collecting bottles, adjusting pillows and taking temperatures. At length one of them noticed me and came over.

'Well,' she said. 'How are you feeling?'

'Where am I?' I asked. 'What am I doing here?'

'You had a bad case of concussion,' she said, inspecting a chart at the foot of the bed. "Your driver brought you in late last night.'

Concussion! Instead of getting Norah I had got myself knocked-out. I looked up at the ceiling in despair.

'You must be washed before doctor's rounds,' the nurse said, briskly. 'Otherwise there'll be trouble. Can you manage to sit up?'

'I'm not sure,' I said.

'Well, try anyway,' she said, bringing over a plastic bowl which she perched on the side-table. Unbuttoning my hospital pyjamas — how had I got into them? — she held me up with one arm while she washed my chest and back. When she got to my stomach she handed me the cloth and let me fall back on the pillows. 'You do down there yourself,' she said, in a matter-of-fact voice. But she stood over me while I did it.

'That's funny,' she said, while I dabbed away. 'My boyfriend's got one just like that.'

I hope he has more luck with it than I do, I thought dismally. Then I realized she was looking at the blue-and-red striped watchstrap on my wrist.

51

'They're so attractive,' she said, taking back the cloth. 'I like a bit of colour on a man.'

She washed my legs and feet and then made up the bed. Last of all she took my pulse.

'I'd love a cup of tea,' I said.

'I'm sorry,' she said. 'Nothing till doctor's been.' She consulted the clock at the end of the ward. 'It shouldn't be long now.'

After she'd gone I lay back with my eyes closed. When I opened them again there was a large policeman standing beside my bed.

'Are you Mr Ram Das?'

For a moment I was so startled I couldn't speak. They'd caught up with me. My father had reported the theft from his tin box, and now here they were. Fate was certainly handing out some cruel blows.

'You *are* Mr Das?'

I nodded.

'I believe you were the victim of some sort of assault on board a bus last night?'

So that was it. I brightened.

'That's right.'

He took a notebook from his pocket and sat down.

'Can you tell me the circumstances in which this attack took place?'

'A bunch of young men set upon me,' I said. 'That's all I know. I never even saw them.'

'You never saw them? How was that?'

'It all took place so quickly.'

'I see.' He scribbled away. 'Did this attack take place on the upper or lower deck?'

'On the upper deck.'

'Was anything said by you which could have provoked the attack?'

'No. I never said a word.'

'How did the attack begin?'

'They kicked me.'

'In what part of your person?'

52

'In the head.'

'In the head?' He looked up for a moment. 'How was that possible? Had one of them forced you down?'

'No. I was on the floor, you see, trying to pick up some money which I had dropped.'

'Had they anything to do with that?'

'No. What happened was I tripped and my money pouch upset. As I began to pick up the money they attacked me.'

'Was any money missing after the attack?'

'I can't tell you. I was unconscious.'

He scribbled on.

'Were there any other passengers on the bus? Did anyone witness this attack?'

'There was a girl.'

'Where was she? On which deck?'

'She was on the upper deck.'

'How near was she to you when the attack took place?'

'She was right beside me.'

He looked up at this.

'Right beside you?'

'Yes. I knew her, you see.'

'You knew her.'

He seemed a shade less sympathetic now. I could imagine what he was thinking. The boys had been coming to Norah's rescue. They were heroes, really. I was the insatiable Indian lout intent on raping a defenceless English girl. I deserved no mercy.

'What is the name of this girl?'

'Miss Plumb. Norah Plumb.'

'P-l-u-m?' He spelled it out.

'No, there's a "b" at the end.'

'And her address?'

'27, Harlequin Road, Gipsy Hill.'

He wrote it down.

'Now,' he said, very slowly. 'Is there anything else you want to tell me about this attack?' He paused, significantly. 'Anything at all?'

I shook my head.

'I don't think so.'

He got to his feet.

'We'll look into it, of course, and we may want to talk to you again. I believe we have your address from London Transport?'

'12 Elm Place, Brixton.'

He consulted his notebook.

'Yes. I've got that.'

For a moment he stood there, looking at me as a director might look at an actor who has just messed up a part. Then he nodded.

'Well, good-day to you.'

'Good-day,' I said, flopping back on the pillow.

The moment he'd gone there was a throaty cackle from the next bed. A white-haired old man was looking at me suspiciously.

'In trouble, are you? Been stealing, eh?'

'I most certainly have not.'

He gave me a toothy grin.

'I know you black buggers,' he said. 'Always thieving. It's in you, like syphilis. Can't keep your hands off other people's things.'

'I was attacked,' I said.

'Attacked.' He let out a hoot. 'You thieving wog. You're all the same. Always after somebody's stuff.'

'Now, now, Mr Parswick.' A nurse came hurrying over. 'You know you're not supposed to get excited.'

'He's a thieving little bugger,' the man said. 'You saw the copper. He came to arrest him.'

'He did nothing of the sort,' the nurse said. 'This poor man was attacked on a bus.'

'Balls,' the old man said. He lapsed into silence.

'What's the matter with him?' I asked the nurse.

'Nothing that a new bladder wouldn't put right,' she said cheerfully.

I lay back, watching the activity of the ward through

half-closed eyes. One of the Indian nurses was really quite beautiful, I decided. She was lighter-skinned than the others and had wonderful legs. In her uniform she looked crisp and clean and deliciously germ-free. I wondered how it would be with her. Would she moan and cry: 'Ram, Ram, you're so wonderful . . .?' I turned my gaze away. Couldn't I keep my mind off it for one minute? I was in hospital because of one attempted seduction. At this rate I'd soon be locked up. They'd find out that my papers were forged and deport me. Back to India. Back to the Undead. Anything was better than that; even abstinence . . .

'Well now: are you feeling any better?'

A dark-skinned young doctor was standing by my bed; the attractive Indian nurse behind him. They were both looking down at me attentively.

'Thank you, doctor. Yes, I am.'

'Concussion can be a nasty thing,' he said, peering into my eyes. 'One has to be careful. It isn't just a question of coming to and going back to work. You must have a rest.'

'Were you here when they brought me in?'

'Indeed I was. Why?'

'I wondered if there was a girl with me.'

'A girl? No; there was no girl. Just your driver.'

He felt my head, very gently.

'Where are you from?'

'Calcutta.'

'Calcutta, eh? That's where I graduated.' Taking my head between his hands he moved it slowly from side to side. 'What were you doing there?'

'Working in a hotel.' I was about to mention the Deedar but decided against it. He might know it; he might even have visited it. 'At the Grand.'

'Ah, the dear old Grand.' He chuckled. 'I was always being called in there. Duodenal ulcers, that's all anybody seemed to have. They have the highest rate of duodenal ulcers in the world in India. Did you know that? It's all that curry.'

'I didn't know that,' I said.

'You see.' He made a note on the chart. 'You learn something new every day.' He patted my shoulder. 'Now just take it easy. We'll soon have you out of here.'

He turned to the nurse who was looking at him admiringly, her lips slightly parted.

'A little sedative, I think, nurse.'

'Of course, doctor.'

'Please,' I said. 'Could I also have a cup of tea?'

'I don't see why not.' He turned to the nurse. 'He can have the sedative after that. All right?'

'Of course, doctor.'

As they moved away, I watched him enviously. It must be great being a doctor, I thought; they had no trouble getting hold of women. Surrounded by nurses, and all of them oversexed — everyone knew that! — life for them must be one long romp. 'Number Six is dying, nurse, and Number Eight needs oxygen quickly but first slip down your pants, there's a good girl ...'

And if it wasn't the nurses in love with them it was the patients. They all fell for the white coat and the cool authority. 'Where does it ache most, Miss Mountjoy? About there?' 'No, doctor, a little lower down. Lower still. Yes, just there. You're right on it now ...'

A doctor. That was the thing to be. But it took years to qualify. Years and years. There were no short cuts. Mind you, a lot of them didn't have to know so much, really. According to a book I'd read in the library more than half the women going to Harley Street had nothing wrong with them. It was all in the mind. What they needed was a bit of attention and a few kind words. I could do that. All you had to do was dress well and look concerned. But what if something really serious came up? That was definitely a problem. You couldn't talk your way out of that? Though you could always recommend a second opinion, and pass them on to someone who really knew what he was doing ...

Locked in my reverie, I didn't hear the beautiful nurse come up. Suddenly, there she was, with a cup of tea in one hand and a tiny plastic bowl in the other.

'Is that my sedative?'

'That's right.'

She smiled, parting her lips. Her teeth were quite perfect.

'He seems nice, the doctor who spoke to me?'

'Yes, he's very nice.'

'A good doctor, too, I'll bet.'

'The best.'

She gave me the sedative and I swallowed it with a gulp, looking up at her for approval. She was still smiling.

'Have your bowels opened this morning?'

I shook my head.

The smile disappeared as she made a scribbled note on my chart. Oh, the shame of it! With one non-functioning of my bowels romance had gone out of the window. Before I could speak again she had gone, sweeping down the ward on those lovely legs of hers. Headed for the doctor's private sanctum, no doubt. 'I'm afraid Number Five is a constipated little bastard, doctor.' 'Oh forget about him, nurse, we've just got time for a quickie before lunch ...'

The white-haired old man in the next bed was staring at me again.

'Thieving little bugger,' he said.

I turned on my side, unhappily.

'Oh get stuffed,' I said.

13

I had been out of hospital three days when the event took place which changed my life. Even now, looking back on it, I get an odd sensation in the pit of my stomach. For it could so easily not have happened.

Since I was not due to report to the depot until the end of the week, I had been spending my time reading and resting. I was still feeling weak from the beating, and sleeping none too well.

Patel, who had taken me home from hospital, urged me to stay in bed as long as possible. 'You don't seem to realize the punishment you took,' he said. But I was bored. And so, on this particular afternoon, I set out for the West End to see a film.

The star of the picture I selected was Omar Sharif, and in the film he played a doctor. Now Mr Sharif, it is true, makes an impression on the ladies whatever part he plays. But even his Middle Eastern charm seemed heightened by the magic of medicine. To see his liquid-amber eyes glancing meaningfully over his face-mask as he muttered 'Scalpel' had the women around me in ecstasy. And why not? Who could fail to be moved by the sight of someone playing God — particularly when he had a good script?

Sitting there, eyes riveted on the screen, my imagination took flight. I could see myself in the role; making the long, lonely walk down the corridor outside the operating theatre, watched by my worshipping staff: 'He tried, heaven knows he tried, but even he is not omnipotent.' Then my strong arm round the sobbing widow's shoulders. How magnificent it all was.

When the film was over I had a cup of tea at a nearby café and walked through the West End. It was a bright, crisp sort of afternoon and the streets were thronged with cheerful-looking people. I walked aimlessly for a while, looking at shop windows, enjoying the feel of sun on my face, and at length found myself crossing Oxford Street.

And at this point what had been a perfectly ordinary sort of day was suddenly transformed into a red-letter one.

I had just turned into one of the small streets north of Oxford Circus when I came upon a crowd of people clustered in front of a stationary bus. A number 12 it was. At their feet lay a girl, her arms flung wide, her blonde hair splayed out on the dark-grey road. At first I was about to walk on, but then curiosity overcame me and I joined the crowd.

'What happened?' I asked.

'The bus knocked her down as she was crossing the street,' someone said.

An anxious-looking conductor was talking to the people in the crowd, taking down addresses, while the driver bent over the girl, holding her head. As I pushed my way forward he got up, pale-faced.

'Get a doctor, someone; please.'

And that's when it happened. There was no time for reflection; no time for anything. It was as though the scene had long been set; all I had to do was speak my lines. Perhaps, had I not seen Mr Sharif at work that afternoon, I might have hesitated. I don't know. All I do know is that my mind was suddenly crystal clear.

'I'm a doctor,' I said quietly.

The effect was remarkable. The crowd fell silent, looking at me. The driver, a small, hairy man, clutched at my arm.

'I couldn't avoid her, doc,' he said. 'I was just pulling into the stop when she stepped out, without even looking. God love us; I've been driving for twenty years without an accident, and now this ...'

He looked at me imploringly, seeking reassurance in my face.

'That's all right,' I said. 'Just keep these people back, if you will.'

'Of course, doctor.'

With the driver and conductor behind me acting as a shield, I bent over the girl. She was quite astonishingly pretty, with a heart-shaped face and an exquisite nose and mouth. Looking at her lying there, I was both frightened and fascinated. But I was committed to a course of action now, and there could be no holding back. Gingerly I reached out my hand. Which side was the heart? For an instant I couldn't think, and panic set in. Then, collecting myself, I unbuttoned her coat and slid my right hand across her chest. With a start I found myself clutching a soft breast. That couldn't be right, surely? Then I felt the beat of her heart.

Without hesitation I straddled her thighs and, bending low, covered her mouth with mine, breathing deeply. It was absolutely marvellous. There she was, this adorable, defenceless girl, with me astride her, kissing her, and it was all in order; so much in order, indeed, that although preoccupied with what I was doing, I could hear the murmurs of the crowd: 'It's the kiss of life.'

I had heard of people giving others mouth-to-mouth resuscitation and always found the prospect repugnant. But then it was usually being given to somebody old and decrepit; never to a young girl whose lips, cold as they were, tasted of honey.

As I continued breathing I felt her move slightly beneath me and had to think quickly of rotting coffins and slimy caves in order that my feelings should not get out of hand.

After a moment or two the girl's eyes opened and, reluctantly, I straightened up.

'What happened?' she asked, in a small voice.

'You had an accident,' I said. 'But everything's all right now.'

Helped by the conductor and driver, I carried her into a nearby shop; a small boutique which fortunately had a sofa in the showroom. While the girl lay back, the manageress went into the rear of the shop to make some tea.

'Will she be all right, doctor?' asked the driver.

I put my hand on his shoulder. It was exactly as I had imagined it in the cinema.

60

'She'll be fine,' I said. 'There's nothing for you to worry about.'

'Thank God,' the driver said. 'Thank God.'

When the manageress brought in the tea, I held the girl's head while she sipped it.

'Golly,' she said, with a small smile. 'That was a silly thing to do.'

'Don't talk,' I said. 'Just drink your tea.'

She looked up at me with wide grey eyes.

'Whatever you say,' she said.

The conductor took out his notebook.

'I'll need her name, doctor. And yours too, of course. For the report.'

The report! I hadn't thought of that. It was one of the first things we learned on joining London Transport: Fill in the report.

'I haven't a card on me,' I said, surprised at my own coolness. 'I'll write it down for you.'

'Thanks, doctor.'

He ripped a sheet from his notebook and passed it across.

'Ram Das,' I wrote, carefully. '12 Elm Place, Brixton.' So what, I thought. It wasn't as if the girl had died or anything. Nobody could prove I'd claimed to be a doctor. The driver had misheard me. I was just a passer-by, giving what help I could.

'And you, miss. Can I have your name and address?'

The girl sat up a little.

'Susan Partridge,' she said. '27 Halliday House, Hallam Street, W.1.'

Susan Partridge! I knew that name. She was a model. I'd seen her picture in the magazines Patel sometimes brought back from the airport.

'Well, doctor, if everything's all right, we'll be pushing off.'

'You do that,' I said. 'I'll make sure the young lady gets home safely.'

'Then we'll say goodbye. And thanks.'

They shook hands with both of us and a moment later I heard the bus pulling away.

As soon as they had gone the girl picked up her purse, which the driver had placed beside her, and took out a mirror.

'Oh, lord,' she said. 'I do look a mess.' Producing a comb, she began fussing with her hair.

'Where were you going when all this happened?' I asked.

'I'd just finished work and was walking home,' she said. 'I wasn't thinking, I suppose. It's so silly, really.'

'It's certainly silly,' I said. 'But it's not something to be taken lightly. Concussion can have after-effects.'

'Really?'

'It's hard to tell. But perhaps I ought to take another look at you later.' I hesitated just long enough. 'Or would you prefer to see your own doctor?'

'Well, no.' She put away the mirror and comb. 'Actually I haven't got a regular doctor.'

'Then I'll look in on you,' I said. I turned to the manageress, who was fluttering behind me like some great crow. 'Madam; would you be so kind as to find a taxi?'

'Of course, doctor; of course.'

She went into the street and I put my arm around Susan Partridge and helped her to her feet. Her body was soft and pliable, and I could feel her breath on my cheek as I walked beside her.

'I'll drop in tonight, then, about eight.'

'All right,' she said. 'It's Halliday House, in Hallam Street. Flat 27.'

'I've got it,' I said.

She got into the cab and I watched it careering away towards Portland Place.

A door had opened ...

62

14

When I arrived at Hallam Street that night, courage almost failed me. The street was lined with huge blocks of flats, all very imposing and splendid-looking.

For several minutes I stood outside Halliday House, looking in at the huge chandelier-dominated foyer. Who could live in such a palace, I wondered. Rajahs, probably. And princes. And lovely models like Susan Partridge. As I stood there, feeling shabby and ill-at-ease, a group of young people came out and got into a maroon Rolls-Royce. They were all laughing. 'Oh, Simon,' one of the girls was saying to a handsome young man. 'You are a scream.' I wondered if Susan knew Simon, and hoped not.

Twice I turned to go, but each time the thought of the girl in Flat 27 held me back. Finally, head down, I walked into the foyer and looked around for the lift.

'Can I help you?'

A large, uniformed porter loomed in front of me, wearing a chestful of medal ribbons and a sneer which would have frightened a herd of Indian battle elephants.

'I wish to see Miss Susan Partridge.'

He looked me up and down.

'Have you an appointment?'

'I have. I'm her doctor.'

The sneer stayed right there.

'Third floor,' he said. 'Turn right when you get out of the lift.'

I turned right when I got out of the lift and pressed the buzzer on the door.

For a moment nothing happened. I buzzed again. Then I heard sounds from within and the door opened just wide enough to reveal Susan Partridge in orange-silk pyjamas and a black silk robe. It was obvious that she'd been asleep.

'Oh it's you, doctor. Please come in.'

Pulling the belt of her robe tighter around her, she walked ahead of me down the hall to the bedroom. A moment later I was staring at the rumpled pink sheets of Susan Partridge's bed. The room smelled deliciously of sleep and girl.

'I'm feeling fine,' she said, taking off the robe and getting into bed. 'I hope this hasn't been a waste of time for you.'

'Better safe than sorry,' I said. 'We'll have a look at you anyway.'

She glanced at me.

'Don't you need instruments, and things?'

'Not for this sort of thing.'

Could that be me talking? So cool; so calm?

She bunched the pillows behind her.

'It's funny. I don't think I've ever seen a doctor without a black bag. I've often wondered what you carry around in them?'

'All sorts of wonderful things.'

Taking her wrist between my thumb and forefinger — the way the nurses had done in the hospital — I consulted my watch. What was it one looked for? A throb a second or a throb a minute? But I mustn't think about throbs at a time like this.

'Your pulse seems fine,' I said. 'Now, if you'll just unbutton your pyjama-top.'

Without hesitation she undid the buttons so that the sides of her orange pyjamas fell away, exposing the most perfectly-shaped breasts. Hurriedly I looked away, trying to think of something else. Then, bending my head to one side, the way the hospital doctor had done, I tested first here, then there.

'Does this hurt? Does this?'

Each time she shook her head.

Her face was so close to mine that, looking up as I asked the question, I could see the tiny blue specks in her grey eyes.

'How do I seem?' she asked.

'Fine,' I said. 'But I'd better check the rest of you.'

Putting her hands on her hips she edged down her pyjama-bottoms. Her stomach, smooth as alabaster, was quite perfect. In the centre, straying over the white cord of her pyjama-trousers was the softest trace of golden down.

'I had a bit of a feel round myself,' she said. 'Everything seems to be in its proper place.'

I could tell that just by looking. I could hardly imagine everything being more in its proper place. And however hard I concentrated on the terrible disaster in South America, and the rows of dead bodies, I could feel small pulses at work all over my body.

Before she could lower her pyjama-bottoms further, I took hold of her right ankle and raised it slowly. It seemed the safest way of coping with a situation which was rapidly getting out of hand.

'That one seems all right,' I said, briskly. 'No pain, I hope?'

She shook her head.

'I'll just try the other one.' Carefully I raised her left leg, looking at her face.

'Nothing,' she said.

'All right,' I said. 'Button up.'

Still looking at me, she pulled her pyjama-top together.

'How long must I stay in bed?'

'Oh, you can get up tomorrow. Take a hot drink now to relax and get to sleep early.'

'What sort of hot drink? Cocoa?'

'Cocoa will do?'

'I think there's some,' she said. 'I'm not sure. I'll have to look.'

'Is there anyone to look after you?'

'No. I'm on my own.'

I was determined to delay my departure as long as

possible.

'Tell me where the kitchen is,' I said. 'I'll make you some cocoa.'

'Golly, doctor, with this sort of bedside manner you could make a fortune ...' The telephone rang at that moment, and she reached to answer it. 'It's the first on the right down the hall,' she whispered.

While I busied myself in the kitchen, trying to make the best cup of cocoa in the history of the world, I heard her talking on the telephone. Her voice was too low for me to make out what she was saying. Who could it be, I wondered. Her lover, perhaps; some handsome, rich, sleek-haired bounder with a huge car and a flat in Mayfair. The very thought of anyone seeing what I had seen sent a shiver of jealousy through me.

When I took the cocoa in to her she was lying back against the pillows.

'Really,' she said. 'You are the most extraordinary doctor.'

'Doctors are human beings, too,' I said.

'I thought you weren't allowed to be,' she said. 'I thought you got struck off.'

'Only if we go too far,' I said.

'And how far is too far?' she said, laughing.

'I don't think we'll go into that,' I said. I handed her the cup. 'Drink this.'

'Listen, extraordinary doctor,' she said. 'I don't even know your name. You wrote it down in the shop but you didn't tell me.'

'It's Ram,' I said. 'Ram Das.'

'Ram Das.' She repeated it. 'And where is Doctor Das from?'

'Calcutta,' I said.

'And now you're working here?'

'That's right.'

'Where is your practice?'

'I've just left St Michael's Hospital,' I said — that was true, anyway. 'Now I'm planning to start up in the West

End.'

'In Harley Street?'

'I hope so.'

'How exciting! Are you going to be terribly expensive?'

'Of course,' I said.

'Oh my goodness.' She put the cocoa down on the bedside table and reached to the floor for her purse. Her pyjama-top splayed open as she did so and I caught another glimpse of her breasts.

'I almost forgot. How much do I owe you?'

'Put that away,' I said. 'I haven't done anything.'

'But your time ...?'

'It's been a pleasure,' I said. 'If you ever find me lying in the road I hope you'll do the same for me.'

'Any time.' She sat up, suddenly. 'Listen, I've just thought of something. There is a way I can return your kindness. I can send our girls to you.'

'Your girls?'

'Yes. From the agency. I'm with the Jenny Abbot Model Agency — you've heard of it, probably. We've got loads of girls, and all of them hypochondriacs. If you'll give me a card or something I'll make sure you've enough clients to start you off.'

'Clients?'

She laughed. 'I mean patients.'

'I can't give you a card because I haven't got my consulting rooms yet, but as soon as I do I'll let you know.'

'All right. But don't forget.'

'It's very kind of you,' I said. 'It's always nice to have pretty girls on one's list. It makes the waiting room look less depressing.'

I took her hand.

'Well,' I said. 'I must be off. Try to get a good night's sleep.'

'I will.'

She watched me to the door.

'I'll tell you one thing,' she said. 'You're going to be a big hit in Harley Street.'

'You think so?'

'With your style,' she said. 'There's no doubt about it.'

She slid down the bed until her chin was just above the top sheet.

'Goodbye, Miss Partridge,' I said.

'Goodbye, extraordinary doctor,' she said softly.

15

When I got back to Elm Place, Patel was waiting in my room. He had cooked himself a meal of baked beans, and the whole place reeked of burned toast. He was never very good at toast.

'How did it go?' he demanded.

I was rather annoyed at finding him there. I didn't want to talk; I just wanted to dwell on what had taken place an hour ago; to keep alive the memory of Susan Partridge snuggling between the sheets.

'It went all right,' I said shortly.

'She suspected nothing?'

'No.'

His face creased into a crooked smile. 'You have been given a sign, my boy, by Ganesa, the god of success. Unwittingly you have stumbled upon the road to more cash than most men get in a lifetime.'

'You can't be serious?' I said. 'You don't imagine I'd take a chance like that again?'

He leaned forward, his eyes fixed on mine.

'I've never been more serious in my life,' he said. 'You're going to set up as a doctor.'

I laughed wildly.

'But I don't know anything about medicine.'

'What's that got to do with it?' he demanded. 'Half the fucking physicians in Harley Street don't know anything about it either. Don't you realize that the majority of people going to the doctor have nothing really wrong with them? I tumbled on to that years ago. If they didn't go, whatever trivial complaint they think they're suffering from would disappear. Most of those Harley Street quacks are taking money under false pretences, since none of them ever says: "Go home — you'll get better anyway."'

He paced the room.

'Most of their patients are middle-aged women with more money than sense; women with time on their hands who crave a bit of attention. If they're suffering from anything it's usually some sort of tension, or a headache. A few soothing words, a bottle of tranquillizers, a little neck massage perhaps, and another four pounds goes into the pot. Why, anybody could do it ...'

He stopped in front of me.

'Come to think of it,' he said, 'perhaps you ought to concentrate on that line — headaches, backaches, that sort of thing. The way osteopaths do. You've heard of osteopaths, I suppose?'

I nodded.

'They're on to a good thing,' Patel said. 'They know that if you stretch most people you only do them good.' He chuckled. 'I read a book once about torture in the Middle Ages. Some man who'd been a cripple all his life was put to torture on the rack. After a couple of sessions, far from crying for mercy, he was relieved of pain for the first time and got up, grinning. Isn't that something?'

I shook my head. 'I still don't think I could do it.'

He wheeled on me. 'Of course you can. And for once your colour is an advantage. Britain is full of Indian doctors.'

'But suppose someone comes to see me who is really ill?'

'I've thought of that,' Patel said. 'And worked out a plan. We'll fix you up with a National Health doctor. There's one just round the corner from here, Dr Stirrup. He's a dried-up old poop but he knows his medicine. The only things he won't touch are tertiary syphilis and terminal cancer. He's funny about those. Otherwise, he'll take anything. So you see, if someone comes to you who's obviously ill you just make a note of their symptoms and describe them to Dr Stirrup. He'll sort out what's to be done.'

'You really think it would work?' I said. Some of his enthusiasm was beginning to wash off on me.

'Of course it will work. As a matter of fact, with that fantastic memory of yours, you could probably study and become a real doctor, if you chose. But it takes years.'

He went over to the sink and flushed away the tea-leaves.

'Incidentally, what was that book you memorized in India?'

'*A Complete Guide to Indian Railways?*'

'No. Not that one. Nobody gives a damn what time the best train leaves Calcutta for Delhi . . .'

'Five p.m.' I said, without thinking. 'Mondays and Fridays. Arrives in Delhi ten-twenty the following night. Fastest train on Indian Railways.'

'Air-conditioned?'

'Sleeper and chair-car.'

'Incredible.' His face broke into a smile. 'We could make a fortune on the halls. The Great Das. Or, perhaps, Patel and Das.' He dried his hands on my dish-cloth. 'But I was thinking of that other book . . .'

'*Newnes' Family Doctor?*'

'That's the one. Did you memorize that one too?'

'Every page.'

He wheeled around.

'Page 259.'

I didn't have to think. I could see it clearly in my

mind.

'Exophthalmic Goitre,' I said.

'Great heavens,' Patel said. 'What's that?'

'A form of goitre or swelling of the thyroid gland in the front of the neck,' I said. 'There is also great protrusion of the eyeballs, rapid action of the heart, and tremulousness ...'

He clapped his hands together.

'Fantastic. Dazzle them with that sort of stuff and how can you lose?'

I sat on the edge of the bed. Patel was right. If I had memorized *Newnes' Family Doctor* page by page without even trying, I could do it with other medical books. And I would be off to a good start, with Susan Partridge's girl-friends. Suddenly I saw the future clear: Ram Das, rich and respected, sought after far and wide for his wise counsel and advice. The fantasy expanded. Perhaps, one day, the Queen herself would come.

'I keep having these terrible headaches,' she'd say. 'I'm at my wit's end. Sir Charles Limpette-West and Sir Laurence Wainscott-Evans and all those other medical layabouts can do nothing. You are my last hope.'

'When do you get these headaches, Ma'am?'

'Oh, usually after some big do,' she'd say. 'The Commonwealth Conference Dinner, or something like that.'

I'd be on to it in an instant.

'Your crown, Ma'am. Was it made to measure?'

An imperious stare.

'Of course it was. You don't suppose I got it off the peg, do you? What sort of Queen do you think I am?'

That was it. She'd been crowned when she was a young girl. Now she was a woman, and her head would have grown. The crown, tight on her head, would be causing the headaches.

'Put yourself in my hands, Ma'am. I will not fail you.'

From then on it would be easy. A discreet word in the ears of the court jewellers, a couple of tugs on the royal neck and — presto! — all would be well. Hauling on the Queen's neck, though. Even in fantasy I felt a twinge of unease. A hundred years earlier I'd have been strung up in chains just for thinking of it.

But she'd be delighted. And one afternoon up she'd roll in the Royal car and get out with a stool in one hand and a sword in the other and dub me, right then and there, on the floor of my consulting room. 'Arise, Sir Ram ...'

'What's the hell's the matter with you?'

Patel was standing in front of me, frowning.

'Nothing, I was just day-dreaming.'

'Well, what do you think?'

'I'll have a go,' I said, determinedly.

'That's the stuff. This is a great day, my boy; a momentous day.'

'How do I start?'

'First we have to find you a consulting-room in the West End,' he said. 'And then get you outfitted with some proper clothes. And we need lots of equipment.'

'Equipment?'

'You know, medical things; scales, an examination couch, lamps, a desk. The more the better. People feel cheered by the sight of lots of instruments.'

'But how do I pay for all this?'

Patel smiled mysteriously and padded out of the room. Minutes later he was back, counting out £250 in ten pound notes.

I sat there, stunned.

'Where did you get all this?'

'Oh, tips and things,' he said, vaguely.

'And you're lending it to me?'

'Only as a business proposition,' he said. 'I shall want interest, of course. Fifteen per cent.'

'Isn't that rather high?'

'You're damn right it's rather high,' he said. 'But see if any other money-lender will chance his arm on a no-good, layabout Indian rascal who plans to set up shop as a phoney doctor.'

I saw his point.

'I agree,' I said.

Patel took a piece of paper from his pocket. 'I owe I.Q. Patel £250,' he wrote. 'I guarantee to repay said sum in full within one year, plus £37.50 interest on said sum in two equal parts of £18.75 every six months.'

'Sign that,' he said, thrusting it at me.

I signed with a flourish and he handed me the wad of money. Solemnly we shook hands.

'Now,' he said. 'Let us celebrate this great occasion. In my room I have a bottle of Algerian wine; putrescent stuff, undoubtedly, full of fungus and filth and made, no doubt, by Arab feet rotten with syphilis. But drinkable.' He glanced at his watch, and heaved a small sigh. 'Thank goodness,' he said. 'I've got a full half-hour before I have to service the old hag ...'

16

I slept badly. For one thing I was keyed up after my conversation with Patel. For another, the wine was lying like acid in my stomach. What could have been in it, I wondered next morning, as the mirror reflected a rim of red sediment around my mouth. Not grapes, certainly. Sand from all those Arab sandals, more likely.

Feeling as I did, it surprised me that Patel had found the strength — let alone the inclination — to go to the hag's room after we said goodnight. My admiration for the man deepened with every passing day.

He had obviously risen early, for on the chair by my bed was a copy of *The Times*, with a note pinned to it: 'Take a look at Page 26 under Property to Let — I.Q.P.'

Eagerly I turned to the page. Half-way down the second column, Patel had ringed an advertisement.

Harley Street, W.1. Consulting suites to let in fine period property recently subject to extensive improvements. Waiting room, receptionist, c.h.; c.h.w.; lift etc. Magnificent room £1,200 p.a. inc. Fine suite with office, £1,750 p.a. inc.

There was a telephone number.

'It is a sure sign,' Patel had scrawled at the bottom of the page. 'This is the first time I have seen such an advertisement. You must telephone immediately.'

No, I thought. What I must do immediately is splash some cold water in my face and make some hot coffee. Otherwise I will never survive the day.

That done, I made my way downstairs to the pay-telephone in the hall.

'About your advertisement ...' I began.

'Yes, yes,' a voice said. 'What sort of accommodation were you interested in?'

It was a good question. What sort of accommodation was I interested in?

'Could you tell me what is available?' I asked.

'It's all in the advertisement,' the voice said sharply. 'It cost a lot of money, that advertisement.'

'I was wondering ...'

'There's a marvellous three-room suite,' the voice said. 'The main room has a superb Adam ceiling ...'

What on earth was an Adam ceiling?

'... The suite is £1,750, inclusive,' the voice added.

'I'm really looking for something smaller,' I said.

'One room?'

'Something like that.'

'There's a nice room on the ground floor,' the voice said. '£1,200 inclusive. With a three-year lease.'

Three years! I almost laughed out loud. One week, I thought, and they'll be coming to get me.

'When could I see it?'

'Any time you like.'

'Would this afternoon be convenient? About four?'

'Four will do nicely,' the voice said. 'By the way, what is the name?'

'Das,' I said. 'Ram Das.'

'I'll see you at four, Dr Das.'

The owner of the voice was waiting at the door when I arrived.

He was a small, beetle-like man with huge ears and an odd way of twisting his neck about, as though he were being strangled by some unseen assailant and was trying to ease the pain.

'I guessed you were Indian,' he said, ushering me into the hall. 'I can always tell by the voice.'

'Oh, really?' I said.

'Now.' With an oddly theatrical gesture he flung open the door to the left and I walked into a large, pleasant room with a high ceiling and a window looking out on Harley Street.

'It's nice, isn't it?' he said, watching my face.

It certainly was nice. Airy and spacious and with an imposing white marble fireplace. Anybody would have been impressed.

'I see there are curtains,' I said, inspecting the dark-red drapes which hung to the floor.

'And they're good ones,' he said. 'Whoever rents the room will be expected to buy them. I'm not about to take them down and it would cost a lot of money to have new ones made.'

'I imagine it would,' I said.

I looked at the parquet flooring, and the panelled door. There was no doubt about it; it was a superb room. But so much money ...

'How much are you asking for the curtains?'

'Fifty pounds,' he said. Seeing my look of dismay he added: 'They're worth a lot more. Beautiful material. Feel them.'

I fingered the heavy drapes. He was right. They were beautiful. They gave the whole room dignity.

'It is just the sort of place I'm looking for,' I said.

'Most of the doctors who've been here have been happy,' he said. 'Smith-Evanson had this room for years. I expect you know him — the neurosurgeon?'

I shook my head.

'You know how it is. We meet so many people.'

'I expect you do,' he said.

He led the way back into the hall, almost tripping over a tall, angular woman in a white coat who was heading for the door.

'That's our Miss Furze,' he said. 'The receptionist. She's included in the rent, of course; as are cleaning and electricity. But of course you know that.'

'Well,' I said. 'Thank you very much. I'll think about it and let you know.'

He gave his neck a sudden twist.

'Don't think too long,' he said. 'The room will probably be gone by tomorrow. Single consulting rooms in Harley Street today are rarer than virgins in the King's Road.'

I stood there, hesistating. He was right, of course. It wasn't a sales pitch. The room would be gone if I waited. 'It is a sure sign,' Patel had written. The fickle finger was beckoning. If I ignored it, there might not be another chance. And Susan Partridge would be gone from my life for ever.

'I'll take it,' I blurted.

'Splendid,' he said. 'Splendid. It's a beautiful room. You will do beautiful work in it. Come —' he said, as Miss Furze came sweeping down the hall again — 'let us go inside and discuss the details.'

We went back into the room — into *my* room — and I stood there, drinking it all in. Yes, it was a great room. I had not made a mistake.

The little man took my arm.

'If a three-year lease does not suit your plans at the moment,' he said, 'we can easily agree on something shorter. Say six months. With a shorter lease, of course,

I would require payment in cash.' He shot me a sly glance. 'Three months in advance.'

'That would be more convenient,' I said.

He smiled understandingly.

'Then if you will let me have £300 by tomorrow morning we can shake hands on it.'

He wrenched his neck savagely.

'Are there any other queries, doctor?'

'How does the telephone work?'

'Miss Furze has an extension in her office at the back, so that if any of the doctors are busy and do not wish to answer their calls, she can take them.'

'That would seem to be a very satisfactory arrangement.'

'Most of the other doctors find it so.'

'Then I can't think of anything else,' I said. 'What time shall I see you tomorrow?'

'At your convenience, doctor.'

'Shall we say twelve?'

'Twelve it is.'

We shook hands and I strode off down the street, elated and happy. What a strange little man. The only thing he'd seemed to care about was the money. Oh, well, I thought, he wasn't so different from everyone else.

Further along the street a Rolls was parked, with a chauffeur standing beside it. As I walked past, a plump man came bounding out of the house to my right, brandishing a black bag. 'Morning, Sidney,' he said cheerfully.

'Good morning, sir,' the chauffeur said. And away they went. He's off on his rounds, I decided. A nod here, a joke there, a pulse taken somewhere else and he'd be fifty pounds better off by the time I got back to Elm Place.

I'd soon have some of that, I thought. I'd taken the plunge. I was on my way. My heart racing, I hurried home.

'You see,' Patel said. 'It was meant to be. I know about these things.'

He stirred his tea with a knife, peering at me as he did so.

'But will I get away with it? The landlord didn't ask any questions, but surely others will?'

'You'll get away with it,' Patel said, 'because others are already getting away with it. Don't you realize that most of those Harley Street quacks haven't increased their medical knowledge one scrap since they bluffed their way through their exams God-knows how long ago? Most of them are still back in the leech-and-poultice era. How can you lose?'

'Quite easily,' I said soberly. 'Someone will come in riddled with disease and I won't know what to do.'

'Yes, you will,' Patel said doggedly. 'We've been through all that. Pull yourself together. We are on to a good thing here. We must pursue it with determination. The next thing to do is to get you outfitted.'

'Outfitted?'

'Well you can't expect them to take you seriously in that rubbish you're wearing.'

'This is my best suit,' I protested.

'I was afraid of that,' Patel said. 'Well, it's just not good enough. You will have to get something more suitable.' He eyed me speculatively. 'A dark-grey number, I think. That should do the trick. Not too formal, not to casual. I will take tomorrow off and go shopping with you.' He paused. 'And what about furniture?'

'Furniture?'

'For your consulting-room, you idiot. What were you planning to do — diagnose their ailments lying on your back? You've got to get the right props.'

'But all this will cost money.'

'Too right it will,' Patel said. He did some rapid calculations in his head. 'I'll tell you what,' he said. 'I will advance you another £250 — at the same interest as before. That should take care of everything.'

Seeing my look of astonishment, he chuckled.

'Don't worry,' he said. 'You may have no faith in your future, but I have.' He sipped his tea, slurping noisily. 'You'll pay me back,' he said. 'Don't worry about that.'

Next day we went to a large men's store in Regent Street where I bought myself a dark-grey single-breasted suit, some grey shirts and a dark-blue tie. Then, clutching my purchases, we took a taxi to a warehouse off Euston Road, where Patel was sure we would find everything we needed. And he was right. An hour later we had it all: a shabby but imposing desk; a large folding screen; a worn leather sofa; a couple of chairs, an electric fire and a square of reasonably decent grey carpet. And, best of all, an ancient traction-couch, which we discovered tucked away at the back; a huge leather thing with straps for attaching around the chest and ankles and a wheel at the side which, when turned, extended bars at either end, tightening the straps. Beneath it was an electric motor which, the assistant assured us, needed only minor repairs to function properly. When working, it vibrated both ends of the couch, producing a massaging effect.

'General Eisenhower used it in the last war,' the assistant said. 'I got that straight from the horse's mouth.'

'And I suppose you got the couch straight from General Eisenhower?' Patel said, cynically. 'I can just see him nipping in here with that thing under his arm. Or perhaps he advertised it in *The Times*. "American General, urgently called home, must sell traction-couch ..."'

'I'm only telling you what I was told,' the assistant said, stiffly.

'And I'm only telling you what I believe,' Patel replied. He thought for a moment. 'Get the motor fixed and we'll take it.'

79

'Done,' the assistant said.

We arranged for the furniture to be delivered within the next few days, and then set off for Harley Street to meet my landlord.

'Is there anything else I should have?' I asked, as we hurried along.

'A name plate,' Patel said. 'Some headed notepaper. Maybe a couple of things to put on the desk. I know a place where we can get all that after we see your man.'

My man, as Patel dubbed him, was waiting for us in the hall, talking with Miss Furze, the receptionist.

'My dear Dr Das,' he said, giving his neck a tremendous wrench, 'I trust everything is in order.'

'Absolutely,' I said.

'Then let me introduce you to your receptionist, Miss Furze.'

'How do you do?' I said.

She smiled thinly.

'I'm well, thank you, doctor.'

I introduced Patel to them both, and then took him into the consulting-room.

As we entered, he gazed around, his eyes wide.

'Well,' I said. 'What do you think?'

He grinned widely.

'Dr Das,' he said, 'I think you have made a very good choice indeed.'

17

The next few days were busy ones. We completed the transaction with Mr Grime, the landlord. We bought the rest of the things for the office. We had a brass plate made. We bought up all the medical books we could get our hands on. And Patel took me along to meet Dr Stirrup.

Outside the entrance to the doctor's house, which lay

some distance up a hill leading towards Streatham, a girl of about fourteen was playing with a dog.

She had shining blonde hair and blue eyes and her teeth were very white.

'Hello,' she said. 'You going in to see the doctor?'

'That's right,' Patel said.

'He's no good,' the girl said, contemptuously. 'My mother's been going to him for months now. He hasn't cured her.'

'What's wrong with her?' Patel asked, guardedly.

'She's pregnant,' the girl said, matter-of-factly.

Patel shrugged and made to open the gate.

'Guess what I was doing when you arrived?' the girl said.

'I've no idea,' Patel said.

'I was pretending that the dog had been run over, and I was making him well.'

'You like dogs?' Patel asked.

She nodded.

'When I grow up that's what I'm going to do. Mend dogs.'

'You want to be a veterinary surgeon,' Patel said.

'No,' the girl said, adamantly. 'I want to mend dogs.'

She followed us to the door.

'Will you be in there a long time?' she asked.

'No,' Patel said. 'Not long.'

'I'll wait for you,' the girl said.

Dr Stirrup was a ruined old rascal with grey hair falling about his shoulders and an odd way of looking at you, as though he was seeing someone standing behind you.

'Well,' he snapped at Patel. 'What's wrong with this one?'

'Nothing,' Patel said. With a glance at me he led the doctor over to the corner and began talking earnestly. From time to time the doctor nodded. At length a wintry smile spread across his ravaged face. When they had finished talking he was almost cheerful.

'That will be all right,' he said to me. 'Come and see me whenever you need advice.'

Patel gave me a long look.

'I was just explaining to the doctor that you were studying medicine in your spare time,' he said.

'I'm grateful,' I said to Dr Stirrup. 'Thank you very much.'

'Don't thank me,' he said brusquely. 'It'll cost you a quid a time.'

'As much as that?'

'Well you don't expect me to help you out on the National Health, do you? It'd break your heart, anyway, sitting out there with all those other poor buggers, coughing their lungs up. Bloody murder, it is. Believe me.'

'All right,' I said. 'Can I telephone you, if I can't get here myself?'

'You can do what you like,' he said. 'Send a carrier pigeon, for all I care.'

He thrust a bony hand through his hair, cascading dandruff over the shoulders of his shiny black suit.

'Is that all?'

Patel nodded.

'I'll see your friend about seven, then. Tomorrow night?'

'I'll make sure she's on time,' Patel said.

I wondered what it was that he and Patel had been talking about. Half-way down the drive Patel enlightened me.

'He's the cheapest abortionist in town,' he said. 'Twenty quid. Can you imagine? They charge one hundred and fifty in the West End. Mind you, his methods are a bit suspect. I think he does it with a knife and fork.'

'But how do you find them?'

'I work at London Airport, don't I?' Patel said. 'You can spot them a mile away. They don't actually look

82

pregnant, coming through Customs, but they do look anxious. A couple of my friends are there, scouting for me. I give them a pound a time.'

At the gate, the young girl was waiting for us. The dog had gone.

'Did you see the doctor?' she asked.

Patel nodded.

'Stinks, doesn't he?' the girl said. 'My mother says that's the worst thing about him; he stinks.'

'Well,' Patel said, 'perhaps she doesn't mean it in the sense of smell; perhaps she means she just doesn't like him.'

The girl considered this.

'Yes,' she said. 'Perhaps that's it.'

She propped herself against the wall.

'Where do you live?' she asked.

'In Brixton,' I said. 'With my friend here.'

Patel grunted.

'Your friend here is going into the Bell for a beer. Can I tempt you?'

'You certainly can,' I said.

But the girl was not to be lost that easily.

'Would you walk me home first?' she asked. 'I only live up the road.'

'What for?' Patel demanded. 'You got here by yourself.'

The girl looked hurt.

'It's getting late, now. I'm a bit scared.'

Patel turned to me.

'You walk the kid home,' he said. 'I'll go over and order a couple of drinks. But don't be long.'

He sloped off to the pub and I walked up the road with the girl.

'What's your name?' I asked.

'Julie,' she said. 'What's yours?'

'Ram,' I said.

'You're nice, Ram,' she said. She slid her hand into mine. Together we walked along in silence.

'Was that your dog?' I asked.

'Which dog?'

'That dog you were playing with when we saw you.'

'Oh, no,' she said. 'That wasn't my dog. That was just a dog. I haven't got a dog.'

'Haven't you got lots of friends to play with?'

'No,' she said. 'There aren't any children I like. Not a lot, anyway. Not that I can talk to.'

'What about your parents?'

'My parents,' she said, scornfully. 'I can't talk to them. They're old.'

'How old?'

She thought for a moment.

'Mum's forty. And dad's older. I don't know how much.'

'That's not so old,' I said.

'It is if you're fourteen,' she said.

Suddenly I felt uneasy, walking along the road holding the hand of this angelic child. 'You'll be all right now,' I said. 'You can't live far from here.'

'I don't.' She pointed across the street. 'It's that house just there.'

Even as my eyes followed the direction of her hand I saw a woman coming out of the house. She was big-boned, with eyes like the barrels of a 12-bore. I tried to disengage my hand, but Julie held on tightly.

'Where have you been?' the woman stormed, coming up with long strides.

'Just down the road,' Julie said.

The woman seized the girl's free hand and pulled her from me.

'Now you listen to me,' she said, spitting the words. 'If you come round here again pestering our kid I'll call the police. Understand? I know your sort.'

She dragged Julie across the street, leaving me standing there. The child looked back only once, a small, conspiratorial smile on her face. Just before the door shut, she winked.

Towards the end of the week Patel decided we should have a celebration to launch my medical career. So he took me to a club called the Number Four. It was a shabby, dark place, but Patel liked it and went quite often. You could get snacks there late at night, and there was always loud music, which he enjoyed.

We selected a table in the corner, from which we had a good view of the rest of the club, and then we got down to some serious drinking.

'Success,' Patel said, pouring the wine, 'is just around the corner. I feel it in my bones. Nothing can stop you now.'

I crossed my fingers.

'I wish I had as much faith in myself as you have,' I said.

'I have to have faith,' he said. 'It's my £500 that's riding on you.'

'You're an incredible man,' I said. 'Not many people could have saved such a lot in your line of work.'

His eyebrows rose a full half inch.

'You don't suppose I saved it working in the loos, do you?'

'Then how did you make it?'

'In business, of course.'

'What sort of business?'

He hesitated.

'It's not a thing I'm particularly proud of,' he said. 'But it made a lot of money.'

'Well, go on. What did you do?'

'I went into partnership with a man who owned a large rat,' he said.

'Great Lord Krishna,' I said. 'What for?'

'You've heard of sitting tenants?' he said. 'People who can't be thrown out of houses and flats because they're protected by law? Well, this friend of mine decided there was a lot of money to be made by providing landlords with a surefire way of getting rid of them.'

He leaned forward.

'He hit upon this great idea, you see. He knew a lot about breeding, so he set about breeding a monstrous rat; the biggest thing you've ever seen; bigger than a Yorkshire terrier, all glossy and black. Then we went into business. Rent-a-Rodent, we called it. We'd get in touch with landlords who wanted to get rid of a sitting tenant and I'd take the rat round in a big box and leave it outside the person's door. Of course when they saw this huge thing sitting there they went absolutely spare, and moved out. It always worked. We charged £25 a time.'

'But wasn't the rat dangerous?'

'As a matter of fact it was quite docile,' he said. 'All the normal rodent viciousness had been strained out of it by the breeding. At night, when it wasn't on duty, it used to sit in front of the fire with us, staring into the flames. In the end I grew quite fond of it.'

'What was its name?'

'Schwartz.'

'That's a funny name for a rat.'

'Oh,' he said. 'What's a good name?'

'Really,' I said. 'That's a pretty silly question. I meant, well, it just sounds odd, a rat named Schwartz. But go on. I'm fascinated. What was your part in all this, apart from taking Schwartz round to the houses?'

'I concentrated on the business side,' he said. 'Every day I'd go through the advertisements for houses without vacant possession and get in touch with the owners. They all went for it. It was an absolute push-over.'

'How long did it go on?'

'Until Schwartz died,' he said. 'It was our fault, I think. We overfed him with cream. He loved it, you see;

86

he always had it for breakfast, with a chocolate biscuit. One day I came home and there he was, dead in a great pool of cream.'

'Couldn't your friend have bred another one?'

'He tried,' Patel said. 'But he never pulled it off again. Schwartz was something of a freak, I suppose. So that was the end of that. We went out of business.'

'How much had you made by that time?'

'Enough,' said Patel. 'Around £3,000 apiece.'

'Sacred cows,' I said, startled. 'That's a fortune.'

'It's not bad,' Patel agreed. 'And we'd have made a lot more, but for that cream.'

He was silent for a moment, gazing round the club. A couple of giant blacks were cavorting on the dance-floor, partnered by pale-faced, spotty girls. Madame Pew, my dancing teacher, never taught me how to do that, I thought.

'You're going to make money too,' Patel said. 'Making money is easy, you know. All you need is a good idea, and the energy to push it through. You know that old saying: "If you can build a better mousetrap …?" Well, we bred a better rat, and look how well we did.'

As he was speaking, I glanced around the club. A couple of not unattractive girls had just walked in and were standing there, looking at us. Both were blonde, one a little taller than the other. And both were wearing shaggy Afghan jackets.

They looked at me, and smiled, so I smiled back, Patel, catching my glance, looked across at them.

'Forget it,' he said.

'Why?' I said, 'They look rather nice.'

'Rather nice,' he mimicked. 'If they're rather nice what are they doing in a dump like this? Do me a favour.'

I looked at the girls again, and nudged Patel.

'They're coming over,' I said.

He groaned.

'It's all your fault,' he said. 'You encouraged them.'

Ignoring him, I kept my eyes on the girls. The shorter one was wearing skin-tight blue jeans, and beneath her Afghan jacket her breasts bounced as she walked. I decided I liked the way she walked.

As they came up, I got to my feet. Patel remained sitting.

'Hello,' the taller one said. 'May we join you?'

'We were actually expecting Raquel Welch,' Patel said, disagreeably. 'But something seems to have delayed her.'

'My names's Joyce,' the taller girl said. 'And she's Glad.'

'But is she happy?' Patel asked.

'Is she what?'

'Oh, never mind,' Patel said. He held up the bottle of wine. 'We're drinking this. You're welcome to a glass.'

'What is it?' Glad asked.

'It's wine,' Patel said. 'You know, made from grapes?'

'I'd rather have a Vodka and tonic,' she said. 'So would Joyce.'

'Vodka's against our religion,' Patel said.

'But you won't be drinking it,' the girl countered.

'We're not even allowed to have it on the table,' Patel said. 'Don't you know anything about Eastern religions?'

'Not that one,' the girl said. 'What is it, then?'

'You wouldn't have heard of it,' Patel said. 'Well, do you want some wine or not?'

The girls exchanged glances.

'All right,' Joyce said. 'What do you want us to do? Drink it out of the bottle? Or can we have glasses?'

Patel hailed the waiter who hurried over with extra glasses.

'What's your name?' Glad asked, as Patel poured the wine.

'Ram,' I said. 'Ram Das. And he is I.Q. Patel.'

'What do you both do?'

'We sit here,' Patel said. 'Waiting for Raquel Welch.'

'No, seriously.'

'Seriously,' Patel said. 'He's a Harley Street consultant and I look after the bogs at London Airport.'

Both girls giggled.

'Come off it,' Glad said.

'You don't believe us?' Patel said. He looked at me and shrugged. 'Shall I tell them?' he asked.

It was a bit beyond me, this repartee. But Patel seemed to be in a strange mood.

'All right,' I said.

'Well,' Patel said, 'I'm a fish expert from Guatemala and Ram is a pilot with Air India.'

'Fancy,' Joyce said. Turning to me she said: 'You look like a pilot, come to think of it. But what's a fish expert?'

'Someone who knows a lot about fish,' Patel said.

'I realize that,' Joyce said. 'But what's there to know?'

'What's there to know?' Patel echoed. 'Have you any idea of what goes on beneath the sea? It's fascinating.'

'All right,' Joyce said. 'Tell me something fascinating.'

'Well, did you know that certain types of shrimps have orgasms lasting for twenty-four hours?' Patel inquired.

The girls shrieked.

'Come again,' Joyce said.

'Pity we can't all be shrimps,' Glad said.

'I thought that would interest you,' Patel said dryly.

I could sleep with Glad, I thought. Take her home and have a few drinks and pounce. She looked all right, Glad!

'Done a lot of skipping, have you?' Patel asked suddenly.

'Skipping? What are you on about now?' Joyce said sharply.

'I'm on about skipping,' Patel said, eyeing her bust. 'There's nothing like it, you know, for strengthening the pectorals.'

'Are you having us on?' Glad challenged.

'Believe me,' Patel said. 'I'm not having you any way.'

His manner had changed. He was no longer being funny. He was just being rude.

'What about you, love bucket?' Glad said to me. 'What's it like, flying Air India? All curry and cuddles, is it?'

As I turned to answer her I accidentally knocked over my glass. It crashed to the floor, cascading red wine over her handbag, a white basket-shaped thing, which she had placed beneath her chair.

She looked at me in blank astonishment. Then at her handbag. Then back to me. Suddenly her face went very pale.

'You clumsy fool,' she snapped. 'You've ruined my handbag. Look at it. Bloody well ruined.'

'I'm sorry,' I said, trying to wipe the wine from her bag with my handkerchief. 'It was an accident. You could see that.' I turned to Patel for support. 'It was an accident, wasn't it?'

Patel looked at me blankly.

'No,' he said. 'You did it deliberately.'

'What?' I could hardly believe what he was saying.

'You knocked the glass over deliberately,' Patel said. 'I saw you.'

'See,' Glad snapped. 'I've a bloody good mind to make you pay for it. My new bag. Ruined.'

'It was an accident,' I said heatedly. 'He wasn't even looking when it happened.'

For a moment we all sat there, glaring at each other, not moving, as if posing for a photograph. Then Glad got to her feet, dragging Joyce with her.

'Come on,' she said grimly. 'Let's leave these two apes to crawl back into their tree.'

With a last, lingering look of fury, she strode away, holding her wine-spattered bag at arm's length. I turned angrily to Patel.

'Thanks very much,' I said. 'Some friend you turned out to be.'

'Better than you know,' Patel said. 'Those two tramps have been with every man in this club. Believe me, I know. I come here all the time.'

'All right. So they're tramps. So what?'

He looked incredulous.

'Do you realize what you'd have got if you'd gone home with that Glad bag? Clap, at the least, or some nameless disease that would have defeated even Doc Stirrup.'

My anger abated as he spoke.

'Anyway,' I said sulkily. 'You should have backed me up over the glass.'

'Why?' he said. 'It was a heaven-sent opportunity to get us off the hook.'

He put a hand on my shoulder.

'My dear friend,' he said. 'If you are truly in love with Susan Partridge you cannot allow yourself to be soiled by rubbish like those two. It is unthinkable.'

Seeing my look, his grip tightened.

'Have faith,' he said. 'If it is written that you and Susan wind up in the sack together, wind up in the sack you will.'

'That's what I like about you,' I said. 'You make everything sound so romantic.'

He chuckled and poured me a fresh glass of wine.

Next day the furniture arrived, and Patel helped me arrange the office. And that afternoon I sat behind my desk for the first time, feeling rather like an office boy trying out the managing director's chair during the lunch break.

Sitting there, I felt a warm glow of happiness. Patel was right. Things would work out. All I had to do was keep my nerve. And stay friends with Dr Stirrup.

Cheered by this thought, I took out a sheet of my new headed notepaper and dispatched a letter to Susan Partridge.

19

Hilda Furze and I were friends from the start. She was a tall, angular woman in her late forties with veal-coloured features and a slit of a mouth which, instead of turning up at the corners when she smiled, stretched backwards, revealing the tips of her upper and lower dentures and giving her a sort of executioner's leer. But she was a good-hearted woman who patrolled endlessly up and down the hall like a tug-boat and took a genuine interest in all her charges.

'We've all been wondering about you,' she said that first week, popping her head round the door.

We, it transpired, were a man named Pike, who specialized in abortions, an ear, nose and throat specialist called Upjohn and an osteopath named Wyatt.

All of them, according to Miss Furze, were very nice and had been there for some time. Occasionally, at the end of the day, sinuses having been punctured, backs manipulated and unwanted foetuses removed, the three of them went out for a drink together before going their separate ways.

'Though I say it myself,' Miss Furze said, 'this is a happy house. And I hope you'll be happy here too.' She broke off, her lips pulled back. 'By the way, doctor, would you care for a cup of tea? I usually make one about this time of day for the others.'

'That's very kind of you,' I said. 'Thank you.'

While she busied herself in her small office at the end of the hall I sat back contentedly. This was the life. Tea in the morning. A smart office. Civilized hours. No more swaying about on the decks of a London bus. Thanks to Patel, my life had changed overnight. Now all I needed were some patients.

'Here we are, doctor.'

Hilda Furze came in with my tea. And at that moment, the telephone rang.

'Shall I?' she said.

'No,' I said. 'I'll take it.'

I lifted the receiver.

'Is that Dr Das?'

'Speaking.'

'This is Susan Partridge.'

My heart did a handspring.

'Well, hello,' I said.

'I got your note,' she said. 'I was wondering if I could make an appointment to see you?'

I was so excited I almost laughed.

'Of course,' I said. 'Just a moment while I consult my book.'

I saw the glimmer of a smile on Hilda Furze's face as she closed the door behind her. But it was an encouraging smile.

'What about four o'clock tomorrow?'

'Four o'clock would be fine. By the way, which end of the street are you?'

'Number 197. The top end.'

'Good,' she said. 'Then I can walk. See you at four, then.'

'Yes, indeed.'

I made a note in my diary, and then reached for my tea. Tomorrow at four. Tomorrow at four.

Quite apart from the fact that I was in love with Susan Partridge, I was delighted that she should be my first patient. It would give me a chance to spread my wings with someone who already trusted me. And, after all, what could she be coming to see me about? Nothing very important, surely?

Promptly at four, she arrived.

'Well,' she said, as Miss Furze ushered her in. 'This is all very impressive.'

'You like it?'

'It's very grand. What do your other patients think?'

'Most of them seem to like it,' I said. 'But we don't want to talk about my consulting-room. Sit down and tell me your problem. No aftereffects from the accident, I hope?'

'Oh, no; nothing like that.'

She perched herself on one of the chairs in front of my desk and crossed her legs. She was wearing a white dress and her blonde hair was spilling over her shoulders and she looked cool and attractive.

'Frankly, Dr Das, I've come to you because I feel I can talk to you without embarrassment.'

She smiled, a little uncertainly.

'Well, I certainly hope so, Miss Partridge.'

'The fact is I've met a man I like very much. His name is Basil Calder. We've become quite close during the past few weeks and I was wondering, well, what to do about it? Most of my friends are on the Pill, and I wanted your advice.'

I sat back, stunned. Oh, foulest of foul fortune. For weeks I had thought of no one but her. Now here she was, sitting in front of me, asking for help in order that some other swine could get at her. For a moment I was speechless. Didn't she know I loved her? Didn't she know she was driving nails in my heart — and using the cruellest of hammers to do it?

'Well, doctor?'

I drew a deep breath.

'I suppose you've thought about this quite carefully?'

'Of course. Why?'

'Because I, for one, am not in favour of the Pill. And many of my colleagues feel the same way. It can be extremely dangerous, particularly if there are circulatory problems.' (I knew I had that right; it came

94

straight out of *The Pill and You*.)

'You can't be serious?'

'Never more so,' I said.

'But everybody I know is on it. And none of them has had any trouble.'

'They won't have any trouble, as you put it, until one of them drops dead. It's happening all the time.'

She looked shaken.

'I've read of isolated cases, of course, but I thought the Pill had now been cleared. I'd no idea it was still considered a risk.'

'Few women have,' I said. 'The propaganda put out by the major drug-houses is disgraceful. We doctors are most concerned.'

'But what about your own country? They've been using the Pill there for years ...'

'They have. And women have been dying from it for years.'

'I'm shocked,' she said. 'Absolutely shocked. I can't tell you ...'

'It's the same with so many modern drugs,' I said, pressing home my advantage. 'They're just not given proper trials. The drug firms seem only interested in making money.'

She thought for a moment.

'Isn't there a weaker Pill I could take? One that isn't so dangerous? I seem to remember reading something.'

'There are several,' I said. 'And the maternity wards are full of women who've tried them.'

'This is incredible,' she said.

'I know,' I said. 'I just wish more people were aware of the dangers.'

'I hardly know what to tell Basil,' she said.

'Tell him the truth,' I said, shortly.

'He's, well, difficult to talk to about that sort of thing.'

'If he's a real man,' I said firmly, 'he'll understand.'

She gave a short laugh.

95

'Oh, he's a real man all right. Otherwise I wouldn't be sitting here.'

I groaned inwardly.

'Does he know you've come to see me?'

'It was his idea.'

'Well, I wish I could have been more encouraging,' I said.

'So do I. But at least now I know what the risks are.'

She hesitated, looking at me with those lovely eyes.

'If I ... if I decide to go ahead anyway, will you prescribe one for me?'

'Frankly,' I said. 'I'd rather not. I've explained my position to you. If you want to go ahead, you'd better consult another doctor.'

'Oh.'

'I'm sorry,' I said. 'But I regard you as a friend. And one doesn't willingly put a friend in danger.'

'I understand.'

She got up.

'Well, goodbye, doctor. Thank you.'

'I'm afraid I've depressed you?'

'That's all right.'

I closed the door behind her, my heart heavy. I hadn't bargained on anything like this. Sitting there at my desk, my head in my hands, I had a sudden mental picture of Susan, naked on her bed, smiling at her lover.

Oh, fiendish fate. Was there no solace?

Well, there was some. In my desk diary, alongside her name, I carefully wrote: £4.

20

At this point Lady Ammanford came into my life. I say that casually. I might just as easily have written: on

Friday Alexander Fleming looked out of the window and discovered penicillin, for the effect on my life was equally momentous.

The letter was lying on my desk when I walked into the consulting-room next morning, stuck in one corner of the blotting-pad.

'Dear Dr Das,' it read. 'I understand from my niece, Susan Partridge, that you are a physician of some skill. I wonder whether it would be convenient for you to call upon me on Thursday, at four o'clock?'

The notepaper was headed: Lady Ammanford, 97 Connaught Square, W.2.

I had never heard of her. But that was hardly important. The thing was, she had heard of me.

On Thursday, though I didn't know it, my life was about to change. ...

Lady Ammanford's house was so richly furnished, so magnificent in every way, than when I first walked in I was stunned. Never in my wildest fantasies had I imagined anyone living in such style.

There were paintings everywhere. And pieces of rare sculpture. And hundreds of books, all leather bound. And masses and masses of flowers.

As the butler ushered me into the drawing-room, a bulky woman in her early fifties rose to greet me.

'So you're Susan's doctor,' she said.

'That's right.'

She glanced at my brown sandals.

'What in God's name are those?' she asked abruptly.

'My sandals,' I said.

'Sandals,' she repeated. 'What are you wearing sandals for? Do you suffer from some curious ailment of the feet?'

'No,' I said. 'I wear them because they are comfortable.'

'But so is a smock, doctor, and that has yet to catch on in popular fashion.'

　　　　97

She stood there, frowning, as if unsure whether to invite me further into the room. Then, with a shrug, she settled herself on the blue velvet sofa, which was lined with coloured cushions.

'Now look here,' she said. 'Tell me straightaway whether you can help. I get these terrible headaches, you see. I have had them for years, and nobody seems able to cure them.

'I've tried everything. X-rays, sinuses punctured, teeth taken out, even the pressure of my eyeballs checked. It's got to be something, for God's sake, but nobody seems to know what. I haven't got a tumour on the brain, and I don't suffer from migraine, and it isn't my eyes or my ears. So what is it?'

I considered the question, assisted by *Newnes' Family Doctor*, pages 276-278. Syphilis? Surely not. She was a titled lady. Bright's disease, then? No, she hadn't got that, if the symptoms were anything to go by. Constipation, perhaps? It could be that. But dare I ask her?

'Well, doctor?'

'I shall, of course, do everything in my power to help you ...'

Perhaps *Stresses and Strains in Modern Society* held the clue? Page 114, the bit about the neck muscles going into spasm, with resultant pressure on the nerves. Aha! 'Can sometimes be relieved by manipulation of the neck, or traction ...'

But first, some questions. I must not forget that line from *Bedside Behaviour* — 'The good doctor asks lots of questions. He is a detective, searching for clues. And it reassures the patient ...'

'May I sit down?' I asked.

'Of course. I'm sorry.'

She indicated a chair.

'To get to the bottom of this,' I said, 'it will help if I ask you some questions. Some may seem irrelevant to you, but I assure you that they are not.'

'Go ahead,' she said, settling back on the sofa.

'Well, for a start, can you tell me something about your day?'

'Starting when?'

'First thing in the morning.'

'I ride in Hyde Park.'

'Every morning?'

'Yes. Unless it's pouring with rain.'

'That's interesting.'

She looked at me, questioningly.

'You think that may be significant?'

'It could be,' I said.

'Then I come back to the house and have breakfast.'

'What do you do after that?'

'I bathe.'

'Do you lie in the bath for long?'

'Yes. I love soaking. Especially after a hard ride.'

'So your head is bent forward for quite some time?'

'I suppose so. Could that have something to do with it?'

'Perhaps. Then what do you do?'

'I get dressed and start my day.'

'What do you do first?'

'I read the papers in my study, and then attend to correspondence.'

'Do you write a lot of letters?'

'Quite a few.'

'So you are hunched over a desk?'

'A writing table, actually.'

'But hunched?'

'Well, yes.'

'For how long?'

'That depends. Half an hour. Sometimes more.'

'Then what?'

'I see various people. My lawyer, my stockbroker, friends. You know ...'

She adjusted her position on the sofa. She seemed to be getting restless. Just a few more questions, I thought, and then I must come up with something clever.

'What do you usually do in the evenings?'

'I have dinner parties. Or go to a restaurant. Occasionally I go to the theatre. Sometimes I stay at home and watch television.'

'Large screen or small screen?'

'Large.'

'Where is the set?'

'In the bedroom.'

'At the foot of the bed?'

'Yes.'

'So you sit propped up in bed and watch it?'

'That's right.'

'Does it ever give you a headache?'

'Occasionally. Since I go to sleep soon afterwards, that doesn't bother me.'

'One last question,' I said. 'Is your bed hard or soft?'

'Soft,' she said. 'I love a soft bed.'

I sat back. I was rather impressed. The questions had sounded really professional. She wasn't to know they came straight out of *Your Patient and You.* The extraordinary thing was — they had given me the clue.

'I think you should try some traction,' I said.

'Traction?' She looked puzzled. 'How would traction help?'

'It can be most beneficial for some sorts of headache,' I said. 'It is my belief that the trouble is coming from your neck. The fact that you ride may be a factor. It does shake up the spine. That is not always a good thing.'

'No other doctor has ever suggested traction,' she said.

'Possibly not,' I said. 'If they were making money out of you, why should they wish you cured?'

'You can't be serious,' she said. 'That last man I went to is one of the most successful doctors in London. Klein. I'm sure you've heard of him. He has hundreds of patients. You can't get to see him in under a week. He doesn't need me.'

I smiled.

'That's where you're wrong, dear lady. He needs you very much. And others like you.'

'But the same, surely, could be said of you?'

I had led up to this. I didn't know if it would work, but if it did I was home and dry.

'Believe me,' I said. 'It is of small importance to me whether you consult me again. My honest belief is that there is nothing wrong with you that some traction and massage would not put right — and frankly that could be done by any competent physiotherapist.'

She gazed at me, eyes wide.

'I'll say one thing for you,' she said. 'You're the first honest doctor I've met.'

'Lady Ammanford,' I said. 'It isn't a question of honesty; it's a question of ethics. I don't like to see people being taken advantage of, particularly when they are in pain.' I paused. 'Let's be frank. A great deal of medicine is simply a confidence trick. The bottle of red stuff the patient takes home from the chemist is often valueless, containing a little iron, perhaps, but nothing more. Yet the patient drinks it willingly, because he believes it will do him good. And, because he believes it, nine times out of ten it works. The power of suggestion is quite extraordinary. I don't know whether you are aware of it but, until a generation or so ago, it was the custom in China for the patient to swallow the doctor's prescription. And if that isn't an intriguing form of cure by suggestion, I don't know what is.'

She laughed aloud.

'Is that what they did?' she asked. 'How marvellous.'

'What's more,' I said, continuing to quote from *Quacks through the Ages*, 'quite often it worked.'

She sat forward.

'This traction,' she said. 'Where would I have it?'

'In my consulting-room,' I said. 'I have a special traction couch.'

She looked disappointed.

101

'There's nothing you can do here?'

'Not really,' I said, looking round. 'Though I might be able to afford you some small relief. Do you have a headache now?'

'Yes. A bad one.'

What had the book said? 'Can sometimes be relieved by manipulation of the neck ...' Right. I'd have a go.

'You'll have to lie flat somewhere.'

She gestured to the sofa on which she was sitting.

'What about this?'

'That will do.'

She lay flat and I kicked off my sandals and crouched behind her on the arm of the sofa, my feet on her shoulders.

'Now don't alarm yourself,' I said. 'You are perfectly safe.'

Cupping her chin in my left hand and holding the back of her neck with my right, I pulled hard.

There was a sudden, audible click.

'Christ Almighty,' she shrieked, twisting out of my grip. She staggered to her feet, moving her neck from side to side and moaning.

'Oh, my God,' she screamed. 'Oh my good God.'

'Dear lady ...'

'Don't you dear lady me,' she choked, holding her head between her hands.

'I only meant ...'

'Get out,' she shouted. 'GET OUT.'

I picked up my sandals and bag and stumbled towards the door. There, towering above me, stood the butler.

'Simons,' she cried. 'Show this — person — to the door.'

'At once, modom.'

With a deft move he stood aside, allowing me to pass. Then, interlocking his steps with mine, he stalked beside me down the stairs.

As we reached the front door his arm reached out to

release the catch. And there I was in the street, like some drunk evicted from a saloon.

I hopped about for a moment, putting on my sandals, watched by some curious passers-by. Then there was a loud crash, and the door to 97 Connaught Square slammed behind me.

21

I got drunk that night. Almost before it had started, my medical career was over. I had taken a foolish gamble, and I had lost. Not only that, but I had squandered £500 of Patel's money, which I was honour bound to repay.

As the demon drink took hold, I cursed myself for my folly. I could so easily have suggested some pain-killer and left it at that. No harm would have been done. But no. I had tugged at the bitch's neck. And now I was in dead trouble. Damn *Stresses and Strains in Modern Society*. I had a good mind to sue the author.

With every drink I saw Lady Ammanford's face, swimming grotesquely before me. By this time she would have been on to the B.M.A., India House and the police. Very soon they would come to get me.

'Pull on a titled lady's neck, would you?' they'd say, kneeing me in the groin. 'You filthy little rat.'

Then they'd check on my papers and discover I was an illegal immigrant and that would be that. I'd spend my best years in prison, or be deported.

It was hard to decide which would be worse. Deportation, probably. For back in India my father was waiting.

Patel kept trying to cheer me up.

'You're making too much of it,' he said. 'So she's mad at you. All right. But she's hardly likely to hunt you down just for pulling too hard on her neck. You couldn't have done her any injury. It doesn't make sense to worry like this.'

'You don't know her.' I said, morosely. 'She's just the kind to hunt me down for pulling too hard on her neck. And there's another thing. She's Susan's aunt. It's the end of that.'

'The end of what?' Patel snapped. 'The end of making a fool of yourself over a girl who only wants your help in getting laid. Good riddance, I'd say.'

It was all right for him. of course. He wasn't in love. His only worry was making sure that people adjusted their dress before leaving. Me; my whole career in Harley Street was down the drain before it had even begun.

'I'm doomed,' I said, my eyes misting.

'You're drunk,' Patel said, glancing at his watch. 'Come on. I'll take you home. I'm due in the hag's room in fifteen minutes.'

Next day I awoke with a splitting headache. I felt sick and ill and awful. Worse, I felt afraid.

A moment later there was a knock on the door and Patel came in, bearing a glass of brown liquid.

'I thought you might need this,' he said. 'You were really crocked last night.'

'What is it?'

'Fernet Branca.'

'What does it do?'

'It makes it possible for you to face your execution with a grim smile on your face,' he said. 'It tastes so awful that, by comparison, even death seems attractive.'

'Please don't make jokes,' I moaned.

I drank the fearful-looking mixture and staggered to my feet.

'What should I do?' I asked. 'Stay here and wait for

them, or go and wait in Harley Street?'

'You should go to Harley Street as if nothing had happened,' Patel said. 'Anyway, I am sure that nothing *has* happened.' He gave me a critical look. 'Really; if you're going to get in this state every time you have trouble with a patient, I don't see much of a future for you in medicine.'

'Neither do I,' I mumbled.

When I got to Harley Street, Hilda Furze was just coming out of her room.

'Good morning, doctor,' she said cheerfully. 'There's a message for you. Lady Ammanford rang' — I winced — 'and said she wants to see you at noon.'

I groaned.

'I'll bring you a cup of tea right away,' she said. 'You look as if you could do with it.'

I went into my beautiful room — the room I had entered a week ago so full of optimism and hope — and slumped behind my desk.

There was the dreaded message, tucked into one corner of the blotting pad: 'Lady Ammanford. 12 p.m.'

The police would be there, of course, huge, burly men, smiling as they dragged me away.

'Attempted strangulation ... Phoney doctor arrested ... The Beast and I, by Lady Ammanford.'

Ganesa, help me.

I walked twice around the square before plucking up sufficient courage to ring the bell. The house seemed even more imposing than it had the day before; a citadel of Anglo-Saxon security against filthy foreigners intent on pulling off women's heads.

When the door opened, I automatically looked up, expecting to see the butler. But it was not Simons who stood there; it was Lady Ammanford herself.

So keyed up was I, so nervous, that I stepped back, expecting her to strike me.

Instead she gave me a wide smile.

'It's fantastic,' she said. 'I can't believe it. My headache has gone. And it's all due to you.'

Beaming, she pulled me into the hall.

'Doctor,' she said. 'I owe you an apology. Nothing, nothing can excuse what I said to you yesterday. But I didn't know, my dear man, I just didn't know what magic lay in your wonderful hands.'

Taking me by the arm, she led me up to the drawing-room, where a large fire was blazing.

'Should you refuse to treat me further after my behaviour yesterday, you would be quite within your rights,' she said. 'But I beg you — I beg you — not to do this. I have had headaches of various kinds for the past ten years. You are the first person who has ever been able to help. And with just one touch.' She moved her head from side to side. 'It's fantastic. I can't get over it.'

Overwhelmed by my unexpected reprieve from the firing squad I stood there, saying nothing.

Her faced clouded.

'You're still angry,' she said.

I shook my head.

'No. Really.'

'Yes you are,' she said. 'I can see it in your face. You think I'm a rude and stupid woman. And you're quite right.'

'Your reaction was understandable,' I said.

'It was hysterical,' she said. 'However, I am in a position to make amends, should you decide to forgive me. I understand from my niece that you have only recently set up in practice. Well, I have a large and varied collection of friends and I shall tell them all about you.'

She went over to the sideboard.

'Please,' she said. 'Won't you join me in a sherry?'

I hesitated.

'Please,' she repeated.

'Very well. Just a small one.'

She handed me a glass.

'Now,' she said. 'When may I see you again? I am entirely at your disposal.'

'If your headache is cured,' I said. 'Of what further service can I be?'

She gazed at me, admiringly.

'Oh, you dear, dear man,' she said. 'Your honesty and integrity overwhelm me. They really do.'

I finished my sherry.

'I just don't want you to waste your money,' I said.

'You are not only a great doctor,' she said. 'You are a modest and most dear person.'

I bowed my head.

'I shall telephone you next week for another appointment,' she said. 'If we are to keep my headache at bay, it seems to me prudent to keep the treatment going.'

'As you wish.'

She walked with me to the door.

'And am I forgiven for being an idiotic woman who didn't recognize brilliance when she saw it?'

'Of course.'

She flung open the door.

'Do you know what I am going to do now?' she said.

'I have no idea, dear lady.'

'I am going to get on the telephone and tell everyone I know about you ...'

Outside, in the square, I stood for a moment on the pavement, feeling light-headed. I had not pulled off her head. On the contrary, I had cured her headache. And now she thought I was wonderful. Now she was going to tell her friends about me, and make me rich and famous.

I walked back to Harley Street, my mind racing. On the way I stopped and bought myself a pair of shoes.

22

Thus began my career in Harley Street. Lady Amman-ford kept her promise. Within a week I had three new patients; all of them friends of hers and all of them, judging by their clothes and appearances, well-to-do women.

Frances Cookson, Norma Blair and Joan Rainsford were all in their sixties and all equally shrivelled-up and wrinkled. But though I groaned inwardly as I fingered their withered limbs and chicken-skin necks — where, oh where, were the honey-skinned lovelies of my fantasies? — I did not despair. For they were Rung Two of the ladder and better things, I felt sure, were just around the corner.

Fortunately, there was nothing really wrong with any of them. Norma Blair suffered from tension headaches, which massage did much to alleviate. Frances Cookson had a cold, for which I gave her Beechams Powders in tablet form — having previously taken the precaution of emptying the tablets into an unlabelled bottle and advising her 'They're the latest thing, dear lady, direct from the laboratory'. And Joan Rainsford, as far as I could make out, came along simply to see what I looked like.

I was happy to see them all, for I knew, if they liked me, they would recommend me to their friends. And I was pleased to take their money, for I was anxious to start repaying Patel.

On Friday, when I came to add up the fees I had earned that week, they came to only twenty-four pounds — rather less than I would have made as a bus-conductor. But I was not dismayed. After all, I had been in practice just over a week and already I had seen five patients — one of them twice. Not bad for a beginner.

Buoyed up by this thought, I opened a bank account in Regent Street. And treated myself to a white enamel cabinet I had seen in a medical store in Wigmore Street.

And, as the weekend approached, and I sat behind my desk reading *Drennen's Guide to Mental Disorders* something rather curious happened.

I began to feel I really was a doctor.

23

Norma Blair was London's most influential hostess. She was also, according to Lady Ammanford, one of its most accomplished gossips. And it was not long before I found this to be true.

Fortunately I liked her. She was a tall, gangling woman married to a man high up in the Foreign Office, Jocelyn Blair, who, judging from the anecdotes she passed on about the Queen's Ministers, was just as indiscreet as his wife.

While I massaged away at her neck, she regaled me with stories.

'Frances Cookson,' she said, the first morning I saw her, 'she's still at it, you know. Can you believe it? Sixty-five if she's a day and still playing kneesy under the table with her male dinner-guests. She doesn't get any from her husband, of course, but I've got my suspicions about that young chauffeur of hers. Always yawning, I've noticed. I'm sure he doesn't get that tired just driving her around. . . .'

On her next visit she said:

'Of course you realize Joan Rainsford's had her face done? You can always tell, can't you? Three hundred it cost her, and in my opinion she should have asked for her money back. She can't smile now, the poor dear. The fool took up so much slack that even the glimmer of a smile pulls her ears down half an inch. . . .'

It was from her that I learned about Lady Amman-ford's husband, Sir George. He had lost a leg in the last war, apparently, and been invalided out. By some shrewd property deals, both during and after the war, he had made a great deal of money, some of which he had donated to the Conservative Party, thereby ensur-ing himself a knighthood. Once he had got it, he retired. Lady Ammanford, born Grace Partridge, daughter of a millionaire Midlands industrialist, soon tired of having him hanging about the house and urged him to take up an outside interest.

'So he took up funerals,' Norma Blair said.

'Funerals?' I echoed, stopping work for a moment.

'That's right,' she said. 'He started going to funerals.'

'But whose? Friends of his?'

'Good heavens, no. Celebrities. Whenever somebody died, George was there. He read obituaries the way most men read the financial index. "There's a good one on Thursday," he'd say to Grace. "Don't wait dinner for me, dear." He liked to make a day of it, you see.

'He even went to America once. That was for some film star's funeral. First-class fare, of course, and three days at an hotel in Beverly Hills. He didn't stint, I'll say that for him. Of course, there weren't many like that. A lot of them were just up the road at Golders Green.'

'But why did he go? Did anyone ever ask him?'

'I asked him many times. But I never got a sensible answer. He wasn't quite normal, I think. Joan Rains-ford always maintained that he was round the bend. And she may have been right. It isn't normal, is it, to

110

enjoy funerals? But he did. He even took coloured photographs of the ceremony, and had them mounted in albums. Once at dinner, when we were talking about a famous author, George said: "I've got the most marvellous snap of his wife weeping at his funeral. I always meant to send it to her, but somehow I forgot."'

She burst out laughing.

'How about that to make your dinner-party go with a swing?'

'Does he still attend funerals?'

'I really wouldn't know,' she said. 'He took off, as perhaps you've heard, some years ago. I don't even know where he is now. But I don't think Grace misses him too much. She seems to occupy her time fairly well, wouldn't you say?'

'I don't know her that well,' I said.

'All you need to know about Grace Ammanford,' she said, 'is that she's fifty-six years old and still N.S.I.T.'

'I'm afraid I don't understand.'

'N.S.I.T.,' she repeated. 'Not Safe in Taxis. When we were all debutantes together that's what they used to write after certain men's names.'

She sighed: 'Still, why not? Better than taking cold showers. Nobody ever thinks about the plight of the older women. Old men can be as randy as they like, but we're supposed to sit at home with shawls around our shoulders awaiting telephone calls from our nephews. The hell with that.'

I finished the massage and she got off the couch and turned her neck from side to side.

'Much better,' she said. 'Grace was right. You're very good. Now, when do you want to see me next?'

'Next week, sometime?'

'Next week it is. I'll give you a call. Meantime, what about coming to dinner? What are you doing on Friday evening?'

'I'm not quite sure,' I said. 'I may have to see a patient.'

111

'Well, if you're free, do come. Jocelyn won't be there — he's got some damn silly Foreign Office function that night — but some interesting people are coming. It could be amusing.'

'May I let you know?' I said.

'Of course.'

24

I felt distinctly apprehensive about accepting Norma Blair's dinner invitation, but Patel insisted that I should go.

'You must,' he said. 'You'll meet some important people. It's a great chance to drum up new trade.'

'But what if one of them sees through me?' I said.

He paused in the middle of opening a tin of beans for our tea.

'Now listen to me,' he said, firmly. 'You've got to stop all this nonsense. You're a doctor. You have a consulting-room in Harley Street to prove it. And some well-to-do patients on your books. So act like a doctor. If you're going to lurk about like an escaped convict expecting arrest at any moment you're never going to get anywhere.' He finished opening the tin. 'Anyway,' he said, 'give me one good reason, why you should be found out?'

'Someone may ask me a medical question and I won't know the answer.'

He cascaded the beans into a pan and lit the gas.

'Listen,' he said. 'Since we decided to go ahead with this caper you must have read close to a hundred medical books and memorized every one of them. If somebody asks you a question the chances are you will know the answer. But they won't, don't you see? It simply isn't done to ask a doctor questions when he's out to dinner. The British pride themselves on that sort of thing. They're very strong on etiquette.'

'I hope you're right,' I said.

'I know I'm right,' he said. 'I haven't been wrong yet, have I? You've been in Harley Street two weeks and nobody's tumbled you.'

'I'm expecting it at any moment,' I said.

'Oh for heaven's sake! If you go on like that somebody *will* start asking questions. Remember, the first thing a burglar learns is to walk through a hotel foyer as though he's a guest in the place. Act like that in Harley Street and you're in for a distinguished career.'

He stirred the beans.

'How many people have you seen so far?'

'Five,' I said. 'Susan Partridge, Lady Ammanford, and three of her friends.'

'And not even a dose of clap between them,' Patel chuckled. 'It's enough to destroy one's faith in the medical profession.'

25

It poured with rain on the night of Norma Blair's dinner-party, bucketing down from a slate-coloured sky. There should be a Government issue of umbrellas, I thought, as I waited for the bus; in England it never stops raining.

I arrived at Chester Square soaked to the skin, and the maid who ushered me into the warm, centrally-heated drawing-room did so with marked distaste.

'You poor dear man,' Norma Blair said. 'Whatever happened?'

'I couldn't find a taxi,' I lied.

'You should have telephoned,' she said. 'I'd have arranged to have you picked up. Anyway, come by the fire. You'll soon dry out.'

While I stood steaming in the splendid drawing-room, which was crammed with expensive paintings and *objets d'art*, I was introduced to my fellow guests; a tall, lean American script-writer named Jerry Margold; a parrot-faced woman named Nancy Harwood, who kept saying: 'Well, for heaven's sake'; a rather pretty girl named Angela Fulton, who owned a boutique in Chelsea, and a newspaper writer named Marc Stevens, who seemed to be very well informed about almost everything.

We ate lumpy, indigestible food washed down with great quantities of red wine, and everybody talked non-stop. Except me. I kept trying to think of devastating remarks to make, things that would have them falling about, but for some reason my mind refused to function. So I sat there, feeling damp and uncomfortable, and listening to the others talking.

'There simply isn't a decent hotel left anywhere,' Norma Blair was saying. 'It doesn't matter how much you pay; the whole concept of good service seems to have gone down the drain.'

'Oh I don't know,' Angela Fulton said. 'The Connaught's pretty good. ...'

'And the Palace at Burgenstock,' Marc Stevens said. 'They've kept up a high standard.'

'I have a friend,' Jerry Margold said, 'who learned the trick of getting good service. He has visiting cards printed with his name on them and, underneath, Executive Editor, Holiday Magazine. Every time he checks into a hotel he gives the card to the receptionist. It never fails. He gets the best room and the best attention.'

'Well for heaven's sake,' Nancy Harwood said.

'There seem to be fewer and fewer advantages to

being wealthy,' Stevens said. 'Once upon a time, if you had money, you could do things that nobody else could contemplate — travel to exotic places, stay at splendid hotels. Now with package tours, everybody can go everywhere. There are no advantages left. Even if you're wealthy, you can't go to a better restaurant than people with less money than yourself. It's a bit of a swindle.'

'Still,' Margold said, with a chuckle, 'I doubt if there's anyone sitting at this table who wouldn't rather be rich than poor. Including our Indian friend here.'

'I'm sure our Indian friend is rich already,' Norma Blair said. 'All Harley Street doctors are rich.'

'Is that true?' Margold asked.

'Absolutely not,' I said, embarrassed by the sudden attention.

'What was your intention when you started out?' he asked. 'To make your name in medicine, or to make a lot of money?'

'That's a silly question,' Angela said. 'It takes years to qualify as a doctor. You wouldn't do it unless you cared about medicine.'

'How long does it take?' Norma Blair asked. 'I never remember.'

She looked at me, inquiringly.

'Much too long,' I said, uneasily aware that I didn't know.

Margold poured himself more wine.

'There's a chap in New York who discovered a short cut,' he said. 'Did you read about it? He practised as a surgeon in American hospitals for twenty years before they found out he had no medical qualifications whatsoever. He was a carpenter by trade.'

I reached for my glass.

'I don't believe it,' Norma Blair said.

'I promise you it's true,' Margold said. 'It was in all the papers.'

'But how could it happen?'

'Oh listen,' Stevens cut in. 'It happened here too. I

read about it. A Pakistani got a job as a Casualty Officer in a hospital in Fulham. He had no medical experience at all. But it was a year before they nabbed him.'

'Well, for heaven's sake,' Nancy Harwood said.

I sipped my wine, praying the conversation would take a different turn. It didn't.

'But isn't there some kind of check?' Norma Blair said, turning to me. 'How can people like that slip through . . .?'

'It's no good asking this nice man,' Angela cut in. 'That's like asking an airline pilot how it's possible for someone with no experience at all to steal a 'plane and fly it. But it's been done.'

'That's true enough,' Margold said.

'Well it's all very unnerving,' Norma Blair said. 'What if you died?'

'They'd bury you,' Margold said. 'And nobody would be any the wiser.'

'If you're buried you can always be dug up,' Stevens said. 'Most doctors who've made a mistake encourage cremation.'

'Oh, you are terrible,' Norma Blair said. 'I'm sure Dr Das doesn't think any of this funny.'

'Please,' I said. 'It doesn't worry me at all.'

'Anyway, I think we've exhausted that subject,' Norma Blair said. 'Who'd like a brandy?'

There was a chorus of assent.

'I've got a good subject for discussion,' Margold said. 'What do we consider to be the second greatest sensation?'

'The second?' Stevens said. 'I'm not even sure we'd agree about the first.'

He looked around the table. Angela Fulton giggled. Nancy Harwood looked faintly embarrassed. Norma Blair narrowed her eyes. 'Oh, well,' he said. 'Perhaps we would.'

'In my view,' Margold said, 'the second greatest sensation is fighting a bull.'

'Who the hell has ever fought a bull?' Stevens demanded.

'I have,' Margold said.

'Well, for heaven's sake,' Nancy Harwood said.

'I have a friend down in Mexico who rears fighting bulls,' Margold said. 'He let me try my skill with one of the young ones. Talk about scary; it looked as big as a house when it charged. But what a feeling afterwards.'

He turned to Marc Stevens.

'Now how about you?'

'Mine sounds tame compared with yours,' Stevens said.

'What is it?'

'Going across red lights late at night at high speed.'

'What do you mean — tame?' Margold said. 'Sounds goddam dangerous to me. I think I'd rather fight a bull.'

'I've worked it out,' Stevens said. 'You've got a 90 per cent chance of not hitting anything if you're travelling fast enough. I don't do it often, of course, but it's quite a thrill.'

Both men turned to me.

'What about you, doc?' Margold said. 'What do you consider to be the second greatest sensation?'

I decided on a little oneupmanship. I had recently come across an article on Graham Greene, and been fascinated to read of his suicide attempts as a boy.

'You really want to know?' I said quietly.

'Of course,' Margold said.

'Then I'll tell you. Playing Russian Roulette.'

Suddenly I had everyone's attention.

'You've played it?'

'Where ...?'

'How ...?'

'Why?'

'Over a girl,' I said quietly.

'What? You and another man?'

'That's right.'

117

Margold looked at me, his eyes wide.

'You mean you and this other man put a bullet in a revolver and spun the chamber?'

'Two bullets,' I said.

'My God,' Stevens said.

'What happened?' Margold asked.

I decided I might as well go the whole way.

'He was killed,' I said.

'Oh no,' Norma Blair said. 'That's terrible.'

'It was upsetting,' I said.

'He blew his head off? In front of you?' Stevens asked, astonished.

'I'm afraid so.'

'Where was this? In India?'

'Yes. He was a medical student with me at Calcutta University. We fell in love with the same nurse.' I was beginning to enjoy myself. They were all staring at me.

'So you won her?' Margold said.

'No. I didn't.'

'Why not?'

'She was so upset over what had happened that she got a transfer to Delhi.'

'So you went through all that for nothing?'

'Not for nothing,' I said quietly. 'I wouldn't have missed the experience for anything. You know what they say — without danger, life has little meaning.'

'Well for heaven's sake,' Nancy Harwood said.

Marc Stevens gave a short laugh.

'Well, one thing is sure,' he said. 'Nobody is going to cap *that* story.'

'No way,' Jerry Margold added.

And no-one did. The curtain calls were all mine. And when I left the Blair house later that night it was on a cloud of good will, handshakes, promises to call and telephone numbers. I had arrived a wet and bedraggled runt; when I left I was a Person of Consequence.

26

I did not, as it happened, gain any new patients from the Blair dinner-party. What I did gain was confidence.

From that evening on my whole attitude changed. Patel remarked upon it. 'You've stopped looking furtive,' he said. And I had. It was as if, until that moment, I had been merely rehearsing the role; now, at last, I was playing it.

My patients seemed to sense this too. They began recommending me to their friends in ever-increasing numbers. Soon I was treating half a dozen people a day. I even began getting men. Among them an M.P. named Toby Downs who — according to Norma Blair, who sent him — was very important indeed.

'I've got a bad back,' he said, when he walked into my consulting-room. 'Tell me right away if there's nothing you can do for me. I've been to dozens of osteopaths and doctors and they've all been a waste of time. But Norma says you're first-rate, so I thought I'd give you a try.'

'Let's take a look,' I said.

I examined his back. Even to my untutored eye it was obvious that the muscles of the lower lumbar region were very tense. Fortunately, I knew quite a lot about the lower lumbar region. I had 'recently memorized *Afflictions of the Spine* page by page.

'There's a great deal of spasm there,' I said.

'Don't I know it,' he said.

'We'll try some traction,' I said. 'If that doesn't help nothing will.'

It was the first time I had used the traction couch, and I was rather nervous. I tightened the straps very carefully, and switched the motor on low.

'Tell me immediately if it hurts,' I said.

'Don't worry,' he said. 'I will.'

I kept him on the couch for fifteen minutes and then gave him some gentle massage.

When it was over he stood up and felt his back with his hands.

'Do you know,' he said. 'I do believe that's helped.'

'I hope so,' I said. 'But you'd better see me again, anyway. Perhaps you'll make another appointment with my secretary.'

Next morning he telephoned.

'I won't be keeping that second appointment,' he said, brusquely.

'I'm sorry to hear that,' I said. 'Is there any particular reason?'

'Indeed there is,' he said. 'For the first time in years I got out of bed this morning without a backache. What do you think of that?'

'I think that's very good news,' I said, relieved.

'You're a good man,' he said, and hung up.

Buoyed up with this news, I rose to greet another new patient.

Her name was Jo Masters, and she worked at the same model agency as Susan Partridge. She was not as beautiful as Susan, but she was quite striking, with tawny hair and blue eyes.

'So you're Susan's friend,' she said, walking into the consulting-room.

'Right first time,' I said, jocularly.

'She says you helped her aunt?'

'I had some success there,' I said.

'You'll need to try hard with me,' she said. 'I had a fall while riding a couple of weeks ago. My back's murder.'

I smiled encouragingly.

'If you'll just remove your blouse,' I said. 'We'll take a look.'

She didn't step behind the screen, as I expected. She unbuttoned her blouse in front of me and then unhooked her brassière. And there she stood, her breasts jutting proudly. I stared. It was difficult not to. After all, they were only the third pair of breasts I had ever seen, and Norah Plumb's hardly counted, since they had never been glimpsed in the full light.

'I'm only going to examine your back,' I said.

'I know that,' she said. 'But you can do it better if there isn't a bra strap in the way. That's what my last doctor said, anyway.'

I walked behind her and ran my fingers down her spine. As I did so an electric shock seemed to go right through me. I felt small pulses beginning to throb.

'Mmmh,' I said.

'What does that mean? Mmmmh?'

'It means I'm thinking,' I said.

'A thinking doctor,' she said. 'Wild.'

'You don't think much of doctors, then?'

'I don't think anything of doctors,' she said pointedly.

I faced her again, keeping my eyes away from her breasts.

'I'm going to try some traction,' I said. 'I think it may help you.'

She looked me up and down slowly, a half-smile on her face.

'That's what I need,' she said. 'Help.'

'If you'll just lie down on that,' I said, indicating the couch.

She clambered on to it, and I strapped her down.

'Comfortable?' I asked.

'You've got to be kidding,' she said. 'When I'm flat on my back I prefer something softer.'

I tightened the straps and switched on the motor, strength two. Then, unable to stand the sight of her pink-tipped breasts swaying to the rhythm of the couch, I went out and had a cup of tea with Hilda Furze in her room.

Fifteen minutes later, when I released her, Jo Masters was smiling dreamily.

'Hey,' she said. 'That was great.'

'Do you think it did you any good?'

She swung her legs off the couch.

'I think it did me a whole lot of good,' she said.

By the end of the month I was able to repay Patel £50.

'This is wonderful,' he said. 'We must go out and celebrate.'

'All right,' I said. 'Just so long as it's not the Number Four.'

'No,' he agreed. 'Not the Number Four. We must go some place befitting your new status.'

He thought for a moment.

'What about the New Bombay?' he asked.

'All right,' I said. 'The New Bombay it is.'

He put his hand on my arm.

'I'm so happy for you, my boy.'

I was happy for myself. Everything was going splendidly. Indeed, there was only one cloud on the horizon. Since that first week in Harley Street I had not seen Susan Partridge again.

27

At the start of my second month in Harley Street, a note arrived from Lady Ammanford. 'I am taking some friends to the New Theatre this Thursday evening,' it read. 'I wonder if you would care to join us? If you are free, shall we say the theatre, ten minutes before curtain-time?'

It was a command, really. Not that I minded. It would be a new experience. For I had never been to a theatre in my life.

On the night in question, I arrived fifteen minutes before the play was to begin, and anxiously searched the crowd in the foyer for signs of my party. They were not there. And as the minutes ticked by, and ushers began shepherding people to their seats, I began to grow anxious. Had I made a mistake about the date? No. She had definitely said Thursday.

'Curtain's up in half a minute,' the commissionaire said, severely.

'I'm waiting for my friends,' I said.

'They're late,' he said helpfully.

'I know,' I said.

Then they arrived. Tumbling out of a taxi. Laughing and smiling. It was abundantly clear that they had been together somewhere, probably having drinks — perhaps even food — and the realization that I had been excluded from this made me feel instantly ill at ease.

'My dear doctor,' Lady Ammanford said. 'I am so sorry we're late. It's all Tony Melbourne's fault. He would insist on showing us his new house.' She half turned. 'Tony, dear, this is the doctor I have been telling you about. Tony Melbourne — Dr Das.'

A slim, handsome young man held out his hand.

'I hope you weren't worried,' Lady Ammanford said.

'I was concerned in case I had the wrong night,' I said. 'Or that we lost our seats.'

She smiled.

'You should have gone straight to the box.' She turned. 'What are the others doing, I wonder.'

I looked beyond her to the man who had just paid the taxi. He was walking in, his arm round a blonde girl. And, seeing them, my heart sank. For the girl was Susan Partridge.

'Well, hello,' she said. 'I didn't know you'd be here. How marvellous. My aunt never tells me anything.' She smiled at me in that same way which had first stolen my heart. 'Oh, I'm sorry. You don't know Basil, do you? Basil Calder — Dr Das.'

'Hello, Dr. Das.'

Six feet one and ruggedly handsome, her escort looked down at me with a mixture of amusement and condescension.

So this was Basil, heir by birth and breeding to Susan's treasured tuck-box? Dressed so immaculately that, just by standing there, he managed to make me feel shabby and second-rate.

'Susan says you're quite a doctor,' he said, with a chuckle. 'Next time I have the sniffles I must look you up.'

I forced my stiff features into some semblance of a smile.

'Please do,' I said.

'Well,' Lady Ammanford said. 'Shall we go up?'

She took my arm and, followed by Tony Melbourne and the others, we trooped up to the box.

I had hoped I might get to sit next to Susan, but that was not to be. In the general confusion of moving chairs around — to a chorus of Ssh's from the audience — I found myself sitting at the stage end of the box alongside Lady Ammanford. And every time I turned to catch Susan's eye, to show her that I had a grasp of what was happening on the stage, she seemed to be conversing with the beast Basil.

At the first interval, while the others went to the bar, Lady Ammanford ordered coffee for us in the box.

'I do hope you are enjoying it, doctor?'

'Indeed,' I said. 'Indeed.'

'Not one of his best, perhaps, but an interesting idea.'

'What do the others think?' I asked.

She shrugged.

'Who knows? Tony Melbourne likes anything, as far as I can make out. And Susan and Basil are so wrapped up in each other they're hardly discriminating.'

'Oh really,' I said, turning to cold putty.

'He's an awfully nice young man,' Lady Ammanford continued. 'Absolutely charming. I'm so happy for Susan. She needs someone like that. It's so easy for a girl to get mixed up with the wrong type these days.'

Indeed, I thought. Filthy-fingered foreigners, for instance. At all costs they must be held at bay. And Basil was the man to do it.

I sat there for what seemed an eternity, while Lady Ammanford recounted his virtues. Was there anything the bastard had not done since leaving Cambridge and the Guards? He had sailed round the world in a small boat, single-handed. He was one of a party that had climbed some mountain, hitherto believed to be unclimbable. He had been twice runner-up in the Monte Carlo Rally. He had broken the record for the Cresta Run. The list seemed endless.

Morale was rock bottom by the time the others returned from the bar, flushed with champagne. What an attractive group they looked. People in the stalls were staring up at us, recognizing Susan, no doubt, from her pictures in the magazines.

'Seen enjoying a joke at the theatre last night are Lady Ammanford, her niece Susan Partridge, Mr Basil Calder and Mr Tony Melbourne. With them is an unidentified man. . . .'

Then Susan flashed me another of her lovely smiles, and my dejection lifted.

'By the way,' she said, 'I forgot to tell you. Jo Masters was terribly impressed with you. When I saw her she was raving about the treatment you'd given her.'

'I'm glad she was pleased,' I said.

'What's this?' Lady Ammanford said. 'I thought I was the doctor's Number One champion?'

Susan leaned across and kissed her aunt on the cheek.

'Wrong darling. I was rooting for him long before you came into the picture. Remember, he's the man who saved my life.' She sighed. 'And when I think of that dreadful Dr Klein we used to go to — ' She broke off. 'Oh, aren't I awful, saying things like that about one of your colleagues?'

I was about to urge her to continue when the house lights dimmed and we were into the last act of the play.

I never did get the true gist of the plot but I joined in the general enthusiasm and applause when the curtain fell.

Then, once outside the theatre, gloom engulfed me again.

'Now, doctor,' Lady Ammanford said, 'Susan and the others are going on to join some friends at Tramp's. I am too old for that sort of thing, quite frankly, so I suggest you and I have a nice quiet dinner somewhere.'

I tried hard to disguise my disappointment. Tramp's, whatever that was, sounded gay and exciting. Dinner with Lady Ammanford did not. But I could scarcely protest.

We said goodbye to the others and took a taxi to a small restaurant just off the Edgware Road, where Lady Ammanford was evidently known. They made a great deal of fuss of her, and there was much discussion about the best table. Only when the menus were produced was I consulted.

'A drink before dinner, sir?'

I shook my head.

'Most certainly we will have a drink before dinner,' Lady Ammanford said. 'I shall have a whisky sour. What about you?'

'Nothing for me, dear lady.'

'I insist. This is our first dinner together. Two whisky sours,' she said, turning to the waiter.

It was my first visit to a proper London restaurant

126

and I was desperately ill at ease. For one thing, every dish seemed to be in some foreign language; for another, a glance at the prices convinced me that I was in for an expensive evening. I might have been a guest at the theatre, but I could hardly expect Lady Ammanford to pay for the dinner too. I hoped I had enough money to cover it.

'Now,' she said, poring over the menu with the concentration of an archaeologist reading the inscriptions on some Egyptian tomb, 'have you decided what to eat?'

'It all looks so tempting,' I said, wishing she would make up her mind so that I could choose the same dish.

'I am of two minds,' she said. 'They do a quite splendid Filet de Boeuf en croute truffe here; on the other hand, their Chateaubriand grille with bearnaise sauce is also excellent.' She turned to me. 'Decide for me. Which shall it be?'

Anxiously I scanned the menu, trying to pinpoint the dishes she had mentioned. Defeated, I decided to brazen it out.

'Actually I am not in the mood for either of those. I think I will try the fish.'

'Fish,' she echoed enthusiastically — I might have been proposing some rare and succulent dish, unobtainable elsewhere. 'What a perfectly splendid idea! Just right for this time of night.'

She looked up at the head waiter, who was hovering deferentially.

'We will both have the Filet de Sole Marquise,' she said. 'That's the one that's poached, isn't it, with tomatoes and mushrooms?'

'Quite right, my lady. May I suggest some creamed potatoes with it?'

'You may suggest it,' Lady Ammanford said. 'But I shall ignore you.'

'As you wish, my lady.'

He swept away.

127

'Isn't it cosy?' Lady Ammanford said, putting her hand on mine. 'I've been so looking forward to our first evening out together.'

'It's very pleasant,' I said.

'Now you must be perfectly honest with me,' she said. 'After all, we are friends now. Did you enjoy this evening?'

'Well, yes,' I said. 'It was an interesting play.'

'Rather too much emphasis on sex, didn't you think?'

'It seemed to lean in that direction.'

'Frankly I'm sick of it,' Lady Ammanford said. 'It's all anybody seems to think about. I think it was better in my day. At least there was some mystery connected with it. Today it's been reduced to a hot-dog stand level.'

'I know what you mean,' I said.

'Does it worry you as a doctor?'

'I think it worries all doctors,' I said evasively.

The drinks arrived. She toyed with hers for a moment.

'I've often thought it must be, well, a bit off-putting, being a doctor. As far as women are concerned?'

'How do you mean?'

'Well, I'm sure you must see a great many naked women every week?'

'Quite a few.'

'Doesn't it put you off, examining them? I mean, how can you look at a woman with any real desire afterwards? Doesn't she tend to become, well, just another body?'

'A doctor doesn't look at it like that,' I said, hoping I was handling the conversation well. 'When a woman comes to you she is just someone with a problem. You switch off your personal feelings.'

'And how do you look at me?' she demanded. 'As a patient, or as a woman?'

I hesitated.

'To me you are a wonderful woman who has been most kind and helpful to me.'

'But not someone to be desired?'

'Of course someone to be desired,' I said hurriedly. 'You must be desirable to a great many men.'

'But not to you?'

'I am your doctor, dear lady. ....'

She sat back, a small smile on her lips.

'I didn't mean to embarrass you,' she said. 'Forgive me if I did. It's just that a woman, whatever her age, likes to feel that she is attractive to a man.'

'I understand,' I said.

'My husband never made me feel that,' she said. 'To him I was just a part of the furniture.'

'Were you married long?'

'Fifteen years,' she said. 'He was an odd man, George. I never really got the hang of him even after all that time. He had such strange habits.'

'What did he do?'

'All sorts of things. One day I came home unexpectedly in the afternoon and heard sounds coming from our bedroom. So I went upstairs and listened outside the door. "Come on, my little darling," George was saying. "Come on, you beautiful thing. Oh, you're so lovely; I'm so mad about you. You can do it." Naturally I thought he had a girl in there, so I burst in. Do you know what he was doing? He was talking to a plant which we kept on our dressing-table. It had been wilting, probably because we kept the bedroom so warm, and he'd read somewhere that if you showed love to your plants and talked to them they responded. Can you imagine? A grown man, talking to a plant?'

'It is odd,' I said. 'But there are many people in my country who believe that plants *do* have feelings. Years ago people believed that certain plants were kindly disposed towards the human race. There are even references in old books to prayers being addressed to the healing spirits of plants. I remember one: 'The fever that is hot and cold and comes in summer — destroy him, O Plant!"'

'What utter rubbish,' Lady Ammanford said severely. 'I hope you don't subscribe to such nonsense?'

'Well, no,' I said guardedly. 'I was merely trying to show that what your husband did would not have been considered odd by some people.'

'Perhaps not,' she said. 'But there were other things. For instance, he had his leg shot off in the First World War and kept it.'

'Kept it,' I echoed.

'Yes. He said he'd grown attached to it and didn't want it to fall into the wrong hands. So after the amputation he brought it home with him. He used to keep it in his study, in the corner. It smelled awfully in the beginning, but after a while it just turned a horrible sort of grey-black. We used to lose a lot of help because nobody liked dusting it.'

'Where is your husband now?'

'The last I heard of him he was living with a retired traffic-warden in St John's Wood. He met her when she booked him outside Woolworth's in the Edgware Road. A common bit, by all accounts.'

She frowned.

'But let's not talk about him,' she said. 'I want this to be a pleasant evening. Let us talk about you. I want to know all about you. Where you come from; what sort of life you've led.'

'There's not much to tell. I grew up in a small village outside Calcutta, where everyone was very poor.'

'And I expect your poor dear father scraped and saved so that there would be enough money to send you to university,' she said.

Well scraped and saved he certainly had. But not to send me to university. At that moment, I felt sure, if he could stretch a withered arm across the sea the only place he'd send me would be prison.

'He certainly worked hard,' I said.

'Was it very difficult, studying to be a doctor?'

'For me it was easier than for others. I have what is called an eidetic memory.'

'What on earth is that?'

'It means I have a photographic mind. I have a screen just above my eyes and if I want to remember anything I have read I extract it from the recesses of my mind and project it on to the screen. I can then see the page quite clearly.'

'What an extraordinary gift,' she said. 'That must have come in very useful with your studies?'

'It was helpful,' I said. 'We have to read a great many medical books.'

Just then a waiter with a small emblem on his lapel came over bearing a leather book which he handed to me with great ceremony.

'The wine list, m'sieur.'

I was in trouble. The only thing I knew about wine was that it came in two colours.

'Listen,' Lady Ammanford said, apparently sensing my embarrassment, 'why don't we just have a carafe of Chablis? It goes so well with fish, I always think.'

'Just what I was about to suggest,' I said, handing the wine list back to the waiter.

When the food arrived, Lady Ammanford was about to taste hers when she paused, the fork half-way to her mouth.

'Oh, good heavens. I've just realized. That was very stupid of me, a few minutes ago.'

I looked at her blankly.

'You are, of course, a Hindu. So it is not possible for you to eat meat. I simply did not think.'

'I'm not a very good Hindu,' I said. 'But you're quite right, I don't eat meat.'

'I am so sorry,' she said, putting down her fork. 'How foolish of me.'

'Please do not concern yourself. It is a mistake anybody could have made.'

131

'But I am not anybody, am I? I am supposed to be your friend.'

'Friends are allowed to make mistakes too,' I said.

'I'm forgiven?'

'Of course.'

'Yours always sounds such a fascinating religion,' she said.

'It has its points,' I said. 'The British would have done better if they had studied it when they were in India. They might have understood us better.'

'In what way?'

'Well, dear lady, Indian mutineers used to laugh when they were hanged by your soldiers, because they thought they were on their way to a better existence. But they cried and fought when your Army tied them to a cannon and blew them to bits because they thought their souls would be blown to bits too.'

'I didn't know that,' she said.

'Not many of your people did,' I said. 'I'm afraid the history of the British occupation of India was one long saga of stupidity.'

'Oh how you must hate us,' she said.

'Not at all,' I said. 'There are so many admirable things about the British.'

'You would say that,' she said. 'A dear person like you would find it hard to harbour bitterness.'

She pushed her plate away.

'I have the oddest feeling about you,' she said. 'As though we were — I hope this doesn't sound silly — destined to become great friends.'

'I feel that too,' I said.

'It's rapport, in the true sense of the word.'

'Indeed it is.'

'And as for your qualities as a doctor, I am constantly astonished. All my friends are talking about you.'

'I hope they say encouraging things?'

'They think you're the best doctor they've ever come across,' she said.

She finished her wine.

'Before Susan told me about you, I had been going to a doctor just down the street from you — Dr Klein. Perhaps Susan mentioned him? He's got quite a reputation with the ladies. His waiting-room is always full of them. But he never gives anybody any time. You always feel you are keeping somebody else waiting, and you usually are. So you rattle off whatever you feel is wrong with you, and he has you diagnosed and prescribed for within five minutes. Sometimes he began reaching for his prescription pad the moment I entered his consulting-room.'

'I know doctors like that,' I said.

'You're so different,' she said. 'Only the other day Norma Blair was saying that you've never once written out a prescription for her. At first, I think, she was dismayed. But not now. Now she's one of your most ardent admirers.'

'I'm glad to hear it,' I said.

Her eyes narrowed.

'I understand you went to dinner at her house recently?'

'That's right.'

'I hope it was an enjoyable evening?'

'Yes it was. There were some interesting people there.'

'Oh,' she said. 'Who?'

I told her.

'Marc Stevens is quite entertaining,' she said. 'I'm not so sure about the others.'

She put a hand on mine.

'I hope you'll do me the honour of coming to dinner at my house some time?'

'I'd like that,' I said.

'We'll do it very soon,' she said.

She squeezed my hand.

'Now be a dear man and ask for the bill. I have to be up very early in the morning for a hair-appointment,

133

otherwise I would invite you back to Connaught Square
for a night-cap.'

'I'll get it right away,' I said, signalling a waiter.

'There will be other nights,' Lady Ammanford said.

'I hope so,' I said.

'Oh there will,' she said. 'Quite definitely.'

28

When I arrived in Harley Street next morning, Hilda
Furze was almost twitching with excitement.

'There's been a call,' she said.

'Who was it?'

She touched her lips, as if to make sure that they
were still there.

'You'll never guess.'

'You're right,' I said. 'Tell me.'

'Number Ten.'

'Number Ten what?'

'Downing Street,' she said, letting it out with a gasp,
'Number Ten *Downing* Street! Don't you understand?
The Prime Minister! His secretary wants you to call
him back.'

I stood where I was, staring at her.

'You're joking?'

She laughed.

'That's just how I reacted,' she said. 'I couldn't
believe it either. The Prime Minister.'

'What am I going to do?' I said anxiously.

'Do?' she said. 'You're going to call him right back,
of course. Oh, isn't this exciting?'

I walked slowly into my consulting-room. There was
an odd twitching in my stomach, as though I hadn't

eaten for a long time. Which wasn't true. I'd had eggs and beans for breakfast, and a couple of pieces of hot buttered toast.

'Can I listen while you telephone?' she asked, breathlessly. 'Imagine; you talking to Number Ten.'

'I don't know the number,' I said.

'It's there,' she said, pointing. 'On the pad.'

I looked down. There it was, written in Miss Furze's neat hand. 930-4433. I added it up. It came to twenty-six. Not one of my lucky numbers.

'Oh do hurry up, doctor.'

Like a man about to jump in front of a train, I dialled the number.

'Ten Downing Street,' a male voice said.

'I want to speak to the Prime Minister's secretary,' I said hesitantly.

'Who is calling?'

'Dr Das.'

'I'm sorry;' the voice was crisp. 'You'll have to speak up.'

'Dr Das.' I spelled it out. 'D-A-S.'

'One moment.'

There was a click and I was connected.

'Dr Das? This is Hugh St Clair. Thank you for calling back. I wonder if I may make an appointment for you to see the Prime Minister?'

'Could you ... could you give me some idea of what it's about?'

'Of course. You treated a friend of his recently — Toby Downs? The P.M. has the same sort of back-trouble and would like you to take a look at it.'

My heart didn't stop altogether, but it did falter slightly.

'I'm not sure when. ...'

'The Prime Minister has only two possible times,' Hugh St Clair went on. 'Either five past four tomorrow or twenty past five on Wednesday. He leaves for Brussels on Thursday, as you probably know.'

'I might be able to manage tomorrow,' I mumbled, looking round for my appointments book. Hilda Furze thrust it towards me. 'Yes. I could manage four minutes past five.'

'Five minutes past four. . . .'

'Oh, yes. Five minutes past four.'

'I'll tell him right away. Thank you so much.'

'By the way,' I said. 'What's the name?'

The blunder was out before I had time to think. I saw a puzzled look on Hilda Furze's face.

'The name?' There was a pause. 'Oh, you mean mine? Hugh St Clair. I'm the P.M.'s private secretary.'

'Thank you, Mr St Clair,' I said.

I put the telephone down and stared at it for a moment, my heart leaping about in my chest.

Then my attention was diverted by the sight of Hilda Furze cavorting about the room, waving her arms.

'He's coming, isn't he? He coming. And I'm the one who'll let him in. Oh, my God. I may faint. I'm mad about him. *Mad* about him. He's so forceful; so dynamic.' She reeled to a stop in front of my desk.

'He is coming here, isn't he? You're not going there?'

'No,' I said, still finding it hard to believe. 'He's coming here.'

'Perhaps we ought to get some flowers?' she said. 'Brighten the place up? I tell you what. I pass a florists on the way in. I'll pick some up then.' She clapped her hands together. 'And what about tea? If he's coming at four he'll want some tea.'

'We can ask him when he gets here,' I said.

'I'll get a decent cup and saucer, just in case,' she said. 'I got a nice one from my Aunt Agnes last Christmas. One with a picture of Buckingham Palace on it. He'll like that; I expect he goes there all the time. Oh, isn't it exciting? Dr Das, I'm so happy for you.' She flounced over to the door. 'I must go and tell the others.'

'So what kind of a day did you have?'

Patel glanced up from the stove on which he was busily scrambling some eggs.

'Nothing special,' I said, trying hard to contain my excitement. 'A bit dreary, really.'

'Any new patients?'

I put the cups and saucers carefully on the table.

'No. But there's one coming tomorrow.'

He brought the pan over to the table and cascaded the contents on to two pieces of toast.

'Who's that?' he said.

'The Prime Minister.'

He stood absolutely still.

'What did you say?'

I laughed wildly.

'Isn't it fantastic? The Prime Minister's coming. I treated a friend of his, Toby Downs, and now the great man himself is coming. I can hardly believe it.'

Patel put the pan down and slumped into a chair.

'Oh you fool. You stupid, blundering fool.'

I looked at him, astonished.

'You're not pleased?'

'Pleased?' He spat the word. 'Pleased that you've just chucked away hundreds of pounds of my money? Pleased that you're about to be sent to jail? Oh, certainly I'm pleased. I'm delighted.'

'Now wait a minute,' I said heatedly. 'He's coming to me for treatment — not to arrest me.'

'Coming to you for treatment, is he?' He sat there, his dark eyes bleak. 'Don't you realize what you've done, you fool? You've laid yourself wide open. This isn't one of your silly matrons, content with a few kind words and a hand on her knee. This is the Prime Minister, one of the greatest hypochondriacs in London. Everybody knows that. He's been to every doctor in Harley Street. He probably knows ten times as much about medicine as you do. He'll be on to you in a moment. And when he gets to Number Ten he'll tell his secretary: "Check on a little wog named Ram Das, will you; I didn't quite care for the cut of his jib." And the next thing you know there'll be two large gentlemen in bowler hats escorting you to Southampton, or wherever the boat goes from. And I'll be five hundred quid down the drain.'

I sat motionless in my chair in front of the rapidly congealing eggs.

'I couldn't have refused to see him. . . .'

'You could have made some excuse,' Patel snapped. 'You could have said you were too busy, or were going away on holiday.'

'My receptionist was there,' I said. 'She'd have known I was lying.'

'Better her than him,' Patel said, grimly. 'As you'll very soon find out.'

'Perhaps I can bluff it through?' I said.

'Oh, sure,' Patel said sarcastically. 'This is the man who told Nixon to get stuffed; who reduced everyone at last month's Commonwealth Conference to a gibbering pulp. He's the most feared English leader since Cromwell — and you're going to bluff it through?' He shook his head. 'You've got as much chance of doing that as winning the Nobel Prize for Medicine.'

I poured myself a cup of thick brown tea.

'What can I do?'

'You could die tonight,' Patel said. 'That would be one way out.'

He shoved back his chair.

'I'm not hungry any more,' he said. 'I think I'll go somewhere and get crocked instead.' At the door he paused. 'Oh, and by the way, before he does kick you out of the country, you might tell him the loos at London Airport are an absolute disgrace.'

I spent a restless night. Patel was right, of course. The Prime Minister would know immediately that I was not a Solid Citizen but an Illegal Immigrant Runt.

Disgrace. Ruin. Deportation. Jail in Calcutta. An early grave.

Tossing and turning in my small iron bed, I eventually fell into a disturbed sleep and dreamed of Susan Partridge. Oddly enough, considering how much she occupied my thoughts, it was the first time I had dreamed of her, although each night before I slept I thought about her. In this dream she and Basil, both clad in immaculate white safari clothes, were walking along a jungle track while I struggled behind carrying an enormous cabin trunk on my back. Every now and again Basil would order me to put down the trunk and, dipping his hand into it, fish out handfuls of beads which he scattered among the bearers who trailed disconsolately behind us. 'Pays to encourage the little sods,' he would say to Susan, giving her a friendly pat on the bottom.

Around four in the morning I woke to the sound of lorries revving in the courtyard below. Usually I did not notice them, but on this occasion they seemed particularly noisy. And one of them was having trouble starting.

Wuuuuurrr ... wuuuurrr ... wuuuurrr ... went the starter. All to no avail.

There were curses from the yard, and the sound of a bonnet being opened. A moment later the engine roared into life and, with a crash of gears, the lorry lurched away into the street.

I gave up all hope of sleep at this point and, feeling like a condemned man awakened early for his execution, got up and made myself some tea.

Around five o'clock, still gummy-eyed, I decided to brave the chilly bathroom on the floor above. I went there only occasionally, since it stank of drains and rotting lino and the black base of the bath was so rough that it was impossible to lie in it in comfort. But a hot bath, I thought, might help to soak away some of my fears. So, with a washcloth placed judiciously under my rump, I lay in the steaming water, pondering my fate.

There was one thing in my favour I decided. I had been recommended by one of the Prime Minister's friends. That being so, he would not be suspicious from the outset. Everything depended on how I behaved. If I could only master my fear, the day might yet be saved. But could I? After all, I had plenty to be fearful about. Was I not a fifth-rate Indian cheat, lusting after a beautiful white girl and, almost as bad, attempting to hoax the Great British Public?

I was!

'We come now to the case of Ram Das, an Indian of low extraction who has held a number of menial posts since leaving his village near Calcutta. He is, in every possible way, a despicable little bounder; at one time the receptionist at a Calcutta brothel, more recently a bus-conductor with London Transport, having entered this country on forged papers. He has now begun masquerading as a doctor in Harley Street in the hope of attracting young women to his consulting-rooms for the purpose of furthering his sexual fantasies and lecherous pursuits.

'We learn to our surprise that by means of a cruel deception he has met and fallen in love with a girl who is in every way refined, genteel and of good character,

Miss Susan Partridge. She has given him no encouragement whatsoever; indeed she would be horrified to know what unsavoury thoughts lurk in the little lecher's mind.

'She herself has met and been attracted to a man who is in every way superior to the man Das, Mr Basil Calder. Mr Calder, a Cambridge man and former Guards officer, is at present engaged in public relations work for one of the major London organizations, holding down a post of £10,000 a year. He is aristocratic and well-bred, and coming as he does from an excellent family — his father and his grandfather both saw service in India — he is in every way a suitable escort for the aforesaid Miss Partridge. Mr Calder is, in fact, unaware of the infatuation that the dark-skinned little swine has formed for his lady. Should he find out, we must suppose that he would treat the matter with the contempt it deserves.

'Far from being deterred by the competition, the man Das still holds out hope of getting his lustful hands on the body of Miss Susan Partridge. She, supposing him to be a qualified doctor, has already sent her friends to him. Others, too, are in danger of falling into the grubby hands of this rascal — one a Very Important Person indeed. So you will see, m'lud, there is not a moment to be lost if we are to prevent this alien filth from defiling the cream of British womanhood. Why, the very thought is enough to make any red-blooded Englishman reach for a whip. ...'

At nine o'clock that morning, thundering into town on a crowded bus, I saw the advertisement.

'Are you lacking in confidence? Do you wish to improve your potential? Would you like to develop your personality? Call the Star Personality Studio at the number listed below. ...'

I read it again and again.

Yes, I was lacking in confidence. Yes, I wished to

improve my potential. Yes, I would like to develop my personality. Could the Star Personality Studio do this for me? And, if it could, might I yet escape the fate that Patel had predicted for me?

When I got to Harley Street I telephoned the number. Of course, a voice said, the Star Personality Studio would be delighted to see me. But the first appointment they could give me was for the following week.

'That's no good,' I said. 'It has to be today. What about lunch-time? Could I come then?'

There was a pause.

Then the voice said, rather grumpily, 'Very well. Come along at one.'

The Star Personality Studio was located at the top of Marylebone High Street, stuck between a hospital supplies shop on the one side and an undertakers on the other. It seemed an unlikely place to gain confidence, improve potential and develop personality.

At the top of a narrow flight of stairs was a glass door on which was stuck a poster showing a handsome young man with blond hair and steely eyes holding forth to an admiring crowd. 'Confidence' said the slogan — 'The Clue to a Great Career.'

A small brass plate to the right announced: 'Star Personality Studio. Director: A. Van-Rhyne.'

I opened the door and found myself in a small office furnished with a shabby desk, a settee and a couple of old armchairs. There seemed to be papers and brochures everywhere; piled on the desk, scattered about the floor, heaped on the armchairs. On one wall was a huge portrait of Benito Mussolini, his jaw jutting. I knew it was Benito Mussolini because it said so, underneath. And I had read about him in the Brixton library.

Behind the desk sat a sharp-eyed little man, even smaller than myself. The skin of his face was white and withered, as though it had been left in a jar of water overnight. His grey hair, straggling over his ears, was sparse and yellowing. But his eyes were quite remarkable; dark and piercing. As I stood there he rose and looked intently at me. He did not speak.

'I telephoned you this morning,' I said. 'My name is Das. Are you Mr Van-Rhyne?'

'Professor Van-Rhyne,' he corrected. He frowned. 'You're the one who keeps getting sand kicked in his face, right?'

'No,' I said. 'That's not me.'

'What's your problem, then? Panic? Keep panicking, do you?'

'I want to gain confidence,' I said.

'Ah,' he said. 'Confidence — that feeling by which the mind embarks in great and honourable courses with a sure hope and trust in itself.'

'I beg your pardon.'

'Cicero,' he said. 'Remember that. It's important to remember that.'

He rustled through some papers.

'Well now,' he said. 'The full course to gain confidence takes twenty lessons.' He looked up. 'At four pounds a lesson.'

'That's eighty pounds,' I said incredulously.

'Quick thinking,' the Professor said. 'That's something in your favour. A man who quick thinks is off to a good start.'

'But I can't get involved in a whole course,' I said. 'I haven't got the time. What I was hoping for was one lesson teaching me how to look confident even though I'm not.'

'Looking confident even though you're not takes five lessons,' he said severely. 'It's not something you can learn overnight. Good heavens, no. Why it took Cary Grant twenty lessons before he was ready.'

'Cary Grant?' I echoed.

'Oh yes,' he said. 'Cary still looks in whenever he's passing. The big stars, they've all been here.'

'I'm sorry,' I said. 'I can't possibly consider a full course. As I say, I was hoping for just one lesson.'

He leaped to his feet.

'All right,' he said. 'But what you hope to learn in one lesson I can't imagine.' He held out his hand. 'One lesson will be five pounds.'

I took five one-pound notes from my wallet and handed them to him.

'I suppose I could teach you the rudiments of Mu,' he said, counting the notes.

'Mu?'

'Don't tell me you haven't heard of Mu?' he said, looking surprised. 'The Five-fold Elapse, guaranteeing long life, health and mental tranquillity? All based on breath control and with one huge advantage — you can practice it while you're stuck in the traffic. . . .'

'But it's confidence I'm looking for,' I said. 'Not mental tranquillity.'

He thought for a moment.

'Perhaps I could hypnotize you,' he said. 'I hypnotized one client so that the moment anyone said: "How do you do?" he imagined himself to be Genghis Khan. Plenty of confidence there, all right, but unfortunately he kept trying to rape the women. They put him away in the end, still with one lesson to go.'

He shook his head.

'No,' he said. 'Perhaps hypnosis isn't such a good idea.'

He indicated the settee standing against the wall.

'Sit there,' he said. 'I like to walk about while I'm talking.' I perched myself on the edge of the settee and watched him as he paced up and down.

'What you've got to understand,' he said, 'is that most men gain their initial confidence from their mothers, who think they are the greatest thing since sliced bread and never stop telling them so. The result is that when they eventually go out into the world they have some sort of ego to protect them. But there are others, such as yourself, who were not so favoured. You were never told by your mother that you were the greatest thing since sliced bread.' He peered at me. 'Am I right?'

I nodded.

'If anything,' he continued, 'your mother made you feel you were a bit of a drag.'

I nodded again.

'And that is what you have taken into life; a deep-seated suspicion that you are a bit of a drag.' He sneezed suddenly into the back of his hand.

'Bugger,' he said sharply.

I sat and waited.

'Of course,' he said, 'it isn't always an asset, mother's admiration.' He glanced at the picture of Mussolini. 'Take Benito, for example. His mother undoubtedly thought he was the greatest thing since spaghetti vongole — and look what happened to him.'

'I wondered why you had his picture on the wall,' I said.

'As a warning,' the Professor said. 'As a warning.'

He went and sat behind his desk and studied me intently for a moment.

'What sort of underwear have you got on?'

'Just an ordinary vest and briefs,' I said.

'But what kind? Silk, nylon or cotton? And where did you get them?'

'They're cotton,' I said. 'I got them at Marks and Spencers.'

'God in heaven,' he said. 'Does everybody in this bloody country have to get their drawers at Marks and Spencers?'

'What difference does it make?' I asked.

'It makes all the difference in the world,' he said. 'It is essential that when you leave this room you go down the High Street to one of the men's shops and buy yourself a set of silk underwear. Several sets, if you can afford them. Put them on immediately. That way, whenever someone wearing less exotic underwear comes into your presence, you can hardly fail to feel superior.'

'But how will they know I'm wearing silk underpants?'

'Oh my God,' the Professor said testily. 'They won't know, of course. But *you'll* know, which is all that matters. *You'll* know you're wearing silk and that will immediately put you in a position of advantage.'

'It will?' I said dubiously.

'Of course it will,' he said forcefully. 'Let me give you an example. I am wearing silk drawers at this very moment. You are not. Therefore I feel superior to you.'

'I understand,' I said.

'The next thing,' the Professor said, 'is to build up your ego at the expense of everybody else's. Find out their weaknesses and exploit them unmercifully.' He paused. 'Curiously enough, being black is to your advantage.'

'In what way?'

'When you meet a white man, he automatically considers you to be his inferior. It is not his fault. He has been programmed to react like that over the years. It has nothing to do with anything you say or do. He doesn't even pause to rationalize his feelings. So his defences are not up. Which is to your advantage. Seek out his defects and frailties, and go for them.'

'And that will make me feel superior?'

'Of course. You can't possibly feel superior unless you make someone else feel inferior. That goes without saying.'

'But is there something I do? Something I say?'

He looked pained.

'I'm coming to that,' he said. He sneezed again. 'Bugger twice,' he said. He hauled a huge handkerchief out of his pocket and buried his face in it. 'Now,' he said, 'where was I? Oh yes. Making someone else feel inferior.

146

'Let us say now that the conversation turns to some subject of which you know nothing. Archaeology, perhaps, or chemical warfare, or painting. What do you do? I will tell you. You smile secretly and turn away. What happens? Immediately the man supposes that you know something that he does not, that you have information you are unwilling to impart. Perhaps, he thinks, you know the Valley of the Kings like the back of your hand. Or hold a very important position in a mustard-gas factory. Or are Assistant Curator of the Tate.'

'And that makes him feel inferior?'

'Of course that makes him feel inferior,' the Professor said. 'Wouldn't it make you feel inferior?'

'What else?' I asked.

'You pick on words. There is no better way of making people feel inferior than picking on words. When someone says: "It's awful", you immediately correct them. "Awful", according to the *Concise Oxford Dictionary*, means: "inspiring awe; worthy of profound respect". Which is not what they meant at all. The same with "terrific". Never let this go by. "Terrific" means: "causing terror; terrible". It does not mean sensational.'

I glanced at my watch. It was half-past one. Just two hours and thirty-five minutes to go.

'But listen,' I said. 'What if I meet someone who is obviously my superior in every way; someone who knows he is superior to me by virtue of the job he holds? How do I handle him?'

The Professor smiled.

'You mentally undress him,' he said. 'It's the only way. Start with the trousers first, of course. Imagine him standing there without them. Then divest him of his other garments, one by one, until he is completely starkers.'

Of all the things the little man had said this struck me as the most sensible. Perhaps if I mentally stripped the Prime Minister the moment he entered my

147

consulting-room we might be able to talk on an equal footing. Perhaps.

'What about developing my personality?' I said.

'You want a hell of a lot for a one-hour lesson,' the Professor said crossly. 'As it is I've given up my lunch-break in order to improve your potential and make you feel superior. You'll have to develop your personality on your own time.'

He got up.

'Well, good luck,' he said. 'Don't forget what I said about the silk underwear.' He looked at the picture of Mussolini. 'And don't forget what happened to that horse's arse.'

As I made my way down Marylebone High Street, trying to remember all that the little man had said, I passed a man's shop.

'I'm looking for some silk underwear,' I said, walking in.

'You've come to the right place,' the willowy young assistant said. 'What size?'

'I don't know.'

He looked me up and down.

'Small,' he said, hauling a drawer from beneath the counter. 'I'd say you were small. What colour?'

'Have you got white?'

'White?' he said. 'Nobody wears white any more. Pink, blue, red, orange. Fake leopard-skin even. But not white.'

'Blue, then.'

He ruffled through the drawer and held up a small packet.

'Yes,' he said triumphantly. 'I can do you blue. And a vest to go with it?'

I nodded.

'Anything else?'

'No thanks.'

'That'll be three pounds fifty,' he said, slipping the packets into a bag.

'Three pounds fifty?' I said. 'As much as that?'

'They're silk,' the assistant said. 'Not your ordinary cotton rubbish.'

As I counted out the money, he eyed me speculatively.

'Been up the road, have you, improving your potential?'

'How did you know?'

'They all come in here,' he said. 'Our sale of silk underwear has trebled since the Professor went into business.'

He handed me the bag.

'And you know something?' he added. 'It works. It really does. ...'

30

By the time four o'clock came round I was feeling decidedly sick. Sitting behind my desk, wearing my blue silk underwear, I tried desperately to compose myself.

What a fool I had been to suppose that I could get away with it. He'd be on to me immediately. I'd be arrested. And that would be the end of it.

In the hall, Hilda Furze had been pacing up and down for the better part of twenty minutes, determined to have the door open the moment the bell rang. Other patients, arriving to see my colleagues, were ushered brusquely into the waiting-room with scarcely a word.

Promptly at five past four, a black limousine drew to a halt outside and through the window I caught a glimpse of a ruddy-faced man leaping across the pavement and up the front steps. The bell rang briefly and I heard the door opening and the sound of muffled conversation. Then, while I rose to my feet, my heart pounding, my door was flung wide and in bounded the British Prime Minister. I fought back an impulse to stand to attention.

'My dear doctor,' he said. 'I've heard so much about you from Toby. We share the same back trouble as I gather you know. All that sprawling about on the Commons benches, I shouldn't wonder. Nothing like that where you come from, eh? Off to Brussels on Thursday, doctor, so I've got to be fit. Got to be fit.'

He flung me a wild smile, showing more teeth than I had ever seen in a human mouth, and strode over to a chair in the corner. Ignoring the screen, he began undressing, throwing his clothes casually over the back of the chair. It was slightly unnerving, seeing the all-too-familiar figure peeling off in front of me. Indecent, somehow; like catching Mrs Gandhi coming out of the lavatory.

'Bloody painful, these backs. Had mine for years. Bent over one day to pick up an oar and bingo, that was it. Thought of having an operation once, but Jack Kennedy advised against it. Good man, Jack Kennedy. He had the op. and was in pain for years. So I've learned to live with it. Apart from sailing, I don't do anything too strenuous.'

He was down to his bikini underpants by this time — ordinary cotton ones, I was pleased to notice — a rather flabby, pink-skinned figure, but still impressive.

'Well,' he said, flashing me a wide smile again. 'Where do you want me?'

'If you'll just stand straight,' I said nervously, 'I'll check the muscle spasm.'

He turned his back to me and I ran my fingers down both sides of the lower spine.

'Well,' he said. 'What do you think?'

'Hard to tell at first glance,' I said.

150

'What about second glance?' he said.

'Seems to be a little trouble around the twelfth thoracic vertebra,' I said hoping to impress him.

'Twelfth thoracic, you think. Not the first lumbar?'

Evidently he wasn't that easy to impress.

'It could be both,' I said.

'That was my impression,' he said.

I felt his spine again.

'Yes,' I said. 'It's definitely both.'

'What do you suggest, then?'

'A little traction, I think. Then some gentle manipulation.'

'Is that what you gave Toby?'

'That's right.'

'Very well. On that thing, is it?'

He heaved himself onto the traction-couch, and I adjusted the straps round his ankles and chest.

'All right?' I asked.

'Absolutely.'

Carefully I turned the handle which stretched the straps.

'Where did you get this?' he asked, his eyes closed.

'I found it in a warehouse not far from here,' I said. 'It's American. They say Eisenhower had it at his headquarters during the war. He must have had a bad back too.'

'Ike, eh? Good chap, Ike. Not much imagination, of course, but sound with people.'

When the handle had been turned three times, I stopped and felt the straps. They were stretched tight.

'Now I'm going to switch on the electric motor,' I said. 'This will give you a series of tugs, which can be very effective. Call out if you're not happy about anything.'

I clicked the switch and adjusted the dial to 3. The table lumbered into life, both ends vibrating.

'Aaaaah,' he sighed.

'Everything all right?'

'Mmmmmmmh.'

'Tell me if you're not comfortable.'

'Ooooooooh.'

I watched him, anxiously.

'Can't it go any faster?'

'A little,' I said. 'There are two more notches on the dial.'

'Turn it up one more,' he said.

I moved the dial to 4. He gave a great groan and appeared to go into convulsions.

'Sir ...' I said.

No answer.

Prime Minister dies in Doctor's Surgery. ... Stretched to Death. ... Inquiries progressing, say Police. ...

The motor was whining noisily and the whole table was juddering like mad. The body of the Prime Minister of Great Britain and Northern Ireland was jolting about like a carcase in the back of a truck, getting redder and redder.

Suddenly he opened his eyes.

'Enough,' he said.

I switched the motor off and released the straps. He lay for a moment, breathing heavily.

'Oh my God,' he said. 'That was marvellous.'

'You feel all right?'

'Never felt better,' he said.

He glanced at his watch.

'Good grief,' he said, swinging his legs off the couch. 'I should be at a Cabinet meeting.'

'I'd feel a lot happier if you had a brief rest,' I said. 'You had it turned up very high.'

'Nonsense, doctor.' He flashed me a shark-like smile. 'It did me the world of good.'

'What about a cup of tea? I wouldn't take a minute.'

'Never touch the stuff,' he said.

He began getting dressed.

'Now look here,' he said, 'I shall come again. Can't

always give much notice, though. Sure you'll understand. Be all right if I get young St. Clair to call you in the morning, say, and nip along in the afternoon?'

'Of course.'

He crinkled his light-blue eyes.

'Knew you'd be helpful. Splendid chaps, all of you. Had a couple of your people as servants in India during the war' — he broke off. 'You are Indian, right?'

'Yes.'

'Thank God for that. Had a sudden suspicion you might be Pakistani. Left the Commonwealth, the idiots. After all we've done for them. Can't understand it.'

He buttoned his shirt.

'Where are you from?'

'Calcutta.'

'Ah, yes. Calcutta. The dear old Grand. How is it?'

'Still there,' I said.

'Splendid place, Calcutta,' he said. 'Ought to clean up the streets, though. All those people sleeping out. Shouldn't be allowed.'

'They haven't got anywhere else to sleep,' I said.

'Then build them some bloody houses,' he said. 'Kill two birds with one stone, don't you see? Give them jobs as builders and provide them with somewhere to live at the same time. Can't understand what the Government is thinking of. Told Mrs Gandhi that.'

He pulled on his coat and shook hands.

'Goodbye, doctor. Delighted to have met you. See you again very soon.'

As he strode into the hall Hilda Furze, hovering about like an anxious fruitfly, whipped open the front door. He flashed her a wide smile and was gone.

She leaned against the wall, sighing.

'Did you see the way he smiled at me?' she said. 'As though he really cared. What a wonderful man. What a truly wonderful man.'

31

My success with the Prime Minister did wonders for my morale. And that night, at supper with Patel, I came to a decision. I would move from Elm Place.

He received the news without enthusiasm.

'Why?' he demanded.

'Because this place is no longer suitable,' I said. 'Surely you can see that? For one thing, there are the lorries. For another, if anybody asks me where I live I can't say here.'

'I don't see why not,' he said. 'I say here.'

'But it's different for me. You must see that. What can I say if the Prime Minister asks me where I live? Brixton? It's ridiculous. He thinks I'm a West End doctor. I've got to have a West End address.'

He eyed me sceptically.

'It seems to me you're getting ideas above your station,' he said.

'Not at all,' I said. 'I'm getting ideas to match my station.'

'Then go ahead,' he said. 'Move.'

'You don't mind?'

'It's got nothing to do with me,' he said.

'But I don't want you to get upset.'

'I don't have to get upset,' he said shortly. 'I've been upset ever since I was fool enough to advance you that money. I've got as much chance of getting it back as I have of becoming head of Air India. . . .'

'You've already had £50,' I said.

'True,' he said. 'That means you only owe me £450

— plus the interest. And what chance have I got of getting that back if you're going to throw your money away on a flat in town?'

'I won't be throwing it away,' I said. 'Don't you understand — the sooner I start living like a Harley Street doctor, the sooner you'll get your money back?'

'I see,' he said. 'You mean by paying £25 a week for a luxury flat in Mayfair you'll have more money to repay me than if you stay here at £2 a week. You ought to be in the Government with those calculations.'

'I don't plan to move into a luxury flat in Mayfair,' I said. 'Just one room somewhere that sounds better than 12 Elm Place. Surely you don't want me to go on rotting here?'

'I'm rotting here,' Patel said peevishly.

'But you've got a good reason for staying. The hag. You've said so yourself. You could have moved out a long time ago.'

'It may interest you to know,' Patel said, 'that I was planning to leave around the time I met you. But I stayed, because I thought we were friends. I enjoyed being with you, and helping you, and doing things for you. Now this. . . .'

He looked away.

'I'll see you all the time,' I said.

'It's this girl, isn't it? You're moving because of this girl?'

'I'm not. Honestly. It's got nothing to do with her.'

'You're ashamed to bring her here. Why don't you admit it?'

'Because it's not true. I wish it were. I wish with all my heart that Susan Partridge cared enough about me to ask me to bring her here.'

He considered this for a moment.

'You'd better move,' he said.

'I was hoping you might come and look at one or two places with me?' I said.

'I'm sorry,' he said. 'I'm too busy.'

155

He shuffled out of the room without a backward glance and went downstairs.

Two days later, with the help of the *Evening Standard* small ads, I found a room in a house in Devonshire Street, not more than a hundred yards from my consulting-room.

It was ideal. Just what I needed. But it was with a distinct pang that I caught the bus back to Brixton to begin packing.

My heart was very full. I was leaving my first London home. A rundown sewer of a place, perhaps, but I had been glad enough of it at the time.

I went up to my little room and sat there for a few moments, looking at the peeling wallpaper and the cracked lino. Then, shrugging, I hauled my old suitcase from under the bed and began throwing things into it.

There was a knock on the door.

Patel stood there, holding something in his hands.

'I bought you a going-away present,' he said sheepishly.

'You shouldn't have done that,' I said, embarrassed.

I undid the wrapping. It was a quite dreadful black marble clock supported by two elderly gilt nymphs and bearing the inscription: 'To Percy Vale, on the occasion of his retirement from the South Lancashire Wool Emporium after sixty years. April 14, 1890.'

'It's lovely,' I said, touched.

'I thought it would do for your mantelpiece,' he said. 'It doesn't work, but it looks all right.'

'It looks splendid.'

'You really like it?'

'Yes I do.'

He grasped my arm.

'You're right to go,' he said. 'This is no place for you.'

'You mean it?'

'Of course. I was just being selfish.'

'I'll be back all the time,' I said. 'I'm only going to

use the other place as an address. We'll still eat together, and everything.'

He nodded, standing there awkwardly. Suddenly he put his arms round me and hugged me.

'Take care,' he said.

It was not much of a room, I reflected, when I awoke next morning. Hardly big enough to swing a cat around, unless you held it unpleasantly far up the tail. And it looked out on nothing but rooftops. But it was quiet; so blissfully quiet. I had awoken at four o'clock that morning with a vague sense of unease, and it was some time before I realized why. There had been no noise. No starting-up of lorries. The great trucks which, even on Sundays, enlivened the early hours at Elm Place with their revving engines and crashing gears were now a thing of the past.

My new room had a red carpet, a small wardrobe, a chest of drawers, a mirror, a single bed and a picture of H.M.S. *Ark Royal.*

The bathroom was next door, and I was to share it with the other tenant on the top floor. He was a dentist, who used his room solely as a *pied-à-terre*, so I would almost have the bath to myself. For all this, plus the joy of constant hot water. I was to send £10 a week — one month in advance — to the landlord, who lived in Devon.

When I gave Hilda Furze my new address and telephone number, she said:

'Oh that is convenient, doctor. What a lucky find.'

'I think I'll be happy there,' I said.

'You'll be able to walk to work.'

'Yes. That is an advantage.'

'And you've got such a pretty neighbour.'

'Oh, who's that?'

She smiled, her face pulled back in that terrible leer.

'Why Susan Partridge, of course. Doesn't she live round the corner in Hallam Street?'

32

Two days after I moved into Devonshire Street, I was invited to dinner by Lady Ammanford. I had assumed — from her conversation on the telephone — that it would be a dinner party, with many distinguished guests. I was wrong. There were just the two of us.

'I thought this would be more cosy,' she said, leading me into the drawing-room. 'I hope you don't mind?'

'Of course not,' I said.

She went over to the sideboard.

'Now,' she said. 'What shall we drink? Shall we be daring and try something different?'

'I don't know much about alcohol,' I said lamely.

'That's no problem,' she said, with a chuckle. 'I do.'

She fiddled about for a moment and then came over with two tall glasses.

'See what you think of this,' she said.

'What is it?'

'It's called a Cold Duck,' she said. 'Champagne and sparkling Burgundy.' She smiled encouragingly. 'Don't look so alarmed. It's quite harmless. My husband George drank nothing else.'

I took a sip. It was good.

'Do you like it?' she asked.

'It's excellent,' I said.

She held up her glass.

'Here's to our continued friendship,' she said. 'And may your practice ever prosper.'

'Thank you,' I said.

She sat down beside me on the blue velvet sofa.

'You've been such a success with everyone,' she said. 'I'm so pleased. And now the Prime Minister. It's wonderful.'

'I've been lucky,' I said.

'It has nothing to do with luck,' she said, firmly. 'You're a brilliant doctor.'

She sat back, eyeing me thoughtfully.

'Do you know what I was thinking last night?' she said. 'I know absolutely nothing about your private life. I don't even know where you live.'

'I have a flat in Devonshire Street,' I said.

'Is it a large one?'

'No. Quite small.'

'Do you drive a car?'

'No, I don't. It hardly seems worthwhile these days.'

'I so agree. There is simply no place to park. Susan is talking about getting herself an E-type Jaguar, but I am doing my best to discourage her. I just don't see the point in paying a lot of money to garage a car that's never used.'

I sipped my drink slowly.

'Have you seen much of her lately?' I asked.

'She was here for dinner last evening,' Lady Ammanford said.

'Is she ... is she still with Mr Calder?'

'I'm afraid so,' Lady Ammanford said. 'I wish she weren't.'

'I thought you liked him.'

'Oh I did. At first. But he's not at all the sort of man Susan should be involved with. For one thing, he's always away — climbing mountains, taking part in rallies, that sort of thing. She never sees him.'

'I'm sure there are plenty of other men who'd like to take her out,' I suggested.

'Indeed there are. But Susan's a funny girl. When she's with one man, that's it. I admire it, but I don't understand it.'

She paused.

'What about you? Do you have a girl-friend?'

'No,' I said. 'Not at the moment.'

'Why is that?'

For one brief moment I thought of blurting out the truth: 'Because I'm in love with your niece.' But the moment passed. Instead I said:

'Oh I don't know. I just haven't met the right girl, I suppose.'

'Perhaps you're too particular?' she said.

'I expect that's it,' I said.

'I was like that once,' she said. 'Only the best would do. Then I married George. That brought me down with a jolt.'

She looked at my glass.

'You've finished your drink,' she said. 'You see, you do like it.'

She went over to the sideboard and mixed me another.

'Can I help?' I said.

'You sit right where you are,' she said. 'I love mixing drinks. Usually Simons does it, but I told him not to bother tonight.'

'Is he a good butler?' I asked.

'Excellent,' she said. 'But he gives me the creeps. Always lurking about the house. I didn't hire him, you know; he was George's choice. I'd get rid of him, but it's so difficult to get good help these days.'

'I'm sure it must be,' I said.

'He's such an odd man,' she said. 'He's got this thing about shoes. Do you know he spends half an hour a day on each pair. You've never seen anything like it. First he puts on the polish and wipes that off, then he puts on some sort of lacquer, and wipes that off. Then he spits on them! I caught him at it, one day, in mid-spit, as it were. "What in heaven's name are you doing?" I asked. "Spitting, Modom," he said — you know the way he talks — "It's the best polish there is". And, do you know, I've found out he's right. Apparently that's what the soldiers do with their boots.'

She handed me my drink. I took a sip. It really was good. I couldn't think how I'd managed to survive for so long without Cold Ducks. I made a note to tell Patel about them.

'Well?'

'It's marvellous,' I said.

She sat back, sighing.

'How pleasant it is, sitting here talking to you. It's not easy for a woman living alone, you know. We're not like men. We're not meant to survive on our own. You've no idea what it's like sometimes, lying in bed, twisting and turning, unable to sleep.'

'Perhaps you should try a cup of cocoa?' I suggested.

'Cocoa?' She gave a short laugh. 'You dear sweet man — you don't understand! I can't sleep because I'm lonely. I want someone there with me.'

'Oh,' I said.

'I'm sure I don't have to spell it out for you,' she said. 'After all, you are a doctor.'

'Have you considered marrying again?'

'No,' she said. 'I haven't. George and I will be divorced shortly, but I don't want to be tied down again. Anyway, most of the men one meets today are so dreadful. They seem to be only interested in twenty-year-old girls. They have no appreciation of the things a more mature woman has to offer.'

'Surely you meet some attractive men?' I said.

She hesitated.

'I hope this isn't going to embarrass you,' she said. 'But I feel I can be honest.'

'Of course,' I said, puzzled.

'I'm attracted to Indians,' she said. 'Every time I've been in an Indian restaurant I've thought to myself: There's something about them. I don't know what it is. The different texture of the skin, perhaps; the marvellous serenity. I don't know.'

Tread carefully, I thought.

161

'Perhaps what attracts you to them is the fact that Indians are by nature more spiritual than sexual,' I suggested.

She burst out laughing.

'Oh come now, doctor,' she said. 'You didn't get to be over five hundred million people by contemplating your navels. And what about the Kama Sutra, and all those sexy temple carvings, and things?'

'But that's only one side of it,' I said. 'On the other you have Gandhi's teaching of Brahmacharya.'

'What in heaven's name is that?'

'Brahmacharya means sexual abstinence,' I said. 'Gandhi encouraged it. He believed in chastity, you see; he believed the expenditure of man's vital fluid, *bindu*, caused physical weakening and spiritual impoverishment. He also thought it gave you a bad skin.'

'You can't be serious?'

'Never more, dear lady, never more.'

'Well,' she said, 'no Brahmawhatever for me. You only live once is my motto.' She put her hand on mine. 'Now drink up, doctor, and I'll refresh your glass before dinner.'

Two days later, or so it seemed to me, we finished dinner, which had been served by the arrogant Simons, wearing a starched white jacket and a sneer which stretched from ear to ear. The sneer, of course, was fully justified. I had to admit it. Full of white wine, which had been dispensed in great draughts, I had done everything wrong. I had dropped food on the carpet, and got my cutlery confused, and while trying to turn over my grilled sole I had allowed it to flop back on to the plate, showering sauce all over the lace tablecloth.

If Lady Ammanford was prepared to ignore this, Simons most definitely was not. With each new mishap his look of contempt grew more marked. There was no question about it; in his eyes I was a Low Person, and destined to remain so.

But I was almost too drunk to care. The wine, coupled with the earlier drinks, had finally got to me. My only fear was that I might throw up over the table-cloth — an occurrence which even Lady Ammanford would be obliged to take note of. And that would be it.

After coffee was served Lady Ammanford, who had been floating somewhere between the floor and the ceiling, came to rest somewhere in front of me.

'Now,' she said. 'Time for a little treatment, I think?'

'Treatment?' I echoed.

'My neck,' she said, 'has been stiff all day. I'm sure all it needs is a little traction. But first I'm going to have a sauna.'

'Good idea,' I mumbled — anything to get her out of the room, so that I could be sick in private — 'I'm sure that will be most helpful.'

'I'll call you when I'm ready,' she said.

After she'd gone I sat still for a few moments, trying to focus on my shoes and decide what to do.

I was in trouble. Whatever I did would be wrong. If I slipped away, she would be enraged. If I passed out, she would be disgusted. Only one course was left to me. To give her the traction. But she would want it in her bedroom, and not even Lord Krishna himself could help me once she got me there.

I sat for a long time with my head in my hands, feeling sick and ill and miserable. When I looked up Simons was standing in the doorway.

'Her Ladyship is ready for you now,' he said. 'In the bedroom.'

He led the way upstairs and there she was, lying on a vast gilt bed, clad in a pink peignoir.

'Oh doctor,' she said, leaning back on the pillows and flinging her arms wide. 'I've had the most wonderful sauna I feel so relaxed, so warm ...'

Krishna, I prayed, don't do this to me.

'... so womanly.'

'Perhaps,' I muttered, propping myself against the

door to avoid swaying, 'we should keep the traction for another time?'

'No, no. I want it now. Now that I'm in the mood.'

She sat up, so that the peignoir fell open, revealing her giant breasts.

Please Krishna, I prayed, pick any penance, and I will gladly do it. Work in a leper colony. Delivering cheques to pools winners. But not this.

'How do you want me?' she demanded.

'The other way round,' I mumbled.

She turned, and as she did so the peignoir opened completely.

'Oh the hell with it,' she said, throwing the robe aside. 'It will only get in the way.'

She placed her feet against the headboard.

'Right,' she said. 'I'm ready.'

Moving with great care to avoid falling, I removed my shoes and, crouching at the foot of the bed, placed one hand beneath her chin and the other behind her neck.

And then it happened.

She reached up and, clutching my head with both hands, hauled my face down beside hers.

'Dear lady,' I gasped. 'What are you doing? I'm a doctor; you're my patient.'

She gave a throaty laugh, and I could feel her breath on my cheek.

'We're people, you dear man. A man and a woman. Don't fight it. . . .'

'But I can't.' Desperately I sought an escape. 'I'll be struck off.'

'Nobody will know. It will be our secret; our own, warm, wonderful secret.'

'Simons will know. Simons.'

'Silly boy. We're not going to let him watch.'

Passionately, she hauled my mouth to hers.

Then the door-bell rang.

'It's the door,' I cried, struggling. 'The door. . . .'

'Simons will get it,' she said, unbuttoning my jacket.

'But it may be for me,' I said. 'I left this address.'

'Don't worry.' She put a hand on my forehead as I attempted to rise. 'If it is Simons will knock.'

She began undoing my tie — no easy feat considering how tightly she was clutching me to her bosom — making a curious hissing sound as she did so. Then, unbuttoning my shirt, she began hauling it of my back. I was being peeled like a banana. And still no knock on the door.

Suddenly there was a commotion in the hall. And an odd stomping sound, as though someone were striking the marble with the top of a broom.

'Oh my God,' Lady Ammanford said, releasing me quickly. 'It's George.'

'George?'

'My husband. What a time to choose!'

At half-past eleven, two minutes away from the rape of Ram Das, I could imagine no better time.

Suddenly there was a shout.

'G-R-A-C-E!'

'Damn him,' she said, pulling on a dressing gown. 'What the hell does he want?'

'Perhaps he wants to patch things up?'

'After six years,' she said, 'he's hardly likely to be coming round at midnight to patch things up. He must want something.'

'Like what?' I said, pulling on my crumpled shirt.

'Who knows? The last time he came back was for his leg. He left it behind when he walked out.'

She went to the door.

'Wait here,' she said. 'I'll go down and take the fool into the drawing-room. Then you can let yourself out.'

'Does it matter if he sees me?' I said, sensing a small advantage. 'After all, I am your doctor. I have a perfect right to be here at this hour.'

'He sounds angry,' she said. 'It's better that he doesn't. Believe me.'

I believed her. The last thing I wanted at that

moment was to be confronted by an enraged, one-legged man.

I finished dressing.

'I'm sorry,' she said. 'But don't worry. There'll be other times.'

Not if I can help it, I thought, picking up my shoes. Even if the success of my practice depends on it, I will not go through this again.

I waited until I heard the drawing-room door close and then, holding my shoes in my hand, crept down the wide staircase to the front hall.

At the foot of the stairs, something made me turn. There was Simons, standing in the shadows.

'May we take it that you are leaving?' he inquired.

'That's right.' I said, feeling suddenly rather ill. 'I'm leaving.'

He glanced disdainfully at the shoes in my hand.

'It might be advisable to put those on,' he said. 'I do believe we are in for a little rain.'

33

The following evening, at supper, I told Patel all that had happened.

'What on earth can I do?' I asked miserably.

'Your only hope is to stall the old bitch as long as possible,' he said. 'Until you have built up such a large practice that losing her and her friends will make no difference. But don't make her mad until then. We need her.'

Sipping my tea, I found myself vaguely resenting his use of the word 'we'. But he was right. 'We' did need her. Patel for the return of his money; me to further my friendship with Susan. She adored her aunt. If I lost Lady Ammanford, I lost Susan too. That I knew. What I didn't know was how to hang on to my virginity with the lustful Lady A. around.

'You could always say you're a poof,' Patel suggested.

'Thank's a lot,' I said.

'I'm only trying to be helpful,' he said.

'Well, try harder,' I said.

He poured me another cup.

'Cheer up,' he said. 'The situation isn't that bad. What's the worst that can happen? You get seduced by the old bag? That's not so terrible.'

'Isn't it?' I said. 'You haven't seen her stripped.' I shuddered. 'She's the end. Even if I wanted to, I couldn't. And that would make her madder still.'

'Listen,' he said. 'If I can do it with the hag downstairs for nothing, you can certainly do it with Lady Ammanford for something.'

'It's easy for you to talk,' I said. 'Yours isn't as bad as mine.'

He stared at me in disbelief.

'You've got to be joking,' he said. 'Mine's got breath like a dead lion and skin like an alligator. She never bathes, she's got hardly any teeth, and underneath that rag she wears round her head she's damn near bald. Not so bad, you say? She's the worst. And now she's beginning to nag. She wants me to marry her. She says she needs security. I've a good mind to tell her that if it's security she wants she ought to go to India.'

'Why India?' I asked.

'Because there we've had the Cow Protection Society since 1882,' he said. 'And, believe me, she more than qualifies.'

He got to his feet.

'Come on,' he said. 'Let's go out and have a drink. We're due for a celebration. I haven't seen you for days. ...'

34

Hilary Pike looked even less like a doctor than I did, which was encouraging. He always wore a crumpled dark-blue suit and a badly ironed shirt and his shoes always seemed in need of a shine. He was, I suppose, in his early forties, but it was difficult to say. Sometimes he looked older than at other times. 'It takes it out of you,' he explained, 'taking it out of them.'

A few days after the fiasco at Lady Ammanford's, I met him as he was dashing along the hall.

'Well now,' he said. 'When are you going to join the rest of us for an evening drink? We usually get together during the week for a pint or two. And I know the others would love to meet you.'

'I'd like to meet them,' I said. 'I've been rather busy up to now, I'm afraid. ...'

'Oh I know,' he said. 'We're all very impressed by the fact that you're treating You Know Who.'

'Oh, you've heard?'

'Yes indeed. Hilda Furze spread the news far and wide. What's he like?'

'He's very nice.'

'I've got a lot of time for him,' Pike said. 'Best Prime Minister we've had for years.'

'That's what everybody says.'

'I'm dying to hear all the gossip,' Pike said. 'What about a drink this evening?'

'I can't manage this evening,' I said.

'How about next week sometime?'

'Yes. Next week should be all right.'

'Try for Tuesday. That's good for me.'

'All right,' I said.

'Give me a ring when you're sure,' he said. 'I'm at the nursing home most mornings — Miss Furze has the number — and here after twelve.'

He gave me a cheery smile.

'Well,' he said, 'must dash. Got a busy morning. Five of the little darlings. Thank God for the permissive society, I say. Don't forget to let me know about Tuesday?'

'I won't,' I said.

Seated at my desk, I read the letter for the third time.

'Dear Miss Partridge,' it began. 'If you are free, I wonder if you would care to drop by for a drink on Tuesday around 6 p.m.? One or two others are looking in, and it would be so nice to see you again. ....'

I tried to imagine her in her flat in Hallam Street, opening the letter. She'd be wearing her orange pyjamas, perhaps, and the black silk robe. She'd have had breakfast, and would be sitting on the edge of her bed reading her mail.

How would she react? Would her lovely face light up with pleasure? Would she cry: 'It's from Ram — at last'? Would she do a little jig around the bedroom, trying to decide what she should wear? The short black crêpe dress with the pleated skirt and large bishop sleeves, perhaps? Or the white trouser suit with lots of gold bracelets? Which was the more suitable? Which would *he* like? He being me!

Or would she merely scribble a quick note: 'So sorry ... a previous engagement ... how kind of you to ask? ...'

I sat back, the letter in my hand.

Only that morning, I had received her cheque for £4. Attached to it was a little card reading: 'Happy Thoughts — Susan'.

Happy thoughts, indeed. It was the first time I had

seen her writing, and the sight of it sent a tremor of pleasure through me. How beautifully rounded it was, compared to my own illiterate scrawl. How well-spaced. How special my name looked the way she had written it.

I sighed.

With Susan Partridge, I was in a fur-lined trap. One from which there was no escape. The only way I could get to her was as her doctor. And that was the only way I could never get to her.

How different it would have been in films. No producer in his right mind would make a picture where the doctor didn't get the girl. 'This phoney Indian doctor bit, it's a great idea,' he'd tell his writers. 'But the way you've angled it, nobody will believe it. Of course he must get the girl. A man in a white coat with a stethoscope dangling from the pocket *always* gets the girl. Anyway, Omar won't do it unless he winds up with Raquel. ...'

'Right, T.J.,' the writers would say, shambling off to write the script again. And this time the girl would be a nymphomaniac writhing in a mucoserous flood while the dusky doctor hovered over her. ...

Why wasn't it like that in real life? Why wasn't I struggling to disengage myself from Susan's arms? Why was I being forced to send her this pathetic invitation?

But if I was unhappy over my failure to make headway with Susan, I was delighted with my Harley Street career. Thanks to Lady Ammanford and the Prime Minister, I now saw a splendid future ahead of me, lined with hitherto undreamed-of rewards, for now my waiting-room was full every day and I was turning patients away.

Of course, I had to be careful. Every now and again I found myself actually believing that I was a doctor. On these occasions, and they were becoming more and more frequent, had some skilfull Q.C. marched me into the dock and flung charges like 'Fraud', 'Charlatan' and

'Rascal' at me, I would have been genuinely bewildered. I was none of those things, I was a dedicated man, helping the sick.

'Ask my patients,' I would say.

'Your patients,' he would thunder. 'You mean those innocents you've duped, you wily Indian villain.'

Yes, I had to be careful.

Sliding the letter into an envelope I addressed it in my best handwriting.

Susan, lovely Susan. Come to the party. Please.

35

'He's on his way,' Hilda Furze said.

I looked up.

'Who's on his way?'

'The Prime Minister,' she said excitedly. 'Mr St Clair telephoned a few minutes ago while you were with Mrs Rainsford. He said he'd be here at eighteen minutes past twelve.'

I glanced at my watch.

'But it's noon already,' I said.

'I know it,' she said. 'He doesn't give you much notice, does he?'

'Who have we got waiting?' I asked.

'Lady Marsh,' she said. 'She's a friend of Mrs Blair's. And there's someone due at half-past twelve.'

'Have a word with Lady Marsh,' I said. 'Tell her what's happened. Say I'm terribly sorry.'

'I've already done that,' Miss Furze said. 'She says she understands completely. You're not to worry.'

I looked at her.

'Really, Miss Furze, I don't know what I'd do without you.'

She looked flustered.

'Why thank you, doctor,' she said.

She stood there, uncertainly, for a moment. 'I'd better go out and wait for him in the hall,' she said.

Prompt to the minute, she opened the door and the Prime Minister strode in.

'Good of you to squeeze me in,' he said. 'Can't tell you how grateful I am. Felt a bit tense, you know, and thought a quick stretch would do me good.'

'Happy to oblige,' I said.

'Got a perfectly ghastly afternoon,' he said. 'A two-hour session with the French. Loathe the blighters. Always breathing garlic in your face. At least de Gaulle didn't do that. Or, if he did, he was so tall it went over your head.'

'How have you been feeling since the last visit?' I asked.

'Frightfully fit,' he said, starting to undress. 'Of course, I make it a rule always to feel frightfully fit. Great believer in bodily exercise, you know; jogs, spins, brisk walks. Play squash, do you?'

'No,' I said.

'Should have a shot at it,' he said. He gave me a wide grin. 'Splendid fun. Good for the legs, too.'

'I'll remember that,' I said.

'Another thing,' he said. 'Not too many hot baths. Make it a rule not to have too many hot baths. Two a week, that's the maximum. More than that weakens a man; saps his strength. Had a Home Secretary once who bathed every day. Bit of an eccentric, of course. ...'

By this time he was down to his jockey-shorts. Almost as an afterthought he took those off too. And there stood the Prime Minister of Great Britain and Northern Ireland — totally naked.

'On the couch, is it?'

'I'd better just check your back first.'

I ran my fingers down his spine. He gave a sudden shiver.

'You're tickling,' he said.

'Sorry.'

'Don't be sorry,' he said. 'Haven't been tickled in years.'

'If you'll just lie on the couch, then.'

Eagerly he clambered on to the traction-couch.

'Love this,' he said. 'Absolutely love it. Wonder if I could get one for Number Ten?'

'I doubt it,' I said. 'As I told you, I found it by chance. It came from the States.'

'I remember. Eisenhower, you said. Must have had a new motor fitted, of course. 110 volts there; 250 here. Still, wouldn't have had much difficulty changing it over. Must have been one competent electrician under his command.'

I adjusted the straps.

'Quite comfortable?'

'Absolutely,' he said.

I began turning the handle which stretched the straps. When the wheel had turned three times I stopped.

'One more turn,' he said.

'I'm not sure it's wise. ...'

'One more,' he insisted.

I turned the wheel again.

'Now switch on.'

I clicked the switch and turned the dial. With a roar the motor leaped into life.

'Aaaaaaagh,' he murmured.

'Is everything all right?'

'Mmmmmmmmmh.'

'It's not hurting you?'

'Oooooooooh.'

Strapped to the throbbing couch, the Prime Minister jolted about like a landed whale.

Then:

'Faster,' he croaked.

'It's on 4 now.'

'Faster, man, faster.'

I turned the dial all the way. With a whine, the motor speeded up. There was a faint smell of burning oil in the air. The table, vibrating madly, seemed about to rend its victim in two.

Fascinated, I stood over the thrashing body while the groans approached a crescendo.

'Aaaaaaghhhh! Eeeeeeeooooooh!'

So loud were his cries that I glanced uneasily towards the door, fearing the imminent arrival of his detective. But nothing happened.

Then the bulky figure in front of me seemed to go slack, despite the tension upon it, and the Prime Minister opened his eyes.

'Enough,' he said.

I switched off the machine. Enough was right, I thought, looking at his body, which was drenched in sweat. He lay for a few moments, breathing heavily. Then, with a sigh, he swung himself off the couch.

'Well,' he said, 'I may not be the greatest Prime Minister this country has ever had, but I may turn out to be the longest.'

He held out a hand.

'Got a towel?' he asked.

I gave him one.

'Feel marvellous,' he said. 'Extraordinary machine. Most invigorating experience.'

'You had it turned up awfully high,' I said.

'Why not?' he said. 'A few tugs can't do you any harm.'

He towelled himself vigorously.

'Try it yourself, do you, sometimes?'

I shook my head.

'I haven't got anyone to attend to the straps and motor.'

'You've got your receptionist.'

'She's not properly qualified,' I said. 'Anyway, I'm fortunate. I don't suffer from back trouble.'

'Who's talking about back trouble?' he said.

He tossed the towel at me and went over to the mantelpiece and inspected the clock Patel had given me.

'That's new,' he said.

'Yes. A friend gave it to me.'

'Poor Percy Vale,' he said. 'Sixty years with the South Lancashire Wool Emporium and that's what they thought of him.'

He began getting dressed.

'Look here,' he said. 'There's a reception at Number Ten on Monday for these French blighters. Would you care to come?'

I brightened.

'That's very kind of you' I said. 'I'd be delighted.'

'You won't have to talk to them, or anything like that,' he said. 'And there'll be lots of other people there.'

'I'll look forward to it,' I said.

'It's at seven o'clock,' he said. 'I'll get young St Clair to send you an invitation.'

I walked with him into the hall. Hilda Furze was waiting by the front door. As soon as she saw him she whipped it open.

'And how are you today?' he asked.

'Exceedingly well, thank you, sir.'

After he'd gone she closed the door and leant against it for a moment.

'He spoke to me,' she said faintly. 'Did you see that? He actually spoke to me. . . .'

36

I bought myself a new suit for the occasion, a dark-blue, double-breasted number which set me back thirty pounds. I was delighted with it, but when I showed it to Patel that night he flew into an immediate rage.

'What in heaven's name did you have to buy that for?' he demanded angrily. 'You've already got the grey one. What's wrong with that?'

'I've worn it every day for weeks,' I said. 'Anyway, this is a special occasion.'

'I see,' he said sarcastically. 'Getting a bit fussy, aren't we? What will it be next, I wonder? A yacht? A house in the country? Well, just remember this. It's my money you're tossing around.'

'I haven't forgotten,' I said, stung. 'But I've got to look smart on an occasion like this.'

'You don't have to spend thirty pounds doing it,' he said. 'You could have hired a suit, come to that.'

'Don't you understand?' I said. 'It's just like investing in myself.'

'Oh is it?' he said, disgruntled. 'Well in that case I'd just as soon you did your investing with your own money.'

I was distressed. Patel's approval was important to me. Particularly when I was so keyed-up.

Not until supper was over and we had consumed the better part of a bottle of wine did he relent.

'Oh, well,' he said. 'Perhaps you're right. I suppose it is important that you look smart. And it is a beautiful suit.'

'You really think so?' I said. 'Does it fit all right?'

'It fits perfectly.'

'What about the back?' I got to my feet and turned round. 'How does it look at the back?'

'The back's fine. It looks as if it were made for you.'

'You're not just saying that?'

'No. It's a nice suit.'

So we were friends again. He even accompanied me to the bus stop.

'I can't wait to hear how it goes,' he said. 'When will I see you again?'

'I'll come to supper next week,' I said, jumping onto a bus.

176

'Don't forget to tell him about the loos,' he said.

When I got in next day there was a message on my desk.

'Miss Partridge rang,' it read. 'She says she'd be delighted to look in for drinks on Tuesday. She's looking forward to seeing you again.'

My heart leapt.

She was coming!

Hurriedly I telephoned Hilary Pike.

'Are we still on for Tuesday?'

'Absolutely,' he said. 'Peter and Frank are joining us. Where do you want to go — the Devonshire Arms?'

'No,' I said. 'Let's have it here. I'll get some drinks in.'

'What a splendid idea.'

'I've invited a girl,' I said hesitantly.

'Then let's make it a party,' he said. 'There's a little swinger come my way recently — three months gone and due for demolition next week — but meantime quite happy to have a giggle. I'll bring her.'

I had a sudden thought.

'What about Miss Furze? Shall we ask her too?'

'It might be tricky if we don't,' he said. 'After all, we can hardly converge on your room singing and dancing and leave the poor bitch in the hall by herself.'

'All right. I'll ask her.'

'And remember — we go four ways on the booze. Just keep a tally of what you spend.'

'I will,' I said.

I put the telephone down and sat for a moment, re-reading the message. I could hardly believe it. Susan was coming. She was looking forward to seeing me again.

I would go out and buy some roses.

37

At seven o'clock on Monday night, confidence dribbling from my toes at an alarming rate, I stood outside Number Ten, Downing Street, clutching my invitation in my hand.

To my surprise, without my knocking or ringing a bell or anything, the door opened immediately. And there stood a white-jacketed person.

'Your name, sir?'

'Dr Das.'

I handed him my invitation.

'Good evening, Dr Das. Please proceed along the hall and up the staircase to the first floor.'

I proceeded along the hall and up the staircase to the first floor. At the top of the stairs another white-jacketed person ushered me into a brilliantly-lit salon. And, suddenly, there they were, my sort of people; all mixed together under the chandeliers. Good-humoured men, sure of themselves, and attractive women, beautifully at ease.

'Champagne, sir?'

A waiter came up with a silver tray laden with drinks.

'Thank you.'

I took a glass and sipped it cautiously, wishing that I had somebody to talk to. Everybody in the room seemed to know everyone else. The air was loud with conversation and laughter.

To my right, an immense woman in a gold caftan, heavily adorned with chains and beads, was talking to a pale, limp young man.

'Last time I came here,' she said in a loud voice, 'the Iranian Ambassador was sick. Right there.' She pointed to the place where the hapless Persian had thrown up and indeed, on inspection, it did appear to be rather lighter than its surrounding.

'Disgusting,' the pale young man said.

'You know the trouble with those sort of people,' the woman said. 'They don't know how to hold their drink.'

She glared sharply at me, and I moved away.

In a corner by the window, a florid-faced man was talking earnestly to a tall woman in horn-rimmed glasses.

'Can you give me one reason,' he was asking, 'why I should suffer because of the stupidity of the masses? Most of the working-class people in this country are cretins — I'm sure we agree on that. Yet their vote carries just as much weight as mine, which is ridiculous. If they chose to put some half-wit into Parliament — and they do, again and again — and that man's decisions affect my way of life — which they do, again and again — what can I do? Nothing. So the lowest common denominator of intelligence rules the country; not the highest.'

'And what's the answer?' the tall woman said.

'I'll tell you,' he said. 'There should be an island somewhere in the world set aside purely for the élite. To get in you would have to pass the stiffest of tests, and they, of course, would be designed to exclude the sort of rabble who are reducing this country of ours to its present pitiful state. We would have only the finest writers, the finest architects, and the finest lawyers. Our doctors would be the best; so would our politicians; so would our artists. Ours would be an oasis of talent in a world swamped by mediocrity.'

'It's a fine idea,' the tall woman said. 'But who would do the dirty work? Who would look after the drains and the garbage collection and the lavatories?'

'Oh, we'd import lesser breeds for that sort of thing,' the man said. 'We'd keep a tight rein on them, of course. They'd have to live in special camps, and all that.'

'But what would happen when they began breeding,

as lesser breeds tend to do? Eventually they'd gain the upper hand, as they have here, and in no time at all you'd have them pulling the switches in the power-stations and immobilizing industry, just as they do here.'

'If they did that,' the florid-faced man said, 'we'd shoot the sods, I should have mentioned: we'd have an élite police force too. Very well armed.'

'Sounds just like South Africa,' the tall woman said. 'Except that the whites there are hardly an élite group. Fascist louts, the ones I've met.'

'Come now,' the man said. 'Don't let's get started on that. You know the P.M. hates politics being discussed at Number Ten.'

People kept moving around, greeting each other, making plans to meet again, searching for friends. But nobody spoke to me.

It was all very different from the way I had imagined it.

'My dear Dr Das,' the P.M. would say striding forward. 'How marvellous to see you.' He'd turn and hold up a hand. 'A moment, please, everybody. I want you to meet the man I've talked so much about — Dr Das.' And then they'd all rush forward, eager to shake my hand. Instead, here I was standing about like some loiterer at a street corner.

Just when I was about to give up hope and leave, a plumpish woman with dark bags under her eyes came over and looked at me searchingly.

'You're Singh, right, from India House?'

'No,' I said. 'I'm afraid I'm not.'

'You look like Singh,' she said.

'I can't help that,' I said. 'I'm not him.'

'Not *he*,' she said reprovingly. 'Not *he*. Not not him.'

I was so low in spirits by this time I could think of nothing to say. So I just stood there looking blankly at the woman while she inspected me as though I were something she had just bought and was not quite sure about.

'If you're not Singh,' she said, finally. 'Who are you?'

'My name is Das,' I said. 'I'm a doctor.'

'Oh.' She looked interested. 'What kind of doctor?'

'A good one,' I said, irritated by her manner.

'I don't doubt that,' she said. 'What I meant was — what do you specialize in?'

'I don't specialize in anything,' I said. 'I'm in general practice.'

'In general practice, eh?' Her eyes narrowed. 'But you know the Prime Minister, apparently?'

'He's a patient of mine,' I said.

'Is he indeed? I always thought his physician was Sir Laurence Wainscott-Evans?'

'I believe he did go to him at one time,' I said, making an effort to move away.

She put a hand on my arm.

'If you're a doctor,' she said. 'there's something I must ask you. Do you believe in blepharoplasty?'

'Do I believe in what?'

'Blepharoplasty,' she repeated. 'I mean — do you consider it a dangerous operation?'

I was fed up with her by this time. Anyway, I was getting into deep water. I had no idea what blepharoplasty was. And if the conversation continued, she would very soon find out.

'Madam,' I said. 'Like you I am a guest under this roof. If you wish to consult me in a professional capacity, I suggest you telephone my secretary in Harley Street and arrange an appointment.'

Her face went deep red. She took a step backward. Fearing that she might slap me, I turned on my heel and walked quickly away, brushing past a beak-faced man in a dreadful green suit who was being horrid to a small bald-headed man.

'You're a twat,' he kept saying. 'An absolute twat.' Leaving them to it I wandered out into the corridor.

Standing with her back to me was a girl in a black velvet trouser suit. An aristocratic-looking man was talking to her. I couldn't hear what he was saying, but whatever it was it seemed to be annoying her. She kept shaking her head and saying, quite audibly, 'No. I won't.'

'Why not?' the man said loudly.

'Because I don't bloody well want to,' the girl said.

The man flung me a furious glance and I moved further along the corridor. A moment later he passed me, breathing heavily. I turned and looked back at the girl. Tawny hair and blue eyes. Of course. It was Jo Masters, Susan's friend.

'You,' she said. She seemed to be having difficulty in focusing.

'Hello,' I said.

'I need a drink.' She held out an empty glass. 'Be a love and get me a drink.'

'What would you like?'

'Oh, God, I don't know. Champagne I suppose.'

I went back into the main room and plucked two drinks from a passing tray. The plumpish woman with the bags under her eyes was still standing where I had left her.

'Thanks,' Jo said.

She took a sip.

'Muck, isn't it?' she said.

'I don't know much about champagne,' I said.

'I do,' she said. 'This is muck.'

She swayed slightly, and took a step backwards.

'You're staring at me,' she said. 'Why are you staring at me?'

'I'm sorry,' I said. 'I didn't mean to.'

'What are you doing here, anyway?'

'I was invited by the Prime Minister,' I said.

'Oh well,' she said, 'I suppose it's as good a way as any of getting into Number Ten.'

'And you?'

She shrugged.

'I come here all the time. It's sort of home away from home.'

'By the way,' I said. 'How's your back?'

'What's that got to do with you?'

'I treated you. Remember?'

She peered at me over the rim of her glass. Suddenly she smiled.

'Of course! You're the doctor. The one with the lovely machine.'

'That's right.'

'What's your name?'

'Dr Das.'

'Mine's Jo Masters.'

'I know. You're a friend of Susan Partridge's.'

'We work together,' she said.

'So I understand. Have you seen much of her lately?'

'I've seen all of her lately,' she said, with a chuckle. 'In the changing-room. She's got a great figure.'

'Yes she has,' I said.

She swayed towards me.

'Have you had Susan?' she asked.

I looked around anxiously.

'Are you mad?' I said. 'I'm her doctor.'

'What's that got to do with it? Don't you fancy her?'

'I like her very much.'

'Then what's holding you back?'

'Well, for one thing, she's already got a boy-friend.'

'Basil,' she said. 'That drip.'

'What's wrong with him?'

'Nothing, if you happen to be climbing the Himalayas. But who's climbing the Himalayas?'

She finished her drink.

'I'm an authority on drips,' she said. 'Anything you want to know, ask me.'

'Was he a drip — that man you were having an argument with?'

'That man I was having an argument with?' She looked puzzled for a moment. 'Oh, *him*! I wasn't having an argument with him. I was just saying No.'

'He seemed very angry.'

'He gets angry once a day,' she said. 'Regular as a bowel movement.'

She leaned against the wall.

'Are you here on your own?'

I nodded.

'Do you know many of these drears?'

'I don't know anyone,' I said.

'If you get really desperate,' she said. 'You can always talk to me.'

'I'm desperate now,' I said.

She giggled.

'You're a funny one,' she said. 'When I came to your consulting-room you hardly said a word. All you did was stare at my breasts.'

I flushed.

'I think we'd better change the subject,' I said.

'Why?' she demanded. 'It's just becoming interesting.'

My eye was diverted by a portrait hanging on the wall behind her. A former elder statesman gazed malevolently down, his glare preserved in oils forever.

'Attractive, isn't he?' Jo said. 'Great one for gunboats, he was.'

She held out her glass.

'I need another drink.'

'So do I,' I said. 'But I think I ought to find my host. I haven't even seen him yet.'

'There's lots of time,' she said. 'This will go on for hours.'

'Are you sure?'

'I'm sure,' she said.

I went back into the salon and collected two more drinks.

'It gets worse,' she said, sampling hers. 'It really does.'

'Where do you live?' I asked.

'Beauchamp Place,' she said. 'What about you?'

'I live in Devonshire Street.'

'Near Susan?'

'Fairly near Susan.'

'That's cosy,' she said.

We were interrupted. An elegantly-dressed young man, looking harassed, grabbed me by the arm.

'Dr Das?'

'That's right.'

'I've been looking everywhere for you. My name's St Clair — the P.M.'s secretary?'

'Oh, yes. How do you do?'

'He's been asking for you.' He turned to Jo. 'Will you excuse us, Miss Masters? I did promise the P.M. I'd take Dr Das straight to the study.'

'You're excused,' Jo said.

'Perhaps I'll see you later?' I said.

'Perhaps you will,' she said.

Hugh St Clair led the way along the corridor to a room at the end.

'Know her well, do you, doctor?'

'Miss Masters? No, not very well.'

'Have to be careful there,' he said. 'Mix Masters, we call her. Great little swinger. But trouble.'

'In what way?'

'Didn't you know? She's the girl the Foreign Secretary left his wife for. Mad about her, he was. They disappeared for three days once. The P.M. went absolutely spare. Guess where they turned up? Frinton, of all places.'

He opened the door and ushered me into a soft-lit room with panelling on the walls. There was a cheerful fire burning in the grate and in front of it four persons were standing about like models in a Men of Distinction advertisement. One of them was the Prime Minister.

'My dear fellow,' he said. 'I was beginning to think you must have had a better invitation.' He strode forward, and without waiting for me to reply, took my arm and steered me towards the men by the fire.

'Gentlemen,' he said. 'I want you to meet someone of whom I think most highly. Didn't discover him myself, to be honest, Toby Downs did that. Good man Toby.

185

But at least I can take the credit for getting him here. This, gentlemen, is Dr Das.'

The three men nodded distantly.

Turning to me, the Prime Minister said:

'This is Sir Lawrence Wainscott-Evans (panic). This is Sir Reeves Mapleton, Commissioner of Police (double panic). And this is His Excellency Dr Jaisooria, the High Commissioner for India, whom you undoubtedly know (treble panic).'

Standing before the three eminent men, it struck me for one fearful moment that I might emulate the Iranian Ambassador and be sick right there on the carpet. So great was my alarm, so frantic the twitchings of my stomach, that it seemed I might be unable to control myself. I uttered a silent prayer to Krishna: 'Not here, please; not in front of this lot.'

Then the door opened suddenly and a tall young man came in, clutching a notebook.

'Sorry to interrupt, P.M, but Washington's on red.'

'Damn,' the Prime Minister said.

He turned to us.

'Sorry about this gentlemen. Shan't be a jiffy. Unless it's nuclear, of course. That may take a little longer.'

He flashed us the now familiar shark's grin and hurried out.

I tried to move, but couldn't. All the strength seemed to have gone out of my legs. Here I was, face to face with Triple Doom, and I couldn't walk. It was the sort of thing that happened in dreams. But this wasn't any dream.

Then, from an immense height above my head, I heard the voice of Sir Laurence Wainscott-Evans.

'So you're Dr Das, are you?'

I looked up. And up. He was the tallest man I had ever seen, a giant of a person, towering above me like a well-dressed street lamp. He was clad in a black jacket and striped trousers and his white shirt, crisp, and immaculately laundered, glistened in the light from the fire.

'That's right,' I said.

'I've been hearing a lot about you,' he said.

'So have I,' said the man in the middle of the group, the celebrated thief-catcher Sir Reeves Mapleton. Tensed like a coiled spring, he stood there glaring at me, as if annoyed at being detained when he could have been out arresting large numbers of people.

'Regrettably the only person who has not been apprised of you is your fellow countryman,' said the High Commissioner, a small pudgy man with black hair and dark muddy eyes.

'I'm afraid I don't mix much in diplomatic circles,' I said.

'You should,' he said. 'You should. There's a lot of free liquor, and always some attractive women.'

'I suppose I ought to be upset that we're sharing the same patient,' Sir Laurence said. 'And I would be, had I not been sharing him with half a dozen other doctors for the past ten years.'

'What was that?' barked Sir Reeves. He seemed to be rather deaf.

'I was saying that we were not the only doctors treating the P.M.,' said Sir Laurence.

'Ah,' said Sir Reeves. 'Both got him, have you? How long have you had him, Rum?'

'Ram,' I said.

'Ram?' he queried. 'That's a damn funny name.'

'It's Indian,' the High Commissioner said smoothly. 'Quite a common name in our country really.'

'Odd,' Sir Reeves said, looking at me suspiciously. 'I've never heard it before. Knew a cat-burglar years ago called Tam. Gone out now. Gone out now, cat-burgling. Thieves don't seem to have a head for heights any more.'

'Are you enjoying yourself, young man?' the High Commissioner asked.

'Yes, thank you,' I said. 'I haven't been here before.'

'I'm not enjoying myself,' Sir Laurence said. 'Just got

187

button-holed by some damn fool woman out there who wanted my opinion of blepharoplasty. ...'

'What in God's name is that?' asked Sir Reeves.

'It's the operation for removing the bags under the eyes,' Sir Laurence said. 'Not wise, unless you go to a good man. You can wind up looking like an exceedingly ancient twelve-year-old.'

'She asked me the same thing ...' I began.

'I trust you told her to get stuffed,' said Sir Laurence.

'Well, not in those words,' I said.

'I always tell those sort of people to get stuffed,' he said. 'Sat next to a woman at a dinner-party not long ago who kept on about her headaches and depressions. "Oh do get stuffed, madam," I said finally. And do you know what? A few days later I ran into her again and she said: "I took your advice, doctor, and the headaches and depressions have completely gone. ..."'

He broke off.

'Ah,' he said. 'Here comes the P.M. now.'

The Prime Minister joined us, looking slightly flushed.

'Really,' he said crossly. 'I don't know what the President is thinking of, using the hot line to ask for someone's address. I don't mind it at Christmas, but he might be a little more considerate at this time of night.' He glanced at his watch. 'Trouble is,' he said 'he's probably just lurched back from lunch.'

'Whose address was it?' asked Sir Reeves. 'A woman, I'll be bound.'

'How did you guess?' asked the Prime Minister. 'God in heaven, I thought I had more womanizers in my Cabinet than any Prime Minister in history, but that lot over there leaves us standing. I wonder they get any work done at all with all those starlets telephoning the White House.'

'Always been like that, the Americans,' said Sir Laurence. 'That's all they think of, crumpet. Ghastly lot.'

'Trouble is,' said the Prime Minister. 'Every time I say anything about it to the President he gets huffy.

Keeps telling me I'm in no position to talk. I once made the mistake of telling him about the Foreign Secretary and that bint Jo Masters.'

'What's that?' barked Sir Reeves.

'I was saying I told the President about the time the Foreign Secretary went off to Frinton with Jo Masters,' the Prime Minister said. 'Since he was supposed to be in Washington at the time I really had no alternative.'

'Nice little town, Frinton,' said Sir Reeves. 'Wouldn't mind retiring there.'

'If you're going to retire anywhere,' Sir Laurence said, 'Bournemouth's the place.'

'What's so good about Bournemouth?' asked the Prime Minister.

'Healthiest town in Britain,' Sir Laurence said. 'Statistics done for the National Health Council prove that a man lives longer in Bournemouth than in any other town in Britain.'

'Stuff and nonsense,' said Sir Reeves. 'It just seems longer. Dullest place I know, Bournemouth. All those dreadful gardens, full of old men.'

There was a sudden commotion outside. The door opened and in came Jo Masters, followed by a red-faced Hugh St Clair.

'I'm sorry, Prime Minister. She insisted. . . .'

The Prime Minister nodded.

'That's all right.' He looked at Jo, who was standing by the door, swaying slightly.

'How are you, my dear?'

'Drunk,' she said.

'I can see that,' the Prime Minister said. 'But how drunk?'

'Stewed to the gills,' she said. 'It's this cheap champagne you're serving. Can't you get them to come up with something better?'

'No one else seems to be complaining,' the Prime Minister said.

'No one else has drunk as much of it as me,' she said.

189

She made no effort to come closer.

'Was there something you particularly wanted?' the Prime Minister said.

'Yes,' she said, looking straight at me. 'Him.'

The Prime Minister looked surprised.

'I was not aware you knew each other?' he said.

'She's a patient of mine,' I blurted.

'Is she indeed?' he said.

I went across to Jo.

'Look,' I said. 'You're embarrassing everybody.'

'Good,' she said. 'They could do with a little embarrassing.'

'Please. For my sake.'

'You said you'd see me later.'

'I know I did.'

'Well,' she said. 'It's later.'

'I meant after I'd finished talking with the Prime Minister.'

'I won't interrupt,' she said. 'Go ahead. Talk to him. I'll just stand here and sway.'

'I promise I'll be out in a few moments,' I said. 'Please don't make things difficult for me.'

She considered this for a moment.

'All right,' she said. 'But five minutes, that's all.'

She reeled out into the corridor.

Hugh St Clair put his head round the door.

'What shall I do?' he inquired.

'God knows,' the Prime Minister said. 'Who's got her now, anyway? Is she still with Environment?'

'Good Lord no,' said St Clair. 'That was weeks ago. She's moved on to Trade and Industry.'

'Well, keep her out of here,' said the Prime Minister. 'We can't have her falling all over my guests. They'll wonder what sort of a house this is.'

'I'll do my best,' said St Clair.

He closed the door behind him.

'What an extraordinary young woman,' said Sir Reeves.

'You've met her before, surely?' the Prime Minister said.

'I don't believe I have,' said Sir Reeves. 'What does she do?'

'Oh, this and that,' said the Prime Minister.

'By the look of her,' said Sir Reeves, 'it's not too much of this, but a hell of a lot of that.'

The Prime Minister smiled sourly.

'She has her uses,' he said. 'And her mother's a damn fine woman. Works for the Party at Orpington.'

'Oh, yes,' said Sir Laurence. 'I believe I treated her once. Jane Masters, right? Tall, willowy woman. ...'

'That's the one,' said the Prime Minister.

'Serves a dashed good sherry.'

'Indeed she does,' said the Prime Minister.

Sir Laurence glanced at his watch.

'Well, Prime Minister. I must be off. I've got to get back to Brighton tonight.'

'Must you Larry? It's only nine o'clock.'

'Afraid so. Enjoyed it, though. Splendid party.'

'It's time I was cutting along, too,' said the High Commissioner. 'I have another reception to attend after this. At the American Embassy.'

'Oh that one,' said the Prime Minister. 'It's for Reagan, isn't it? Ambitious fellow.'

'Handsome, too,' said the High Commissioner.

'That's the trouble with the Americans,' the Prime Minister said. 'Always voting people into power because of their looks. They don't give a damn about their policies, only their profiles. Soon the whole country will be run by former movie stars.'

'I'm afraid you're right,' the High Commissioner said.

Sir Laurence turned to me.

'Well, young man, I'll say goodnight. I expect we'll meet again.'

'I hope so,' I said

'Give me a call if I can be of any help,' he said, smiling thinly. 'You never know. There might be something I know that you do not.'

'I'll say goodbye too,' the High Commissioner said. 'Let's see something of you from now on. You must come to our next reception.'

'I'd like that,' I said.

He nodded and followed Sir Laurence from the room.

'Well,' the Prime Minister said, finishing his drink. 'I suppose I ought to circulate a little. ...'

'I'll come with you,' Sir Reeves said.

The Prime Minister put a hand on my arm.

'See you presently, then. Make yourself at home.'

I waited until they had gone and then wandered out of the room. I felt curiously elated; almost heady. I had talked with the giants, and not been defeated.

Propped against the wall was Jo Masters.

'Well,' she said, 'is the Four Power Conference over? What did you decide? To take the tax off iron-lungs?'

'Something like that,' I said.

She lurched towards me.

'You haven't got a drink.'

'I've had quite enough,' I said.

'I haven't,' she said. 'Get me another, there's a good boy.'

'I don't think you should. ...'

'I do,' she said firmly.

I got her another drink. When I returned she was leaning against the wall again, smiling at no one in particular.

'Thanks,' she said. She leaned forward and kissed me on the cheek.

'Have you ever had two girls?' she demanded.

'Two girls?'

'Yes. At the same time.'

Suffering swamis, she was something this one.

'No,' I said. 'I haven't.'

'Would you like to?'

I took a deep breath.

'I could always get my friend,' she said. 'Fiona. You'd like her. She loves threesies. What do you think? Shall I call her?'

'No,' I said.

'I told her about your traction-couch,' she said. 'She's dying to try it out. She's going to ring you.'

'You keep on about that couch,' I said.

She giggled.

'Can't you guess why?' she said.

'I think I will have another drink,' I said.

She leaned heavily against me.

'Forget about the drink,' she said. 'Let's go back to your place.'

'Devonshire Street?'

'No. Harley Street.'

'At this time of night?'

'Why not? Do you only rent the room by the day, or something?'

'No, but. . . .'

She touched my cheek lightly with the back of her hand.

'Come on,' she said.

She took my hand and led me along the corridor to the stairs. Walking beside her, conscious of her swaying hips and smell, my head began to swim.

At the door one of the policemen saluted politely.

'Goodnight, Miss Masters.'

'I hope you didn't move my car,' she said.

'It's just where you left it,' he said, nodding towards a small red sports coupé parked a few yards along the road.

'Shouldn't we take a taxi?' I said. 'You've had a lot to drink.'

'I drive better like that,' she said.

'But what about the police? Won't they say anything?'

She paused, half-way into the car.

'Of course not. They're friends of mine.'

She gunned the motor and we shot out into White-hall with a great screech of tyres.

'For heaven's sake be careful,' I said, holding on tightly.

'Have no fear,' she said, accelerating towards Trafalgar Square. 'I haven't killed anyone yet.'

We made Harley Street in a matter of minutes, having driven up Regent Street at 80 miles an hour, mounted two kerbs, narrowly missed running down a drunk and forced a number 3 bus to mount the pavement.

'Which building is it?' she demanded.

'The grey one on the left.'

'The first grey one on the left or the second grey one on the left?'

'The first.'

She braked to a stop so fiercely that I had to fling out my hands to stop myself being thrown against the dashboard.

'Your reactions are dreadful,' she said. 'You ought to see a doctor.'

'Do you always drive like that?' I asked incredulously.

'Only when I'm anxious to get where I'm going,' she said, brushing a wisp of hair back from her forehead.

She looked at me for a minute and then leaned over and kissed me on the mouth. My passion, which had abated considerably during the nightmare drive, re-kindled. I made a grab for her, but she jumped from the car and ran up the steps.

My consulting-room was very dark. There was just a faint glow from the street-lamps outside. She looked around for a moment. Then, without a word, she unbuttoned the top of her velvet outfit and dropped it to the ground. When she stepped out of her trousers she was naked. She kissed me, thrusting her body against mine.

'I want the machine,' she said.

'The what?'

'The traction-couch.'

'We can't use that now,' I said. 'It makes too much noise.'

194

'Who else is here?'

'Nobody. But someone in the street might hear.'

'Sod them,' she said cheerfully.

She groped her way to the couch and slid into it, shivering slightly as her skin made contact with the cold leather.

'Now strap me down,' she said. 'Not too tightly.'

I fastened the straps, my hands trembling.

'Helpless in the clutches of the mad doctor,' she intoned, 'the innocent virgin writhed and struggled.'

She tested the straps.

'Actually,' she said, 'I don't feel much like writhing and struggling.'

I pulled off my jacket.

'Now turn it on. Gently.'

'I'm not quite ready.'

'Turn it on.'

I switched on the motor and turned the dial to 1. The couch began vibrating.

For a moment she lay there, her eyes closed, her breasts swaying gently. I undid my tie and took off my shirt.

'Well, go on,' she said.

'I won't be a minute,' I said, removing my undervest.

She reached out a hand and grabbed me behind my neck, drawing my face down to hers. Undoing the belt of my trousers with my right hand and using the left for support, I kissed her passionately.

'That's better,' she said.

Hurriedly I slid my trousers to the floor and began to step out of them. But they were not to be stepped out of so easily. My right shoe caught in the trouser-bottom and I half-tripped. My face fell against her taut stomach. She held it there while I struggled with my trousers. And she kept on holding it there, while the couch vibrated steadily.

Then it happened. A shock wave seemed to ripple through her body, starting at her feet.

'Oh God,' she moaned, her head jerking from side to

side. 'Oh God.'

As suddenly as it had started, it was over. She released her hold on me and lay there, sighing.

Hastily I bent down and untied my shoes.

'Wow,' she said.

I hauled off my trousers.

'Let me out of these straps,' she said.

Swiftly I undid them.

'I'm dripping wet,' she said. 'Have you got a towel, or anything?'

I groped my way towards the washbasin. There was always one there. Then I remembered. Hilda Furze took it away each night and replaced it with a clean one in the morning.

'There's one in the cloakroom at the end of the hall,' I said. 'I'll get it.'

'No. Let me.' She slithered off the couch and padded her way out of the room, pausing for a moment beside her clothes.

I removed my underpants and took her place on the couch, my pulses racing. What a truly sensational girl. No wonder the Foreign Secretary had run amok. She was the *Playboy* fantasy come to life; sensuous, erotic and wild. I'd been foolish to waste my time thinking of Susan. There was nothing there for me, Jo was the one to aim for — this bonfire of a girl whose passions were equal to mine.

Suddenly the room was flooded with light. Startled, I sat up, covering myself with my hands.

She was standing by the door, her hand on the switch. She was fully-dressed.

'You know what I've been thinking?' she said. 'You ought to be on the National Health.'

She was fully-dressed!

'Because if you were,' she said, 'this place would be knee deep in groaning girls.'

SHE WAS FULLY DRESSED!

She laughed softly and turned on her heel. A

moment later I heard the front door shut and the sound of her car accelerating away down Harley Street.

I sat there for a long time, stunned.

Naked Indian Seen in Harley Street Window. ... Neighbours Raise Alarm. ... Check on Mental Hospitals.

Oh Great Lord Krishna, why have you forsaken me?

38

I was still in a state of shock next morning. When Hilda Furze came in with my tea I was sitting at my desk, my head in my hands, going over and over the events of the night before. Where, where, where did I keep going wrong?

'Are you all right, doctor?'

I looked up.

'I didn't sleep very well,' I said.

'I'll make you a second cup when you've finished that,' she said solicitously. She rearranged a couple of things on my desk. 'By the way, Lady Ammanford has been calling.'

I groaned. I was in no mood for Lady Ammanford.

'Did she say what it was about?'

'No. Only that she'd like you to call her.'

I waited until I'd had a second cup of tea and swallowed two aspirins, and then made the call.

Lady Ammanford sounded agitated.

'I'm so glad you called,' she said. 'I've been so upset.'

'What's happened?'

'That maniac George has taken leave of his senses. Do you know what he came to see me about that night?'

'I've no idea.'

'He's changed his will.'

'Well, lots of men do that. Who's he left his money to?'

'He's left it to nobody,' she said sharply. 'He says he's going to take it with him.'

197

'I don't understand. . . .'

'*You* don't understand,' she said. 'How do you think I feel? He's left instructions that his money is to be buried with him.'

'In the coffin?'

'Yes.'

'But that's insane.'

'He is insane,' she said.

'Can he do that? Isn't there some law?'

'I don't know. I don't suppose anyone in the history of the world has ever left such crazy instructions. He's told a solicitor friend that this money — which is all in the bank, by the way, not even on deposit — is to be cashed and the notes buried with him.'

'Are you going to fight it?'

'Nobody can fight it until after he's dead,' she said. 'By that time it'll be too late. He'll be down there with all his loot. You'd need a Home Office order to have him exhumed, and you wouldn't get that unless you could show he might have been poisoned.'

'It's unbelievable,' I said.

'I know it,' she said. 'We'll be divorced by then, of course, unless he keels over during the next week or two. And I don't give a damn about the money; I've got plenty of my own. That's not what's upsetting me. It's just that it's such an insult. There'll be stories in the papers, and everything. People will know he's done it to spite me. I'll be the laughing stock of London.'

'Perhaps he'll change his mind . . .?'

'George never changes his mind,' she said. 'He's the most obstinate sod I've ever known. I sat up with him half the night trying to make him see sense. It was a waste of time.'

'What about this woman he's living with? Maybe she can help?'

'Help who? Me? I wouldn't be caught dead taking a parking ticket off her.'

'Perhaps not. But she can't be too pleased with what

he's doing.'

'Oh, he'll probably take care of her beforehand. He looks after his own, does George. And she's his own.'

'I'm sure there must be something you can do,' I said.

'I intend to see my solicitor today,' she said.

'You must let me know how you get on.'

'I'll tell you tonight. Come to dinner.'

'I'm sorry, dear lady. Tonight is impossible.'

'But I so desperately need your comfort, doctor.'

'I understand that, but. . . .'

'Please come. If not for dinner, at least for a drink. There is something else I wish to discuss with you. Something important.'

Oh well, I thought, perhaps I could drop by after the party.

'All right,' I said. 'But just for a moment.'

39

Had I not already known that unkind Fate held a grudge against me, I found out at the party. It was as if, by spurning dinner with Lady Ammanford, my benefactress, and courting, instead, a girl whose hand was pledged to another, I had been singled out for a particularly savage blow; as if whoever was manipulating the strings had decided 'Right — now we'll really fix the little bugger.'

Until the moment disaster struck, everything had gone so well. Drink flowed freely, the mood was gay, and — pushing aside the memory of the night before — I was really enjoying myself.

Peter Wyatt had been the first to arrive. I had been wary of meeting him — since he was a practising osteopath and the one person in the house likely to question my credentials — but he turned out to be a jolly little man more interested in talking about India than the medical profession.

Apart from a cursory glance at the traction-couch — 'Haven't seen one of those before' — he showed no interest at all in my work.

'India's been my passion for years,' he said, helping himself to a large whisky and soda from the tray of liquor that Miss Furze had arranged on my desk. 'My father was there, with the police, and I grew to love it. I've read every book that Kipling ever wrote — but so have you, I expect?'

'Most of them,' I said.

'A lot of people don't realize he was born in India, do you find? I've talked to lots of people about him, and they don't know that. Remember what he wrote after he'd been here in England at school and then went back to India? "My English years fell away, nor ever, I think, came back in full strength." He really loved your country. I've always felt that India to Kipling was what Italy was to Byron — a place to recover innocence. Do you know what I mean?'

'Absolutely.'

'I'm going back one day. I'm determined on that. Who knows? We might go together. . . .'

'That would be nice,' I said.

At that moment Frank Upjohn came in, accompanied by a statuesque blonde girl. I had run into Upjohn in the hall on several occasions, and liked him. He was a good-looking man, with a fund of good anecdotes.

'Well, well,' he said. 'How nice to see you again. Haven't met Carol, have you? Darling, this is the doctor I've been telling you about: Dr Das.'

She held out a limp hand.

'Frank says you're the most successful doctor in the house,' she said. 'He's quite jealous.'

'I'm afraid he exaggerates,' I said.

'Not at all,' Upjohn said. 'His consulting-room is

always knee-deep in people; beautiful models, not so beautiful Prime Ministers. I don't know how he does it —' He broke off, his eyes widening. 'Oh my God,' he said.

In the doorway stood Hilda Furze. She was wearing black boots, a bright red tartan skirt which reached below her knees, and a black velvet jacket, adorned with pearl buttons.

'What *has* she got on?' breathed Upjohn. 'She looks like a reject from the Dagenham Girl Pipers.'

I hurried forward.

'My dear Miss Furze. How nice to see you.'

'Why thank you, doctor.' With the air of a head girl on a privileged visit to the teachers' common-room, she sidled shyly in.

'Come on, Miss Furze,' Wyatt said. 'What's it to be? Something potent?'

'No thanks, doctor. Just a plain gin and tonic.'

'Coming up,' Wyatt said.

Miss Furze went over to inspect the tray of drinks. She had bought all the liquor for the occasion, and arranged the bottles carefully on the small tray which she used for our teas in the morning. She had also provided the glasses, which she had brought from home.

'Now all we need is old Pike,' Wyatt said. 'I suppose he's still busy reaming them out.'

'Dr Pike did say he might be a little late,' Miss Furze said. 'I gather he had to drive somewhere to collect a friend.'

'Ah yes. That'll be the bird he was talking about yesterday,' Wyatt said.

'Hilly and his birds,' Upjohn said. 'I don't know how he does it. Where does he find them all?'

'He doesn't,' Wyatt said shortly. 'They find him.'

At that moment Susan Partridge arrived. And as she appeared at the door my heart turned over. She was wearing a green trouser suit which so complemented her hair and figure that it seemed to have been designed just for her. Seeing me, she walked over, both hands extended.

'How lovely to see you,' she said.

'It's been ages,' I said.

I stood for a moment, holding her hands, drinking in her beauty.

'How have you been?' she asked.

'Fine. Working hard.'

'I hear you're doing terribly well?'

'Not bad,' I said.

'I always knew you'd be a big success.'

'Did you?'

'Yes. Don't you remember that night you came round to the flat? I told you then.'

'I don't think I believed you.'

'That's because you don't know how awful other doctors are.'

I laughed happily.

'Careful,' I said. 'The room is full of them.'

She looked around.

'Are they both doctors?'

'Yes. They're two of the men who share this house with me.'

'I bet they're not as good as you,' she said.

'They're both good in their own fields,' I said.

'But you're the one who's treating the Prime Minister.'

'Did Aunt Grace tell you?'

'Who else?'

I realized I was still holding her hands. And she was making no move to pull away.

'What about a drink?' I said.

'I'd love one,' she said. 'But shouldn't I meet your friends first?'

'Oh, I'm sorry.' I turned. 'Miss Furze you know' — Susan flashed her a brilliant smile — 'and this is Frank Upjohn and Carol ... I'm sorry I don't know your last name.'

'Hill,' the girl said.

'Carol Hill. And this is Peter Wyatt.'

Susan shook hands.

'Now let me get you a drink,' I said. 'What would you like?'

'Oh I don't know. I don't care really. Is there any vodka?'

'Plenty.'

'Then I'll have vodka. Just by itself.'

'No tonic?'

'No. I don't like tonic.'

While I busied myself with her drink, she glanced at the bunch of roses lying on the settee.

'Those are pretty,' she said. 'A gift from some grateful patient, I suppose?'

'No,' I said. 'I bought them for you.'

For a moment her lovely grey eyes held mine, questioning.

'That was kind,' she said. 'Thank you.'

I gave her the drink.

'What's happening in your life?' I said. 'How's Basil?'

Her face clouded.

'He's away,' she said.

'He seems to go away rather a lot?' I said.

'Yes he does,' she said.

'Where is it this time?'

'Japan,' she said. 'He's climbing Mount Fuji.'

'That's quite a dangerous one, isn't it? Do you worry about him . . . ?'

'Do you mind?' She put a hand on my arm. 'I don't mean to be rude, but I'd rather not talk about him.'

'I'm sorry. Of course not.'

There was a sudden burst of laughter from the group in the corner. Frank Upjohn had just told a funny story. Even Hilda Furze was giggling.

'Your friends seem nice,' Susan said.

'I don't know them well,' I said. 'To be honest, this is our first get-together.'

'It was nice of you to invite me too,' she said.

Three drinks had given me confidence.

'It wasn't nice at all. I've been trying for weeks to think of an excuse to see you again.'

Her eyes widened.

'Why did you need an excuse? Why didn't you just telephone me?'

'I wasn't sure. ...'

'Oh, I wish you'd called,' she said. 'I had tickets for the ballet the other night, and no one to go with.'

I took the plunge.

'What are you doing for dinner tonight? I have to see your aunt for a while, but then I'm free.'

'Oh.' She pulled a wry face. 'Tonight's the one night I'm busy. I'm having dinner with daddy.'

I tried to mask my disappointment.

'That's my bad luck,' I said.

'I can't let him down,' she said. 'He's retired now, and lives in Devon. He only comes up now and again to see me.'

'I understand.'

'And with mummy dead he relies on me.'

'Of course.'

She hesitated.

'I'll tell you what,' she said. 'I'm staying in town this weekend. Why don't we have dinner on Saturday? Come to the flat. I'll cook you something.'

'I'd love to,' I said.

'I'm not a marvellous cook, or anything,' she warned.

'I don't care if it's a boiled egg,' I said. 'Just as long as you're there.'

'I'll be there,' she said, laughing. 'I'm having tea with Aunt Grace, but I'll be back around six. What time would you like to come?'

'Any time you say.'

'What about eight o'clock?'

'Perfect.'

She finished her drink.

'What about your family?' she asked. 'Where are

they?'

'In Calcutta,' I said.

'Have you got brothers and sisters?'

'I've got an elder brother named Ranjit and a sister named Deepali.'

'Deepali,' she said. 'What a pretty name. Is she a pretty girl?'

'She's ... well, appealing.'

'It must be hard having them so far away,' she said. 'Do you get to see them often?'

'Not at all, I'm afraid. I haven't seen them since I came to London.'

'But that's terrible. Why don't they fly over to see you? It's so easy now, with the jumbos and everything?'

'Oh you know how it is,' I said. 'Everyone's busy.'

At that moment Peter Wyatt came over.

'Now look here,' he said. 'Why don't you stop monopolizing this beautiful girl and let someone else say Hello. It's not often we get a famous model in this place.'

'I'm not so famous,' Susan said. 'And I have been here before.'

'Well I just hope you were satisfied,' Wyatt said. 'If you weren't, my consulting-room is on the second floor. I'll be delighted to see you at any time.'

'I'll remember,' Susan said, laughing.

Over Wyatt's shoulder I caught a glimpse of Hilda Furze standing alone by the fireplace.

'She looks a bit lost,' I said. 'Will you excuse me if I talk to her for a moment?'

'Talk to her all night as far as I'm concerned,' Wyatt said. 'I'm delighted to be left alone with Susan.'

I went across to Miss Furze.

'What about another drink?'

'No thank you, doctor.'

'But you hardly had anything. Let me refill your glass?'

'No. Really.'

'You're not enjoying yourself?'

'Yes I am. It's lovely, seeing you all here together.'

'We must do it again.'

'I hope so.'

She hesitated for a moment. Then she said:

'She's very beautiful, Miss Partridge.'

'Yes she is.'

'You obviously like her. I saw the roses.'

'Yes I do.'

'It's none of my business, doctor. But I'm so fond of you. And I don't want to see you hurt.'

'I don't understand.'

'She's *engaged*.'

'I know that, Miss Furze.'

'Oh.' She seemed taken aback. 'I wasn't sure if you knew.' She became flustered. 'I know people don't take engagements very seriously these days, but I get the impression that Miss Partridge is different.'

'She is,' I said.

'I'm always seeing pictures of her and her fiancé — he's the mountaineer, you know, Basil Calder. So I just thought I'd mention it.'

'I understand,' I said.

'I've come to care so much for all of you,' she said. 'I haven't got a family of my own, so I tend to think of you as my family. You mean a great deal to me.'

'You mean a lot to us,' I said.

'I sense that,' she said. 'It's more than just a receptionist-doctor relationship, isn't it? I feel real warmth there.'

'There is warmth there,' I said.

'That's why I brought it up,' she said. 'I didn't want you to get hurt. I hope you'll forgive me?'

'There's nothing to forgive,' I said.

'If I ever said anything to upset you I'd never —' She broke off. 'Oh, here's Dr Pike.'

I looked towards the door.

There stood Hilary Pike. On his arm was Norah Plumb.

40

'You,' Norah said, staring.

Run, I thought. Disappear. I tried to moisten my lips, but there was nothing to moisten them with.

'Why hello,' I said, mustering a sickly smile.

She came towards me, the one girl in all the world who could pull everything down around my ears. She was slimmer than when I had known her, and better dressed. The acne round her chin seemed to have cleared up.

'I can't believe it,' she said. 'Fancy seeing you again.'

'It is a surprise,' I said.

She stood, a step or two in front of Hilary Pike, looking me up and down.

'You know each other, then?' Pike said.

'Oh yes,' Norah said. 'We know each other all right.'

'But not Miss Furze, I think. Miss Furze,' he said. 'This is Miss Plumb.'

'How do you do,' Miss Furze said, extending her bony hand.

'Quite well, thank you,' Norah said.

I glanced across at Susan. She was talking animatedly to Peter Wyatt. I prayed that she would stay right where she was.

'What about a drink?' Pike asked.

'I'd like a sherry.'

He examined the tray.

'You're out of luck there. No sherry.'

'What is there then?'

'Vodka, Gin. Whisky.'

'I'll have a vodka. And lots of tonic.'

Pike went over to the drinks tray. I saw Peter Wyatt

introducing him to Susan. Then I drew Norah to one side.

'Listen,' I said. 'Do me a favour. They don't know anything about my past here.'

She looked at me blankly.

'What do you mean — your past?'

'You know. Brixton. The buses. All that.'

'Why not?'

'Well, for one thing, they wouldn't understand.'

'What's there to understand?' she said. 'There's nothing wrong with being a bus-conductor.'

'Of course there isn't,' I said. 'But you see, I was doing that while I was studying for my exams. You remember how hard I was studying? You were always commenting on it.'

'I still don't see,' Norah said.

'Well, doctors are snobbish about that sort of thing. You're not supposed to work while you're studying.'

'But you've got to live. Everybody's got to live.'

'Of course they have,' I said. 'But if they ever found out that I'd been a bus-conductor they'd, well, look down on me.'

She frowned.

'I think you're wrong there, Ram. Really I do. I think they'd admire your determination.'

'They wouldn't, Norah. I know them. They'd think it very odd.'

She thought for a moment.

'When we met you said you were twenty-three.'

'I know I did.'

'But you couldn't have been twenty-three. It takes years to study to be a doctor.'

'It's clever of you to have spotted that,' I said. 'You're absolutely right. I'm really thirty.'

'Thirty?'

'That's right.'

'Why did you say twenty-three, then?'

'Because I thought you'd think thirty a bit old.'

208

'That's ridiculous. I've been out with men twice that age.'

'I didn't know that, did I? In my country thirty is quite old not to be married. I thought you might think there was something strange about me.'

She looked round for Pike.

'He's taking his time,' she said.

'He's talking to the others. He won't be long.'

Her eyes rested on Susan.

'Isn't that Susan Partridge, the model?'

'That's right.'

'Who invited her, then?'

'I did.'

Her eyebrows rose.

'Well,' she said. 'You really have come up in the world.'

She looked puzzled.

'There's something else I don't understand. You told me you'd only been in the country a few months?'

'I had.'

'Where did you do your studying, then?'

'I thought you understood. I was a doctor already in India. But when I came here I had to pass further examinations in order to practise in Britain. So I took that job on the buses while I studied for them.'

'When did you pass your exams?'

'Shortly after I last saw you.'

'And you came straight to Harley Street?'

'That's right.'

She looked at me, mystified.

'I can't get over it,' she said. 'It seems — well — incredible. A few months ago you were a bus-conductor. Now you're a doctor in Harley Street.'

'Not so loud,' I said, looking round uneasily.

'Remember the last time we saw each other?' she said.

'On the bus.'

'Yes. Wasn't that something?'

'They took me to hospital,' I said.

'I know. But they wouldn't tell me which one. I

209

didn't find out until later.'

'You weren't hurt, or anything?'

'Me? Oh no. The driver stopped the bus when he heard the noise and the boys ran off. Then he called an ambulance.'

'They'd have told you where they were taking me.'

'I didn't wait for it, Ram. I was scared, after what had happened. I ran the rest of the way home. In the rain, too.'

'So you didn't know what happened to me?'

'Not till the police came next day. They said you were all right.'

'It must have been a shock, the police coming, and everything?'

'I was really worried. And you know my dad. He was there when they came. He went mad.'

'I'm sorry.'

'It wasn't your fault, was it?'

'Are you still living at home?'

'Yes. Worse luck. I keep meaning to get a place of my own, but every time I mention it dad gets furious.'

'But you're a big girl now, Norah. You've got your own life to live.'

'I know it. But he's still my dad. And I'm still petri- fied of him.'

'How's the dry-cleaners?'

'Oh, I've got a better job now. In the rag-trade. Just round the corner in Great Portland Street. I meet all the buyers.'

'How did you come to meet Hilly?'

She pulled a face.

'I got myself knocked-up, didn't I? And someone in our firm recommended him.'

'Knocked-up?'

'Pregnant, silly.'

'Oh.'

'I was an idiot. He was a buyer from Birmingham. I didn't know he was married.'

'That was bad luck,' I said.

'Not to worry. It'll all be over in a couple of weeks. And Hilly's good fun. We've had a lot of laughs. ...'

She broke off as Pike came over with her drink. Susan was with him, happily clutching her roses. I introduced her to Norah.

'I'm so pleased to meet you,' Norah said. 'I've read so much about you.'

'Why thank you,' Susan said. 'I'm just sorry there isn't more time to talk. Unfortunately I've got to go.'

'Already?' I said.

'I'm afraid so. I'm meeting daddy, as I told you. I don't want to be late.'

I decided to leave with her. If Susan was going, the whole point of the party was over. And I had no wish to give Norah the opportunity of asking further questions.

'I'll share a taxi with you,' I said.

'Oh don't break up the party,' Norah said. 'I haven't seen you for ages. There's so much to talk about. ...'

'I'm afraid I must,' I said. 'I have to visit a patient.'

'Well let's all get together soon?'

'We will,' I said. 'I promise.'

We said our goodbyes and I took Susan out into the street.

'You told a fib,' she said. 'You're not going to see a patient.'

'It wasn't really a fib,' I said. 'I am going to see your aunt. But I'd had enough, anyway.'

'Is she an old girl-friend?'

'Who?'

She smiled.

'Norah.'

'No,' I lied. 'Why?'

'I just wondered.'

A taxi came by, and I hailed it.

'Give my love to Aunt Grace,' she called. 'And don't forget about Saturday.'

'No chance of that,' I said.

41

'Oh, doctor,' Lady Ammanford said. 'I'm so glad you came. What a good friend you are.'

She rose from the chair where she had been reading and embraced me warmly.

'I'm afraid I can't stay long,' I said.

'I understand,' she said. 'You're so busy, yet you found time to see me.'

'That's what friends are for,' I said valiantly.

'And you're a true friend,' she said.

She pressed the bell by the side of the fireplace. It was answered, a moment later, by a rather pretty maid.

'What would you enjoy, doctor? Champagne?'

'Champagne would be nice.'

She turned to the maid.

'You'll find a bottle in the refrigerator, Josie. But be careful how you open it. The glasses are in the cupboard by the door.'

The maid bowed and scurried off.

'Is she new?' I asked.

'Yes. She came two days ago. Simons has been complaining for months about getting extra help. We have a daily, you know, but that's all.'

'Is she going to be satisfactory?'

'Simons says he's quite satisfied,' she said. 'I'm not exactly sure what he means by that, of course.'

I sank down amid the soft cushions of the sofa.

'Are you still upset about the business of the will?'

'I'm getting over it. But it was upsetting. Did I tell you I was seeing my solicitor today?'

'Yes. What did he have to say?'

'There's nothing I can do about it, apparently. We'll

be divorced any day now, and it's George's money so he can do what he likes with it. Chuck it in the sea, if he wants to.'

'I do sympathize, dear lady.'

'The whole thing has worried me dreadfully. That's why I was so anxious to see you tonight. I've told my solicitor I'm redrafting my own will and going abroad for a while.'

I sat forward.

'Going abroad?'

'Yes. I have only a few good years left, doctor, and I've decided to enjoy them. I'm going round the world. The Far East. China, perhaps. The Pacific. Tahiti. All the magical places. I've seen them before, of course, but I want to see them again.'

'Will you be away long?'

'I'm not sure. Six months, perhaps.'

'That is a long time.'

'It passes quickly, you know, when you are on the move. And Susan is joining me for part of the trip. She's flying out to meet me in Hong Kong.'

It was like being pole-axed.

'Susan?'

'Yes. It will help her get over things. I don't want her sitting around here brooding over the break-up.'

My heart missed a beat.

'The break-up?'

'Oh, didn't she tell you? She and Basil Calder have ended their engagement.'

'She ... she never mentioned it.'

Lady Ammanford shrugged.

'It was inevitable,' she said. 'He was quite impossible. Always away climbing some wretched mountain. This last trip to Japan was the final straw. I'm not unhappy about it myself, to be honest. I liked him well enough at first, but I soon came to realize he wasn't at all the sort of man Susan ought to marry.'

So that was why Susan had declined to discuss it. It

was finished. Over. Done with. That was why I had been invited to dinner on Saturday. She wanted me as her new lover. At last. At long last. Then the realization sunk in. She wouldn't be in Hallam Street. She'd be in Hong Kong or Tahiti.

'You don't seem very enthusiastic about my news,' Lady Ammanford said, watching my face.

'It's not that,' I managed a feeble smile. 'It's just, well, I'll miss you both.'

'It's kind of you to say that,' she said.

'Well, it's true,' I said. 'London won't be the same.'

'Which brings me to the reason I asked you here,' she said, her eyes boring into mine. 'How would you like to come with me? As my personal physician?'

'Come with you? As your personal physician?' It was a magic echo time. 'You mean — *travel* with you?'

'Precisely. As my doctor and companion.'

'But how could I? My practice. ....'

'Take six months off.' She bounced forward on the chair, her eyes gleaming. 'Why don't you?'

'Well for one thing I could never afford it.'

She held up a hand.

'I'm sorry,' she said. 'I should have made that quite clear. You'd be my guest, of course.'

I'd be her guest, of course.

Sitting there on the sofa, my imagination took off. Hong Kong. Tahiti. The dream places. And this woman was offering to make those dreams come true. And Susan would be flying out to join us. I could imagine the scene ... Lady Ammanford, tired after a busy day's sight-seeing, retiring early and leaving Susan and me alone in the sampan, or whatever they called it. Alone with the stars, the music and the swish of oars (Did they have oars in sampans?). And Susan saying: 'I love you, Ram. It's always been you. ...' And me, immaculate in my new Hong Kong suit, smiling down at her. ... But wait. I had no passport. No papers. I couldn't go. There was no way. Unless — unless Patel

214

could fix it? Yes, that was it; Patel could fix anything. He'd get me a passport. ... The day-dream returned in full colour. Lady Ammanford, realizing at last that Susan and I loved each other, giving us her blessing. And everyone living happily ever afterwards. ...

'What do you say, doctor?'

I didn't stop to think.

'I'd love to come,' I said.

She closed her eyes and rocked gently to and fro.

'Oh you dear, dear man,' she said. 'You don't know how happy you've made me.'

'It is I who should be thanking you,' I said excitedly.

'No, no. I shall feel so much better having you there, just in case anything happens. Oh, isn't this wonderful. We must start making plans.'

'I'll need some time to clear things up,' I said.

'How long, do you think? A month?'

'Yes. A month should be just right.'

There was a knock on the door and Josie came in with the champagne. Lady Ammanford beamed.

'Oh,' she said. 'This is a happy day.'

42

I could hardly believe it. I was going around the world. And with the girl of my dreams. After years of dealing me hammer blows, Fate had finally relented.

I had only one worry. How would Patel take the news? It meant, of course, that he would have to wait longer for the return of his money. But he could hardly fail to see that it was the opportunity of a lifetime. Would he help me get a passport? Or would he tell me I was mad?

I worried about this next morning as I listened to chests, tapped knees, looked into eyes and inspected tongues. For Patel held the key. If he said No, that was the end of it.

I was still worrying about it when Miss Furze put her head round the door, just before noon.

'Miss Plumb telephoned,' she said. 'I have the number. She'd like you to call her back.'

'Did she say what it was about?'

'No. And since she's Dr Pike's patient, I wasn't sure what to say.'

'I expect it's personal,' I said reassuringly.

She came over and put the number on my blotting pad.

'The other doctors were asking how much they owed for last night,' she said. 'I told them it came to £2 each.'

'Is that all?'

'Eight pounds altogether,' she said. 'You gave me ten. I owe you eight.'

'It was a nice party, Miss Furze. Thank you for organizing everything.'

'I enjoyed it,' she said. 'It was kind of you to invite me.'

'I hope you'll come to the next one?' I said.

'I'd like to,' she said. 'There's even some vodka left, for next time.'

She smiled girlishly, and retreated back into the hall, closing the door behind her.

I dialled the number.

'Merrywear,' a voice said.

'I'd like to talk to Miss Plumb.'

'One moment.'

I waited.

Finally she came on the line.

'Hello.'

'Norah, this is Ram.'

'Oh hello. I called you earlier.'

'I know.'

'I'd like to have a word with you, Ram.'

'Of course,' I said. 'Is it something you can talk about on the telephone?'

'Not really,' she said. 'Are you free for lunch?'

'I wasn't going to have any lunch,' I said. 'I've got no more patients today. I was planning to go home around one.'

'Could we meet for a little while?'

'I suppose so. If it's important.'

'It is important,' she said.

'All right. Where do you want to meet?'

'I tell you what,' she said. 'I'm going to Apsley's in Bond Street to buy a handbag. They have a nice coffee bar. Why don't we meet there at one-thirty?'

'All right,' I said. 'I'll see you then.'

When I arrived she was standing at one of the counters, examining a handbag.

'It's lovely,' she said to the salesgirl. 'Hello,' she said to me. She held out the bag. 'How do you like it?''

'It's very nice,' I said.

'It's fine quality ostrich,' the salesgirl said knowledgeably,

Norah held it in her right hand and turned to admire herself in a long mirror.

'The only trouble is the colour,' she said. 'It won't really go with anything I've got.'

'Would you like to see it in black?' the salesgirl said.

'That's a good idea,' Norah said.

The girl foraged among some boxes under the counter.

'What did you want to talk about?' I asked.

'Yes,' the salesgirl said, holding up a black bag. 'Here we are. See how you like this.'

Norah inspected the bag.

'It's really lovely,' she said. 'It's beautifully made.'

'It's French,' the salesgirl said. 'Very fine quality skin.'

'I can see that,' Norah said.

'You said it was important,' I said.

'It is,' Norah said.

'Then perhaps we could look at the handbags later?'

'I won't be long,' she said.

She turned to the salesgirl.

'Could I look at the crocodile one again? The one you showed me earlier.'

'Certainly, madam.'

The girl moved to the other end of the counter.

'You mentioned something about coffee,' I said.

'We will have coffee,' she said.

'Here it is,' the salesgirl said, returning. 'I think this is the one.'

Norah examined it carefully.

'No,' she said. 'This isn't the one. It was squarer, the one I looked at, with a sort of horseshoe clasp. This clasp is different. And the bag is bigger. Mind you, it is nice.'

'I'll see if I can find the other one,' the salesgirl said.

She moved away again.

'You're a phoney,' Norah said, smiling at me.

I looked at her. Stunned.

'What did you say?'

'You heard,' she said. 'You're no more a doctor than I am.'

'You don't know what you're saying.'

'Come off it, Ram. Do you think I'm a complete idiot? Giving me all that rubbish about not wanting them to know you were a bus-conductor.'

'Was this the one, madam?' the salesgirl said, coming back.

While I stood there stricken, Norah took the new bag and fondled it lovingly, inspecting the inside, turning it upside down, opening and closing it. 'Yes,' she said, 'this is the one. I love this one.'

'It's a beautiful bag,' the salesgirl said. 'That's the last one we've got in that style.'

'It's so hard to make up my mind,' Norah said. She picked up the first crocodile bag and examined it carefully. 'This one is nice, too. I don't like the clasp so much, but I think I prefer the shape.'

She held up both bags.

'What do you think Ram? Which shall I take?'

'They're both nice,' I said, my mouth dry.

'Have they both got the same sort of inside?' Norah asked.

'Yes,' the girl said. 'They're identical.'

'The lining is beautiful,' Norah said.

'You can't beat the French at that kind of thing,' the salesgirl said.

'And they're so well made,' Norah said.

'Oh yes, madam. Some of our customers have had their handbags for years. And you can use them for almost any occasion.'

'I can see that,' Norah said.

She continued to examine the bags, detail by detail.

'It's so difficult,' she said. 'It really is. I wish I could make up my mind.'

'I'll leave you for a few moments, shall I?' the salesgirl said.

'Thank you,' Norah said.

The salesgirl moved to the other end of the counter.

'Listen,' I said, my voice shaking. 'I don't know where you got this insane idea. But you're wrong.'

She looked at me without expression.

'You're a fake,' she said.

She picked up the ostrich bag and opened it.

'This one's got a nicer comb and mirror,' she said.

'Norah, you've got to believe me. . . .'

'And I really prefer the clasp on this bag. It seems to open better than the others.'

'Can we go and talk somewhere?'

'This won't take long,' she said.

She called after the salesgirl.

'I suppose there's no chance of finding a crocodile bag with a clasp like this, is there?'

The girl looked doubtful.

'It's a different make,' she said. 'It's French, too, but a different make. I don't think they do this clasp on the crocodile.'

'Could you have a look?' Norah said.

'Of course, madam.'

She dived under the counter again.

'You haven't seen me for ages,' I said, close to panic. 'You know nothing about what I've been doing.'

'I know exactly what you've been doing,' Norah said.

The salesgirl straightened up.

'I'm sorry, madam. I'm afraid they don't do a crocodile bag with that clasp. I might be able to order one, of course.'

'Would that take long?'

'About a month. We'd have to get on to Paris.'

'Oh I don't want to go to all that trouble,' Norah said. 'I'll make up my mind between one of these. Can you tell me the different prices?'

The salesgirl examined the tags on the bags.

'The ostrich bag is £60,' she said. 'And the crocodile bags are — where is it, now? — £155 and — oh, this one hasn't got a tag. Just a minute, madam, I'll find out.'

She went to consult a ledger further along the counter.

I looked at Norah, aghast.

'Surely you're not going to pay all that just for a handbag?'

She turned, a small smile on her lips.

'I was hoping you might be able to help me,' she said quietly.

I shut my eyes. This couldn't be happening to me. It was a nightmare.

'What?' I said.

'I was hoping you'd lend me the money,' she said.

I almost laughed with nervous terror.

'Are you mad, Norah? I haven't got that sort of money.'

'What,' she said. 'A successful doctor in Harley Street and you can't afford to buy a girl a handbag?'

'But I *can't* afford it,' I hissed. 'Don't you understand? I had to borrow the money to start the practice. I owe hundreds.'

'Well, now you'll owe a bit more, won't you?'

I wanted to kill her. To take her white neck between my hands and strangle her, right there in Apsley's.

'Why are you doing this to me?' I said.

'I'm not doing anything to you, Ram. I'm just asking for a little help over a handbag.' She paused. 'And I think I will have the one with the horse-shoe clasp.'

The salesgirl came back.

'I'm sorry to keep you waiting, madam. That larger bag is £200.'

'I've made up my mind,' Norah said. 'I'm taking the other one.'

'You've made a good choice,' the girl said. 'It's lovely. You'll get lots of use out of it.' She smiled. 'Shall I put it in a box, or would you prefer a carrier?'

'A carrier will be fine,' Norah said.

'Do you have an account, madam, or will you be paying cash?'

Norah turned to me. It wasn't a nightmare. It was really happening.

'How will you be paying?' she asked.

Indian Drops Dead in Bond Street Store. ... Foul Play Not Suspected. ... I Saw It All, Says Salesgirl. ...

'Cheque.' I barely managed to get the word out.

'If you'll make it payable to Apsley's,' the girl said. 'And put your name and address on the back.'

I took my cheque-book from my inside pocket. My lovely, new cheque-book. With a trembling hand I wrote the cheque and gave it to the salesgirl.

A moment later she returned with the receipt and the carrier.

'Thank you very much, madam. Good day, sir.'

Clutching her prize, Norah turned to me.

'Now,' she said. 'What about that coffee?'

'I don't want any coffee,' I said.

'Oh,' she said pouting. 'I was looking forward to it.'

'How did you know about me?' I demanded fiercely.

She smiled triumphantly.

'Because of something Hilly said last night, after you'd gone. He said they were crying out for doctors in this country. If you'd been a doctor in Calcutta you could have walked right in and been greeted with open arms. You wouldn't have had to be a bus-conductor or anything. ...'

'I wanted to specialize,' I said. 'Don't you see? I didn't just want any old hospital job. That's why I needed further studies. ...'

'Come off it,' she said.

I glared at her, hate rising within me.

'You blackmailing bitch,' I said.

'Now don't start calling me names,' she said. 'Otherwise I might turn nasty. And I can think of quite a few people who'd be interested to hear about the bus-conductor who set up in practice in Harley Street and treated the Prime Minister. The General Medical Council, for one. The Sunday papers, for another. ...'

'They wouldn't listen to you,' I said desperately.

'You want to bet?'

Pushing through the crowd of lunch-time shoppers, she walked into the street ahead of me and hailed a taxi.

'Just as soon as I've got rid of my little problem,' she said, 'you and I must have a quiet dinner together. Then we can talk about what we're going to do.'

I stared at her.

'You mean the bag isn't the end of it? You're going to go on with this?'

She got into the taxi, smiling.

'Remember me to Susan,' she said.

43

I did not go back to Harley Street that afternoon. Despair sitting like a giant bird on my shoulders, I went into a restaurant in Oxford Street and had a plate of fish and chips. Then I went through Selfridges. I started at the top floor and worked my way slowly down to the basement. Assistants kept saying 'Can I help you' and I kept saying 'No.' Nobody could help me, unless they knew a fool-proof way of removing the blackmailing, big-breasted Norah Plumb, three months gone by a married man in Birmingham.

It took me an hour to go through Selfridges, and then I moved on to John Lewis. In the basement, among the refrigerators and cookers, it occurred to me that the simplest way out was to kill myself. But by the time I had reached lamps and shades and ornate mirrors that course had lost its appeal. After all, if anyone was going to be killed, it should be Norah Plumb.

Standing beneath a gilt chandelier, decorated with metal flowers and leaves, I let my mind dwell upon the idea. I would take her to dinner, as she suggested, and invite her back to my consulting-room. I'd show her the traction-couch, and tell her how popular it was, and suggest that she try it. Then, once she was strapped down, with the motor running full pelt, I would choke her. ...

I shook my head. This was madness. I must view the situation calmly and decide on a realistic course of action.

There was only one person who could help me. Patel. I looked at my watch. It was four o'clock. If I caught the bus immediately, I could be at Elm Place by a quarter to five. He would be back from London Airport by that time.

I hurried from the store.

Patel was hunched over a table when I arrived, writing in a ruled notebook. The remnants of his tea were still in evidence; a dirty plate with a few baked beans on it; an empty yoghurt carton, raspberry-flavour; a half-drunk glass of milk.

Despite the whirlpool at my own feet, I felt a rush of sympathy for him, closeted in this bleak cell.

When I walked in he jumped to his feet.

'This is a surprise,' he said. 'I wasn't expecting you.'

'I just came on the off-chance,' I said.

'If I'd known I'd have waited supper.'

'It's all right,' I said. 'I'm not hungry.'

'Some tea, perhaps? I was just about to make a cup.'

'All right.'

He shuffled over to the stove.

'Well,' he said. 'Don't keep me in suspense. How did it go?'

'How did what go?'

'The reception of course. At Number Ten?'

Good grief, I'd forgotten all about that!

'It was fine,' I said. 'Fine.'

'Was the new suit a success?'

'I think so.'

He peered at me.

'You look a bit low,' he said. 'Is everything all right?'

'No,' I said. 'Everything's all wrong.'

'I won't be a moment with the tea,' he said, fussing about. 'Then you can tell me all about it.'

I looked around the dreary room. On the chest of drawers was a photograph in a cheap wooden frame. It showed a large rat with intelligent-looking eyes. Schwartz, of Rent-a-Rodent fame. Standing behind it was Patel.

'It's nice, isn't it?' he said, following my gaze. 'I often wish we'd taken it in colour. He had lovely colouring, you know, a sort of sheeny grey-black.'

He brought me my tea.

'Now,' he said. 'What's the trouble?'

'It's Norah Plumb,' I said. 'She's found out about me.'

His face registered nothing.

'How did it happen?'

I told him about the party. Pike's arrival with Norah, and the affair of the crocodile handbag.

'£155,' he said, his eyes widening. 'She's very sure of herself, isn't she?'

'I'm afraid she is.'

He shook his head.

'I never liked her,' he said. 'I think I told you at the time.'

'I know you did.'

'But this.' He sighed. 'This is hitting below the belt.'

'What do you think I should do?' I asked.

'Frankly,' he said, 'I don't know.'

'If she goes on asking for money,' I said, 'I'll never be able to pay you back.'

'That fact had not escaped me,' he said.

He gazed into his tea.

'Of course, this is the chance one always takes when one embarks upon a career based on deception. There is always the danger that someone will turn up from the past.'

'I got such a shock when I saw her,' I said. 'When she walked in with Pike.'

'How did she meet this man Pike?'

'She's pregnant — I forgot to tell you. She came to him for an abortion.'

'Has she already had it?'

'Not yet.'

'But they struck up a friendship?'

'Yes. He's been taking her out.'

'And he knows nothing of what she is doing?'

'I shouldn't think so. She'd be hardly likely to tell him.'

'Probably not.'

He thought for a moment.

'Who is the father of this child?'

'Some businessman in Birmingham.'

'Does she still see him?'

'Apparently not. He's married.'

'So he's out of the picture?'

'That's what she says.'

Patel's eyes seemed to grow darker.

'Pike's a good doctor, of course?'

'I suppose so. Why?'

His voice lightened.

'I was just thinking. A slip of the knife — or whatever they use — would solve everything.'

'That's hardly likely to happen,' I said.

'No,' he said. 'I suppose not. What a pity she didn't go to our friend Doc Stirrup. She'd have had blood poisoning within a week, and been gone in a fortnight.'

'It's too late for that now,' I said.

'You don't think you could wean her away from your colleague?'

'What could I say? She'd be immediately suspicious.'

'You could say that Doc Stirrup was cheaper. That might work.'

'I don't think it would. Pike may not even be charging her. After all they're going out together.'

'Ah, yes, I'd forgotten that.'

He looked at me with sad eyes.

'I had dreamed of you going home, rich and respected. The envy of all those unfortunate beings in their mud huts and stinking villages. I saw it quite clearly. Part of that glory would have been mine ,since it was I who got you started on the road to success. That thought gave me contentment and pleasure during the long night hours. Now this has happened.'

'I owe everything to you,' I said. 'I'll always be grateful for what you did.'

'I got the rocket fuelled,' he said. 'But I did not get it into orbit.'

'That's my fault,' I said.

'Yes,' he said, 'I'm afraid it is.'

He poured himself a second cup of tea.

'What about you?' he said. 'Would you care for another?'

'No thanks. This is fine.'

'It's a little strong for you, perhaps?'

'It's fine. But I've had enough.'

'Did you eat yet?'

'I had a late lunch,' I said. 'I'm not hungry.'

'I've got beans here,' he said. 'And eggs. I can easily fix you something?'

'No,' I said. 'Really.'

He showered sugar into his tea.

'This girl has parents, has she not?'

'Yes. They live in Gipsy Hill.'

'You visited them once, I seem to remember? And found them not to your taste?'

'They're dreadful people,' I said. 'Particularly the father.'

'What is he like?'

'A bully. Norah is frightened of him. She'd like to leave home and get a place of her own, but every time she mentions it he gets angry.'

'Does he now?'

He sipped his tea.

'Presumably he knows nothing about his daughter's condition?'

'I'm sure of it. He'd kill her.'

'And if he knows nothing of the pregnancy, he can hardly know anything about the intended abortion?'

'Of course not.'

'So, just as you have something to hide, so has she?'

'I see what you're getting at. I can threaten to tell her father?'

He shook his head.

'That would be too crude. And when she was no longer pregnant, you would still be vulnerable. No, the approach must be more subtle.'

He was silent for a moment. Then he leaned forward.

'Now listen carefully,' he said. 'This is what we are going to do. . . .'

44

My first patient next morning was Norma Blair. When she walked into the consulting-room she looked worried.

'There's something I have to talk to you about,' she said, as I began the neck massage. 'Did you know that Grace Ammanford is planning a trip around the world?'

'Yes. She told me.'

'Well, you've got to stop her,' she said. 'She's not a well woman.'

'What do you mean?'

'She keeps fainting. Didn't she tell you?'

'No. Not a word.'

'We were having tea at Fortnum's the other afternoon and she fainted clean into the éclairs. I was horrified. She said it had happened quite often recently. I told her she must get in touch with you.'

'I saw her the other night,' I said. 'She never said a word.'

'How very odd.'

Fainting, I thought? *Newnes' Family Doctor*, page 264 sandwiched charmingly between Faeces and Fainting Sickness: 'Fainting, or sycope, is due to a temporary anaemia of the brain ... weak action of the heart is the commonest cause ... this may be due to actual heart disease. ...'

Heart disease?

'Of course it could be those damn saunas she keeps taking.' Norma Blair said. 'It can't be good for you, surely, baking yourself like that?'

'Not if you do it too often.'

'She has one every day,' she said.

I finished the massage and helped her into her coat.

'I'm glad you told me,' I said. 'I'll look into it.'

'I wish you would,' she said. 'I say terrible things about her, as I do about all my friends, but I'm really devoted to her.'

'I know that.'

And it was then that I remembered what Lady Ammanford had said when I thanked her for the invitation. 'I shall feel so much better having you there, just in case anything happens.'

That evening I went to see Dr Stirrup.

He had just finished surgery when I arrived, and the last patient was wheezing and coughing her way down the steps.

'Pitiful,' he said, watching her go. 'Lungs like lavatory brushes. Smokes one hundred cigarettes a day. "Give it up," I said to her. "I can't," she said. "It relaxes me." "Relaxes you," I said. "It's killing you." "So it's killing me," she said, coughing phlegm all over my tie. And she lit another fag while I was talking to her.'

He thrust back his straggling grey hair.

'It's bloody murder this place,' he said. 'Like working in a zoo, except they vomit ale on the floor instead of nuts. I get girls of twelve who're knocked up and boys of fourteen riddled with clap and old women who smell like sewers and kids of fifteen who're heroin addicts and men with their ears torn off in gang fights. Lovely.'

'Is it all like that?' I said, appalled.

'No,' he said. 'Sometimes it's a little more intriguing. I had an air-hostess in here not long ago. You know what was wrong with her? She couldn't come under 30,000 feet. The first time she got screwed was by the steward in the galley of an air-liner during a night-flight. It happened half a dozen times on other flights, and then they tried it on the ground. Nothing happened. At ground-level she couldn't come. How do you treat that, eh? You tell me?'

The door at the side of the surgery opened slightly and a pale-faced girl of about fifteen looked round the door. She was wearing a short skirt and very high heels.

'Oh, sorry,' she said. 'I thought you was through.'

'What is it?' Stirrup said sharply.

'I was wonderin' whether we was goin' out to eat tonight or stayin' in?'

'We can decide that later,' Stirrup said.

'Only if we're goin' out I mustn't be late,' the girl said. 'I promised mum I'd be home by ten. She thinks I'm at the pictures, see.'

Stirrup sighed.

'Then we'll eat in,' he said.

'There's only eggs,' the girl said.

'We'll have scrambled eggs,' Stirrup said.

The girl shrugged and went out.

'All right,' Stirrup said, catching my eye. 'So I'm not exactly your clean-cut Dr Kildare. What of it?'

'I didn't say anything,' I said.

He went over to a brown cabinet by the wall and took out a bottle of whisky and two glasses.

'You'll join me?' he asked.

'Not just now,' I said.

He poured himself a large drink.

'I need this,' he said. 'It's been a fucking awful day.'

He sat down, put his feet on the desk and swirled the drink round in the glass.

'All right. What do you want to know?'

'What does it mean when a woman in her fifties keeps fainting?'

'Any other symptoms?'

'Not that I know of.'

'You'd better wheel her in,' he said. 'I can't possibly diagnose without seeing her.'

'That's out of the question,' I said. 'Just tell me what could it be?'

'It *could* be a lot of things,' he said, looking at his drink. 'It's no good talking about what it *could* be. The thing is to find out what it *is*.'

'I know that,' I said. 'But can't you give me some idea . . .?'

'She could be anaemic. She could have a bleeding ulcer. She could be suffering from heart disease. There are several things it could be. It's useless speculating.'

He swigged down his whisky.

'Do yourself a favour,' he said. 'Get someone competent to examine her. Don't bugger about.'

I took a pound from my wallet and gave it to him. He stowed it away in a drawer of the desk.

'Anything else?' he said.

'No.'

'You look bloody awful,' he said. 'Sleeping all right?'

'No. I've been worried about a couple of things.'

He fished around in the cabinet beside his desk and tossed me a small bottle.

'Take two of those at night,' he said. 'Put you out like a light.'

'What are they?'

'Mandrax,' he said. 'Don't worry. They won't kill you.'

He saw me to the door.

'What was your name again?'

'Das,' I said. 'Ram Das.'

'Whatever it is you're up to,' he said, 'for God's sake be careful.'

45

I telephoned Norah early next morning.

'Listen,' I said. 'I'd like to have another talk with you. Are you free for dinner tonight?'

There was a pause.

'What's this all about?' she said.

'You wanted to have dinner with me,' I said. 'I'm suggesting tonight.'

'I was going to have an early evening,' she said. 'Hilly's away.'

'I know. He's gone to Brighton.'

'There's a conference on, or something.'

'That's right.'

Another pause.

'Well, all right. What time?'

'Why don't you come to Harley Street at half-past seven?'

'You'll still be there, that late?'

'Yes. I've got some things to clear up.'

'Where are we going to have dinner?'

'There's a good place round the corner in Devonshire Street,' I said.

'I won't have time to go home and change.'

'That's all right,' I said. 'Come just as you are.'

'Actually,' she said, 'I was going to ring you.'

'Oh.'

'I may have to borrow some money. For the operation.'

I waited a moment before replying.

'Shouldn't that come from the man responsible?' I said.

'I don't know where he is,' she said. 'I told you that.'

'You know his name,' I said. 'You could find out his address.'

'I don't want to,' she said.

'Well, we'll talk about it when I see you.'

'It'll have to be in cash,' she said. 'Hilly says he wants cash.'

'Has he said how much?'

'A hundred pounds.'

'That's a bit steep?'

'That's what he's asking,' she said.

'We'll discuss it tonight,' I said.

'There's nothing to discuss,' she said. 'I need the money.'

'All right,' I said. 'I'll see you tonight.'

When she arrived I let her in and flicked back the catch on the front door, as Patel had instructed.

'I hope this is all right for where we're going,' she said.

I looked at her. She was wearing a dark-blue coat with a fur collar and black boots with very high heels. She was carrying the crocodile handbag.

'You look fine,' I said, leading the way into the consulting-room.

She removed her coat and draped it over one of the chairs.

'It's been quite a day,' she said.

'You've been busy?'

'Very.'

'What can I get you to drink?'

'Have you got any vodka?'

'Yes. There's still a drop left over from the party. No tonic though.'

'It doesn't matter. I'll take it neat.'

She sat down and looked around the room.

'You'd fool anyone with this set-up,' she said, with a short laugh. 'No wonder you get away with it.'

'It's a nice room, isn't it?' I said, measuring out the vodka.

'Hilly says you've got some fantastic patients.'

'I've been lucky,' I said.

'It's hard to believe,' she said. 'I don't think I'll ever trust a doctor again.'

I handed her the drink.

'I'm sorry there's no ice.'

'That's all right,' she said. She tasted it. 'It's fine,' she said.

I poured myself a short drink.

'There's something I forgot to ask you,' I said. 'Hilly himself doesn't suspect anything?'

'Of course not. Why should he?'

'I just thought ... well, that you might have said something.'

'I'm not daft,' she said.

Taking my drink, I went and sat behind my desk. She laughed.

'You look just like a real doctor.'

'That's the idea,' I said.

'I still can't think how you've managed,' she said. 'What with people being ill, and everything.'

'I've managed,' I said.

'It must have taken a lot of nerve.'

'Not really,' I said. 'Not compared with what you're doing.'

She looked at me sharply.

'What do you mean?'

'Blackmail takes a lot of nerve,' I said.

'You keep using that word,' she said. 'It's not that at all. It's just an arrangement between the two of us. I say nothing. You help me financially.'

'What makes you think I'm able to do that?'

She looked around the room again.

'With all this? You must be making a fortune.'

I glanced at my watch. Two minutes to go.

'Well I'm not,' I said. 'There's a great deal of money to be repaid to the syndicate.'

'What syndicate?'

'The one I borrowed the money from. Where did you think I got it?'

'I don't know. Some friend, I suppose.'

'I don't know a friend with that sort of money,' I said.

She leaned forward.

'This syndicate,' she said. 'Do they know what you used the money for?'

'Of course. It was their idea.'

She frowned.

'You mean they suggested it?'

'That's right.'

'But that's incredible,' she said. 'You mean there's this group of people and they said: "We'll put up the money for you to pose as a doctor".'

'That's right.'

'Come on,' she said. 'You're pulling my leg?'

'I'm not,' I said. 'Honestly.'

'But what do they get out of it?'

'It's business,' I said. 'They charge a huge interest on the money.'

'But if there's several of them they can't be getting that much from what you earn?'

'It's not just from me,' I said. 'There are all the others.'

'What others?'

'The other doctors.'

She gaped.

'You mean there are other phoney doctors about?'

'Lots of them.'

'I can't believe it,' she said.

'It's true,' I said.

She gulped her drink.

'Does this ... this syndicate know that I've found out about you?'

'Yes,' I said. 'I told them.'

She laughed nervously.

'What did they say?'

I looked at my watch. It was time.

'You'll find out in a moment.'

'What do you mean? Is this some kind of ...' She broke off at the sound of footsteps in the hall. It was Patel. Right on time. 'What's that?' she said, her voice rising.

'You'll see,' I said.

A moment later Patel entered the room. He was wearing a black suit and a black shirt and a white tie. He had on huge sunglasses which completely hid his eyes. He had one hand in his pocket.

235

'Is this her?' he demanded.

'This is her.'

Norah got up.

'What is this?' she said. 'What's happening?'

Patel stood in front of her, black and menacing.

'Sit down, pig,' he said. He shoved her with his free hand and she fell back into the chair.

'I thought we were going to dinner,' she said, suddenly scared. She turned to me. 'You said we were going to dinner.'

'Shut up, pig,' Patel said harshly.

With an air of quiet menace, he walked over to the desk and perched himself on the edge. When he took his hand out of his pocket he was holding a revolver. Norah's face went the colour of dirty paper.

'What's that?' she whimpered.

'What do you think it is, pig?' Patel said.

For a moment I thought she was going to faint.

'I'm three months' pregnant,' she blubbered. 'You shouldn't frighten me like this.'

Patel put the revolver on the desk and spun it round with his finger.

'So you're the blackmailer?'

'It was only a bit of fun,' Norah wailed.

'A £155 handbag is your idea of a bit of fun?'

She burst into tears.

Somewhere, in the back of my mind, I seemed to have seen all this before. A man in black, sitting on the edge of a desk. A girl in a chair, pleading. Then I remembered. It was from an old George Raft film Patel and I had watched on television.

Patel swung his right leg to and fro.

'You're having a child, right?'

Norah nodded dumbly.

'And you're planning to get rid of it?'

'I can't keep it,' Norah blubbered. 'I'm not married.'

'Spare us your excuses, pig. You should have thought of that before.'

236

He got off the desk and stood in front of her.

'Your father will be told about the child,' he said. 'He will also be told that Ram is the father.'

Norah gaped at him.

'Ram?' she said. 'But he isn't.'

Patel ignored her.

'Knowing the way your father feels about the coloured races, his reaction should be interesting. ...'

Suddenly Norah understood.

'Oh,' she wailed. 'He'd kill me.'

'That's your problem, pig.'

Norah reached out, clutching at Patel's legs.

'Please,' she said. 'Don't do that. Don't tell my father. I'll never do this again. I promise.'

He shook her off. Taking some sheets of paper from the top of the desk, he handed them to her.

'Sit there,' he said, indicating the other side of the desk. 'And write this.' He flung her a pen.

'I, Norah Plumb, admit to being pregnant with the child of Ram Das, with whom I have been having sexual intercourse for many months. I intend, against his wishes, to have an abortion carried out by Dr Hilary Pike, with whom I have also been having sexual intercourse. ...'

She wrote quickly, brushing the tears from her eyes with her left hand.

'Have you got that down?'

'Yes,' she whimpered.

'Let me see it.'

He inspected the note.

'Right,' he said. 'Now should you ever again attempt to blackmail my client — or even see my client — this note will be sent to your father. Should he not, in our opinion, deal harshly enough with you, the syndicate will. I will turn the boys loose on you.'

Norah covered her face with her hands.

'Oh God,' she wailed.

'Understood?' Patel rasped.

Her reply was barely audible.

237

'Understood,' she whispered.

Patel leaned forward and picked up the crocodile bag from the chair. Opening it, he turned it upside down and cascaded the contents to the floor.

'Now pick those up.'

Norah scrabbled around on the floor, collecting lipstick and powder and loose coins.

'Is that everything?' Patel demanded.

She nodded blindly.

'Now get out,' he said.

She stumbled to the door without a word. A moment later the front door slammed.

For several minutes neither of us spoke. Then Patel tossed the toy revolver across to me.

'I told you it would work,' he said.

46

When I got in that night, relieved and happy, the telephone in the hall was ringing. It was Hilda Furze.

'Doctor,' she said accusingly. 'I've been trying to reach you for hours. Mr St Clair telephoned this evening in a great state. The Prime Minister has had a bad fall. They want you to go down immediately.'

'Down where?' I said.

'To Poole,' she said. 'In Dorset. he's been sailing there. I've looked up the trains. There's a good one in the morning at ten-thirty. It gets in around lunchtime.'

I sank into the chair by the hall-table.

'Listen,' I said. 'It's out of the question. I've got appointments tomorrow. I can't just take off.'

'Oh but you can,' she said briskly. 'I took the liberty of cancelling them. Anyway, there was only Mrs Crane and Miss Seddon.' She hesitated. 'I felt sure that's what you'd have wanted me to do.'

So there was no escape. I'd have to go. And the prospect alarmed me. The Prime Minister relaxing on my mechanical couch was one thing; the Prime Minister prostrate with pain in Poole was quite another.

'Did they say what was wrong with him?' I asked.

'Only that he'd hurt his back.'

'How did he do it?'

'He fell in his boat. The *Dawn Breeze*.'

I groaned.

'What time was that train?'

'Ten-thirty,' she said. 'From Waterloo. Shall I say you'll be on it?'

'All right,' I said resignedly. 'Say I'll be on it.'

At nine-thirty the following morning I was at John Bell and Croyden, the Wigmore Street chemists. I bought a suspension harness, complete with metal arm for attachment to the top of a door, and a packet of Radox, pine-scented.

The belt cost more than I had anticipated, and when I got to Waterloo I found I had only enough money left for a single ticket. Which was slightly embarrassing. It meant I would have to borrow from Hugh St Clair when I got to Poole. For in my hurry that morning I had left both my wallet and cheque-book in my other suit.

But it was not Hugh St Clair who met me at Poole Station. It was a strange young man.

'Where's Mr St Clair?' I asked.

'He had to go back to London,' the young man said. 'I'm Auberon Fawcett-Greene.'

I dumped my black bag on the rear seat of the car.

'What happened?' I asked.

'Know anything about sailing?'

'A little,' I said, without thinking.

'We were ooching,' he said. 'As the wave was about to take us we surged towards the stern and he tripped.'

I gazed at him blankly.

'The whole day was fraught,' he said, taking a corner

239

fast. 'We shouldn't have gone out at all.'

'Bad weather?'

'It was gusty,' he said. 'As you know, in a gusty wind, blowing slightly too much for driving full with full sail, the usual rule is to carry the right sails for the lulls, and to luff and pinch her through the puffs.'

'Really?' I said.

'Of course there are two schools of thought about this. The first advocates sheeting everything very flat, and then feathering her to the edge of a luff through the puffs, with both the main and jib going aft together —'

He braked sharply.

'Damn,' he said angrily. 'Did you see the way that fool cut in?'

'I think it was a woman,' I said helpfully.

'Stupid bitch,' he said.

We shot forward again.

'The second school feels that the jib should be cleated home, hard in, and the main used like an accelerator let out to luff in the puffs while the boat drives along largely on the jib. Of course this works better with synthetic sails than with cottons.'

I nodded vaguely, wondering what in heaven's name he was on about.

'It's six of one and half a dozen of the other,' he said. 'We chose the latter. Then the P.M. tripped.'

'Where is he now?'

'At the hotel,' the young man said. 'The Falcon. he's anxious to see you.'

'Is he in a lot of pain?'

'Seems to be,' he said. 'I wanted to call in the local quack to give him a shot, but he insisted on waiting for you.'

We squealed to a stop outside the hotel.

'Follow me,' he said, leaping from the car. 'He's in the Ocean Suite on the first floor.'

The Ocean Suite turned out to be two vast rooms, decorated with floral wallpaper, and cluttered with

240

shabby leather furniture.

The Prime Minister lay flat on his back on a large brass bed, wearing an orange dressing gown.

'Thank God you're here, doctor,' he said, extending a hand. 'This is a devil of a thing to have happened.'

I put down my bag.

'Where does it hurt most?'

'In the lower back. I fell forward, you see, and wrenched myself. Bloody painful, I don't mind telling you.'

The young man, hovering behind me, said:

'I'll leave you, P.M. Ring if there's anything you need.'

'There's something I need,' I said. 'A flat board of some sort. Or some planks. I want them to go under the mattress.'

'I'll have a word with the manager,' he said. 'They should be able to come up with something.'

He went out, carefully closing the door behind him.

'This has been such a let-down for the boys,' the Prime Minister said. 'We're in training for Cowes, and things were going so well. Now this. ...'

'Can you stand?'

'I can try.'

He swung his legs off the bed and I helped him to his feet. A sudden twinge made him wince.

'Damn,' he said.

I helped him out of his dressing-gown and ran my fingers down his back. He was standing with a decided list to port.

'I think we should try suspension,' I said.

'What the devil's that?'

'We suspend you by means of a belt from the top of the door,' I said. 'It takes some of the pressure off the spine.'

'It sounds diabolical,' he said.

'I know,' I said. 'But it does help.'

He winced again.

'All right,' he said. 'Anything you say.'

I strapped him into the body harness and led him to the door, against which I placed a chair.

'Stand on that,' I said. 'And I'll attach the straps of the harness to this steel support.'

I wedged this metal bar over the top of the door and linked the straps of the harness through it. Then, very carefully, I removed the chair. A moment later he was suspended, his feet a few inches from the floor. He went rather red, and the skin above the harness puckered, but that was all.

'I do feel a fool,' he said. 'What if someone came in?'

'They can't,' I said. 'The door's jammed by the bar.'

He dangled in silence for a few minutes.

'Shouldn't I sway from side to side, or something?'

'No,' I said. 'Keep quite still.'

'This reminds me of a horror film I saw on the box the other night,' he said. 'Watch horror films, do you?'

'Sometimes.'

'I love them,' he said. 'They help me relax after dealing with all those fools in the Commons. Anyway, there was this man hanging from his thumbs in some torture chamber while the jailer lit matches under his feet. Terrific giggle, really. . . .'

'Try not to talk,' I said.

'I just hope it works,' he said. 'I've got to meet the bloody TUC at Number Ten tomorrow morning. There'll be hell to pay if I don't turn up.'

'Your health comes first,' I said firmly.

'That's true,' he said. 'Can't think properly if you're in pain, can you? Liable to make the wrong decision. Bring the whole country to a grinding halt.'

I looked at my watch. He'd been hanging there for ten minutes. Enough, I thought. I put the chair under his feet and helped him down. He stood for a moment, massaging his body where the belt had pinched.

'What now?' he asked.

'A hot bath, I think.'

He moved his body from side to side.

'Do you know,' he said, 'I think that's helped. I can move a bit without hurting.' He leaned from side to side again. 'Yes, dammit, I can.'

I went into the bathroom and dumped half a packet of Radox into the hot water.

'Try that for five minutes,' I said. 'Then we'll lie you flat for a while.'

I let him stay in the water for ten minutes, during which time the young man returned with a large board which I slid beneath the mattress.

Then I put the Prime Minister to bed.

'I'll give you a couple of pills to help you sleep,' I said. 'I want to make sure you lie perfectly still.'

'Nothing potent,' he said. 'Half an aspirin puts me out for the night.'

'These won't hurt you,' I said.

I got him a glass of water from the bathroom and handed him two of the Mandrax tablets that Dr Stirrup had given me. Five minutes later he was asleep.

I sat in a chair watching him for a while, and then packed away my things and went downstairs.

The young man was standing at the bar, drinking a Pimms.

'How is he?' he demanded.

'Asleep,' I said. 'I think we'll let him rest for the remainder of the day.'

'What about an X-ray?'

'I don't think that's necessary,' I said. 'He's responding well to manipulation.'

'How long will he have to stay here?'

'It's hard to say. We'll know when he wakes up. He may feel a great deal better.'

'Let's hope so,' the young man said. 'He's simply got to be back in town tomorrow morning.'

'I'll do my best,' I said.

'Good man,' he said.

He didn't offer me a drink.

47

The Prime Minister slept all afternoon, and I made sure that the Do Not Disturb notice stayed on his door.

At length I began to feel hungry, so I set out in search of a cheap restaurant. I had less than a pound on me, which was unfortunate, but the strange young man did not seem particularly friendly so I decided to make the best of it.

I had a dreary meal in a nearby café and then set off for a brief walk around the town before returning to the Falcon. The wind had freshened and it was raining slightly but I welcomed the exercise after being cooped up all day. There were few other people about, just a handful of holiday-makers, half-hidden under umbrellas, struggling along the sea-front, and a huddled group queueing outside a cinema.

Everything was dismal and grey, but I felt strangely light-hearted. The Prime Minister would certainly be no worse for the treatment I had given him, and lying flat on his back, with a board under the mattress, would help a lot. By the time I got back I fully expected him to be awake and refreshed. I would give him a little more traction, I decided, and then put him to sleep for the night.

Turning a corner into what seemed like a gale-force wind, I found my thoughts turning towards the morrow. I had dreamed for so long of being with Susan Partridge that the idea of actually dining with her in her flat almost overwhelmed me. By now, of course, she would have been told that I was coming on the trip. She would be keyed-up, eager and gay. We would have candles on the table, and wine. The evening would be a huge success. We would wind up in each other's arms.

I wished there was someone I could speak to about her. I wanted to detail her qualities; to talk about her hair, her eyes, the way she looked. I wanted to explain how the promise of seeing her again made all the setbacks and the disappointments of the past worthwhile. But there was no one.

Walking along, head down, beside the angry sea, I realized I had strayed further than I intended. I was almost on the outskirts of the town. And suddenly the rain began coming down hard, striking the surface of the sea like pellets.

Turning my jacket collar up, I looked around for shelter. Fortunately there was a pub on the corner, so I ran for it.

The bar was full of dreary-looking men standing around in mud-coloured raincoats and holding pints of beer in their hands. Two soldiers were sitting by the fire, and along one wall, on a long, red-leather couch, sat a group of crumpled-looking women. When I walked in, dripping, everyone looked up.

'Evening,' the girl behind the counter said. 'What'll it be?'

I examined my change. There was just enough.

'Vodka,' I said, 'with tonic.'

She poured the measure.

'You're a bit wet, aren't you?'

'Yes. I got caught in the rain.'

'You should be wearing a coat on a night like this. You'll catch your death.'

'I didn't bring one,' I said. 'Stupid of me.'

'It looks as if we're in for a nasty night,' she said.

At the other end of the bar somebody turned on the radio.

'Cyclonic, variable two to four, becoming south-westerly later . . .' a voice intoned.

I sipped my drink.

'Staying here, are you?' the girl said.

'Just for the day,' I said.

245

'You mean the night, don't you?' she said with a smile.

'Humber, Thames, East, three or four, veering South; sundry showers, moderate or poor with fog patches . . .' the voice went on.

'Ever been to Poole before?' the girl said.

'No,' I said.

'It's nice,' she said. 'When the weather's good.'

'Dogger, Fisher, German Bight, north-east veering south-east, four or five, increasing five or six, perhaps locally seven,' the voice continued.

'I'm not too sure where Poole is,' I said. 'I only arrived today. How far are we from London?'

'London?' she said, 'Oh, that's a hundred miles away. Bournemouth's the nearest big town. That's only five.'

'I've heard of Bournemouth,' I said.

'It's lovely there,' she said. 'A proper seaside town. You know, lights, gardens, that sort of thing.'

The shipping forecast stopped at this point and the announcer began reading the news.

It was the usual encouraging stuff. An airliner in America had been hi-jacked and was on its way to Cuba. . . . Some ambassador had been shot dead in South America. . . . Five people had been burned to death in a multiple car crash on the M4. . . . There had been an earthquake in Turkey and hundreds were feared dead. . . .

None of the people in the bar took the slightest notice. Bugger the hi-jackers and the dead ambassador and the human torches and the earthquake victims; all they cared about was getting enough ale down their gullets before they were thrown out onto the wet streets.

'Meanwhile, here at home, union leaders said today that there was little hope of a settlement in the latest docks dispute. . . .'

'Same again, miss,' someone called. Bugger the dockers too, it seemed.

Then:

246

'News is just coming in from Dorset of the arrest of ten Pakistanis who landed illegally from France. Local police say that their boat had drifted miles off course, due to gale-force winds, and broke up on the rocks. Most of the men, who scrambled to safety, were arrested, but one of them is believed to have escaped. . . .'

Poor sods, I thought. What a way to end up after coming all that way. I looked at my watch. It was time to be getting back to the Falcon.

I put my glass on the counter.

Then I realized that the girl was looking at my wet clothes. The two soldiers were staring, too, and some of the crumpled-looking women.

It took a moment for it to sink in. The news broadcast. The escaped Pakistani. My soaking clothes. Surely they couldn't . . .? Then I looked down at my shapeless trousers and sodden shoes and knew, with an awful certainty, that they could.

Trying to look casual, which wasn't easy. I said goodnight to the girl and began making my way back to the Falcon. But I had barely got half-way before I heard the wail of a police siren and a blue car came racing along the street towards me. I looked around quickly. There was an alley-way to the left, so I dodged down it and hid behind a cluster of dustbins, waiting for the car to pass. But my luck was out. It screeched to a stop at the entrance to the alley and three burly men jumped out.

'Down here,' I heard one of them shout.

I leaped to my feet and, rain slanting into my face, scrambled over the wall at the end. There was wasteland on the other side, and I streaked across it.

'There he goes,' a voice cried.

I looked back. The three men were there, right behind me. Gasping for breath, I clambered over a wooden fence which ran alongside a path bordering the rear gardens of a row of houses. On the other side an elderly man was stumbling along, an umbrella held in front of him. I saw him too late. As I collided with him he went slithering into the mud.

'Bastard,' he yelled.

I raced on.

At the end of the path was a street. I stood there for a moment, teetering, trying to decide which way to run, and then another police car — or was it the same one? — raced up. And suddenly I was surrounded by burly men, holding me, pinioning my arms.

'Gotcha,' one of them said.

'Little bugger's dripping wet,' someone else said, forcing me into the rear of the car. 'Watch out for the seat.'

'There's a plastic mac on the floor,' the driver said. 'Put him on that.'

Wet and shivering, I cowered in the corner.

'All right,' the man beside me said. 'Let's have it. Where did the boat leave from?'

'I'm not a Pakistani,' I said. 'I'm an Indian.'

'What were you doing with the others, then?'

'I wasn't with the others,' I gasped. 'I'm a doctor. I practise in Harley Street.'

Still breathing hard from the chase, he wiped his wet forehead with the sleeve of his uniform.

'Is that a fact?'

'I'm serious,' I said. 'This is all a mistake. I'm not the man you're looking for. ...'

'How do you know who we're looking for. ...?'

'I heard it on the news. That's why I was running. I realized I could be mistaken for this man.'

'Too bloody right you could,' the man said.

'Listen,' I said, pushing back my wet hair. 'I know this sounds ridiculous, but I'm down here treating the Prime Minister. He's staying at the Falcon. He fell and hurt his back while sailing yesterday. You can easily check.'

The man laughed.

'You've got to believe me,' I said, urgently.

'That's just where you're wrong,' the man said. 'We don't.'

Nothing more was said until we reached the police-station.

'Got him, have you?' a man in plainclothes said, coming out of an office marked Private. 'That's the lot, then.'

'This one's a real scream, Inspector,' one of the burly men said. 'Says he's a Harley Street doctor. And guess what he's doing in Poole? Treating the Prime Minister.'

The plainclothes man looked at me bleakly.

'Is that right?' he said.

He put his face close to mine. He seemed to have blue teeth.

'What's your name?'

'Das. Dr Ram Das.'

'And what do you say you're doing here?'

'I came down from London to treat the Prime Minister.'

Without warning, he pushed me, so that I fell back against two of the burly men. One of them pushed me back.

'Stand still,' the plainclothes man snapped.

He walked round me, as though I were some sort of animal in a cage.

'You'll be staying with him, no doubt?'

'Yes. At the Falcon.'

One of the burly men laughed.

'Little bugger's got his nerve,' he said.

'He has that,' said one of the others.

The plainclothes man looked at me thoughtfully and then went over to a desk and dialled a number.

He spoke very quietly into the telephone. When the conversation was over he looked at me, his face expressionless.

'They don't seem to know you there.'

'They wouldn't,' I said excitedly. 'I'm not registered, you see. But I've been there all day, treating the Prime Minister. He's there. All you've got to do is check.'

'Oh he's there all right,' the plainclothes man said.

'We know that. It's been in all the newspapers. . . .'

'Check with his secretary,' I said. 'He'll confirm my story.'

'What's his name?'

'St Clair. Hugh St Clair.' I looked at him hopefully. 'I wouldn't know that, would I, if I was a Pakistani?'

He lifted the receiver and dialled again.

'I'd like to speak to Mr St Clair,' he said. He listened for a moment. 'I see,' he said. 'Thank you very much.'

He replaced the receiver and came and stood in front of me.

'He hasn't been there all day,' he said.

Oh, cursed fate. Of course. It was the other man — what was his name? Aubrey something? I almost wept with frustration.

'I'd forgotten. Mr St Clair went back to London. It was another man who met me here. But call the Prime Minister. He'll vouch for me. I swear it.'

He hit me hard in the stomach. As I doubled over he hit me again.

'You know what I think,' he said. 'I think you're a lying wog bastard. And I don't like lying wog bastards.'

'I'm not lying,' I groaned. 'Do you think I'd make up a story like this?'

'Yes,' he said. 'I do.'

'How would I know all these things if I were a Pakistani?'

'All what things?' he said. 'All you had to do was read an evening newspaper.'

I started to shake.

'I'm telling the truth,' I said.

'You came down on the train this morning, you say?'

'That's right.'

'Which one?'

'The ten-thirty.'

'Where did it leave from?'

'Waterloo.'

'What time did it get in?'

250

'About half-past twelve.'

'Then you'll have a return ticket to London?'

'No. I only got a single.'

'Why?'

'I didn't have enough money with me.'

'How much was the return fare?'

'I don't remember exactly. Four pounds fifty, I think.'

'And you didn't have that much?'

'No.'

'You're a Harley Street doctor and you didn't have four pounds fifty on you. Not doing very well, are you?'

'I'd spent more than I meant to at the chemists. I had to buy some things for the Prime Minister.'

'What sort of things?'

'A belt, for traction. And some Radox.'

'Radox? The stuff you put in the bath?'

'That's right.'

'You were going to give the Prime Minister a bath?'

'He'd hurt his back. It helps to soak in Radox.'

'Does it now?'

He smiled thinly.

'How were you going to get back, then?'

'I was going to borrow from somebody.'

'Who? The Prime Minister?'

'No. His secretary.'

'The one who isn't there?'

'I didn't know he wasn't there.'

'You didn't, did you?' he said.

He looked me up and down.

'Turn out your pockets.'

I handed him my keys and what little change I had left.

'Coin of the realm, eh?' he said. 'Got rid of the baksheesh, did you?'

'I don't know what you mean.'

'You know what I mean,' he said.

He examined the keys.

'What do these fit?'

'My flat in Devonshire Street and the front door to my consulting-room.'

'You've got to hand it to him,' one of the burly men said. 'He's got a good cover story.'

'But not quite good enough,' the plainclothes man said, turning his back on me. 'Take him down.'

'Wait,' I cried, thoroughly alarmed. 'There'll be repercussions over this. . . .'

One of the burly men pushed me down some steps.

'Take it easy,' he said. 'Inspector Bean can be a mean sod when he chooses.'

'Just you wait until the Prime Minister finds out what's happened,' I choked.

'Inside,' he said, giving me a shove.

I stumbled forward and collapsed on a wooden bench. Then the cell door slammed shut behind me.

48

I was having this extraordinary dream. I was back in my village in India and Susan, dressed as a nurse, was urging me to try a new treatment she'd heard about.

'It's something they developed in America,' she said. 'It turns you white in half an hour. That way it'll be easier for us to get into hotels and restaurants, and that's what you want, isn't it? I've mentioned it to Aunt Grace. She thinks it's a great idea.'

'I thought she liked me the way I was?' I said.

'She says that, of course, because she doesn't want to hurt your feelings. But she'd much rather you were white.'

So I agreed to try the treatment and Susan accompanied me to a clinic outside Calcutta where I was examined by a doctor, given a cup of tea, and then plunged into a giant vat of whitewash.

'Forget all that Black is Beautiful rubbish,' the doctor said. 'That's just a lot of junk dreamed up by those underprivileged American niggers who're tired of being second-class citizens. Repeat after me, now: "White is right. White is Right".'

'White is right,' I shouted, struggling to prevent myself from drowning in the vat.

'And again.'

'White is Right,' I yelled.

He kept me in the vat for half an hour, occasionally reaching over with a giant paddle and dunking me under completely. Then he hauled me out and led me over to a mirror. And, sure enough, there I was, whiter than white. The only trouble was that, with the white wall of the clinic behind me, you couldn't see me at all. Only my eyes.

When Susan came in to inspect me she let out a shriek.

'My God, you look ill,' she said.

'It's because I've just had the treatment,' I explained. 'It's turned me white.'

'Well it doesn't suit you,' she said. 'What you need is a little colour. We must go some place where you can lie in the sun and get a nice, dark tan. Right now you look like some sort of clown.'

I closed my eyes in despair.

'Now you've disappeared altogether,' Susan said. 'Where are you?'

She reached out a hand to touch me and. . . .

I awoke. There was a hand shaking my shoulder. I sat up, stiff from sleeping on the wooden bench, to find the plainclothes inspector standing over me with something in his hand. Instinctively I flinched. Then I realized it was a cup of tea.

'Good morning, doctor,' he said hesitantly.

For a moment it didn't register. Where was I? What had happened? I blinked my eyes, and it all came back.

I looked up at the Inspector's face. All the bullying swagger of the night before had vanished.

'Good morning,' I said, and swung my legs off the bench. I felt sore all over.

'I just don't know what to say,' he began. 'It's one of those dreadfully unfortunate things. The Pakistanis landing ... you running ... and everything.'

I rubbed the sleep out of my eyes with my hands; my beautiful, coffee-cream hands.

'I understand completely,' I said.

'Here,' he said. 'Your tea.'

I tasted it. It was hot and sweet. I began to feel better.

'We've got a difficult job to do,' he said.

'I realize that.'

'Everything pointed to you. ...'

'Naturally.'

'You were running. ...'

'That was stupid of me.'

'It made us suspicious. ...'

'It would. Of course.'

I drank some more tea.

'Anyway, I expect we all look alike to you?' I said.

'Well, it is difficult to tell some of you apart.'

'Catch all the others, did you?'

'One's still adrift,' he said. 'But we nabbed the rest. Shoved them off to Bournemouth, actually. No room for them here.'

'Good work,' I said.

He began to look less anxious.

'I'm so relieved you're taking it like this,' he said. 'I can't tell you how worried I was.'

'I don't understand.'

'Well, you're entitled to be upset.'

'Why should I be upset, Inspector?'

He shifted his weight from one foot to the other. I was enjoying this. Just a little more, I thought, and then let him have it.

'Well, after all, I did hit you.'

'But that's standard police procedure, I expect, when you're trying to get someone to talk?'

'Actually, no, it isn't. I'm afraid I lost my temper. Your story was so incredible.'

'I expect it did sound rather far-fetched, so you were fully justified in hitting me. I'll tell Sir Reeves that.'

'Sir Reeves?'

'Sir Reeves Mapleton.'

He looked anxious again.

'You know the Commissioner of Metropolitan Police?'

'Very well. He's a personal friend.'

'Why didn't you say so last night?'

'What difference would it have made? You didn't believe I knew the Prime Minister?'

'But lots of people knew the Prime Minister was in Poole. That's why I didn't believe you.'

'Oh, I see.'

He began to get very agitated.

'Look, doctor, if you could just explain to them how this mistake came about. . . .'

'Tell the Prime Minister it was understandable — is that what you mean?'

'That's it.'

'Seems a reasonable enough request to me.' I finished my tea and handed him the cup. 'You want me to go back to the Prime Minister and say: "Guess what happened to me last night? I was grabbed by three yobs in a police-car and taken to the station where I was beaten up. But it's understandable."'

He laughed nervously.

'Not quite like that, I hope.'

'Why not like that, Inspector? Isn't that what happened?'

'You have exaggerated a bit.'

'In what way have I exaggerated?'

'Well, you weren't exactly beaten up, were you? I hit you twice, that's all.'

255

'I'm so sorry. You're quite right. All you did was hit me twice and call me a lying wog bastard.'

'I'm sorry about that, doctor. I'm afraid I got a bit carried away.'

'You get carried away quite often, don't you? The man who brought me down to the cells last night said you could be a mean sod.'

'What? Who said that?'

'"Inspector Bean can be a mean sod when he chooses" — those were his very words. That is your name, right? Bean?'

'That's right.'

'Have you been an inspector long?'

'Just promoted, as a matter of fact.'

'How nice for you.'

'I worked for it, you know.'

'I'm sure you did.'

I put on my shoes and smoothed down my hair and went up the steps to the station room. A group of men were standing about, some in uniform, some not. One of the uniformed men saluted.

'There's a car waiting to take you back to the hotel, sir.'

'Before I go,' I said, 'I'd like the names and ranks of the men who arrested me last night.'

The inspector went over to a desk and consulted a roster.

'Sergeants Bushy and Jones; Constables Parkins and Everett,' he said.

'Write them down,' I said. 'And add yours to them.'

He gave me an uneasy look and scribbled down the names.

'Now perhaps you'll give me back my things.'

'They're here, sir.' One of the uniformed constables handed me an envelope.

I opened it and checked the contents.

'Everything in order?' the inspector said.

'Nothing seems to have been stolen,' I said.

One of the constables laughed.

'Well, goodbye doctor,' the inspector said, holding out a hand. 'No hard feelings I hope. There'll be a proper apology, of course.'

I glared up at him.

'Apology?' I said. 'For being shoved around by your potato-faced goons and then bunged into a stinking cell? If you think an apology is going to wipe that out you're even stupider than you look, Bean.'

His face went very red.

'What can I say, doctor?'

'You could start with Sorry,' I said.

'What else was I to think?'

I looked around at the startled faces of the assembled police.

'What else, indeed? How could one expect your pygmy minds to cotton on to the fact that a newly-arrived and half-drowned Pakistani immigrant was hardly likely to bandy the name of the Prime Minister about. ...'

'Some of them concoct fantastic stories ...' he said weakly.

Secure in the knowledge that I had the most power-ful man in Britain behind me, I faced up to him.

'Bean,' I said, 'you're a bullying bastard. And far from getting you off the hook as far as the Prime Minister is concerned, I shall take enormous pleasure in sinking it right into your thick neck. For, believe me, they'll have your head on a platter for this. ...'

'You said you understood.'

'Oh I do understand,' I said. 'I understand com-pletely. And I hope you'll be equally understanding when they come and take away your inspector's uniform.'

With that I turned on my heel and, closely followed by the police-driver, stalked out to the waiting car.

Ten minutes later, not one word having been spoken en route, I was back at the Falcon.

It was just after seven in the morning, and the night porter who opened the door looked at me suspiciously.

'What do you want?' he said.

'Not you for a start,' I said rudely, and shoved past him. I went straight to the downstairs washroom to clean myself up. I looked a sight. My hair was matted, my eyes were blood-shot and I was unshaven. I had to admit it. I didn't look much like a Harley Street doctor.

When I walked into the Ocean Suite the Prime Minister was sitting in a chair, reading some documents. The young man whose name I had been unable to remember was packing a bag.

'Thank God you're safe,' the Prime Minister said, jumping to his feet and grasping my hand. 'We were so worried. ...'

'The police arrested me,' I said. 'They thought I was an illegal immigrant.'

'I know,' he said. 'Dolts. Auby here called Poole police at five-thirty this morning and they began making inquiries. Found you'd been held at Ross Point.'

'It was a frightening experience,' I said.

'I can imagine,' he said. 'And I couldn't be more sorry. But rest assured I'll have their guts for garters. They'll be back on the beat for this.'

'I've got all the names,' I said. 'A bastard named Bean was the worst. He hit me.'

'They won't get away with it,' he said. He broke off. 'Would you like some coffee, or something?'

'I could do with it,' I said.

He turned to the young man.

'Auby. Roust up that old fool downstairs and get him to make the doctor a cup.'

The young man nodded and went out.

Then I realized.

'Your back,' I said. 'It's all right?'

He flashed the full shark smile.

'Perfectly. You fixed it. Had the best sleep I've had in

258

years and woke up feeling splendid. Looked about for you and found nobody had seen you. Knew you had to be about somewhere — your bag was still here — so Auby started making inquiries.'

'I'm glad he did,' I said.

The young man came back.

'He's making some coffee,' he said. 'It won't be long.'

'It's bloody awful stuff,' the Prime Minister said. 'But it'll keep you going. We can stop on the road for a bite of breakfast if you like. There's a good place in the New Forest — what's it called, Auby?'

'The Red Barn,' the young man said.

'That's it. The Red Barn. They do marvellous bacon and eggs. And fried bread. Love fried bread, don't you?'

'Right now,' I said, 'what I'd really like is a bath.'

A look of concern crossed his face.

'Of course,' he said. 'Use my bathroom, Make yourself at home. Auby will lend you a razor.' He went across to his briefcase and took out a green packet. 'And here,' he said. 'Use the rest of the Radox.'

49

We got back to London around ten and I went straight to bed and slept for the rest of the day.

There were fresh sheets put on by Annie, the withered crone who came in every Friday and did mysterious things about the house, and after the misery of the night before, my bed felt deliciously cool and inviting.

Around six I had a bath and began preparing for dinner with Susan.

It took me some time. There was so much to be done. Different suits to be tried on, shirts and ties to be laid out for matching, shoes to be shone, deodorant to be applied, teeth to be cleaned, nails to be trimmed.

But at length I was ready. And I set out for the brief walk round the corner to Hallam Street. This time I had no qualms about crossing the huge foyer of Halliday House under the suspicious glare of the beribboned porter.

'Dr Das,' I said sternly. 'Miss Partridge expects me.'

He gave me a half-hearted, never-thought-I'd-find-myself-doing-this-to-wogs salute.

'Third floor,' he said. 'Flat 27.' No 'Sir' or anything. Not that I expected it. His grandfather had probably fought at Cawnpore.

As I rode up in the lift, adjusting my tie for the last time, I wondered whether to tell Susan about the night before. By the time I reached her flat I decided against it. Whichever way I told the story it showed me in a poor light. Her respect for me was bound to diminish if she knew I had spent the night in a police cell.

I pressed the bell.

A moment later she opened the door. She was dressed in black. And she had been weeping.

'Oh, Ram. Where have you been?'

With a cry she fell into my arms, sobbing uncontrollably. I held her tightly, conscious of the thudding of my heart.

'What's the matter?' I said, feeling frightened.

'She's dead,' Susan said.

Oh Great Lord Shiva!

'Dead?'

'Yesterday, in Connaught Squre. Simons took her tea up as usual, and she was ... just lying there. She'd been dead for some time. He telephoned you immediately, but they said you were away in Poole. When he tried the hotel there they didn't seem to know anything about you. So he rang me. I didn't know what to do. I was so shattered. But then I contacted Dr Klein, whom she used to attend. Someone had to see her. For the death certificate, and everything.'

I stood there, saying nothing, picturing Grace

260

Ammanford, cold and dead, in that huge bedroom. Gone was my trip around the world; gone my dreams of bliss with Susan; gone everything.

'She had been reading,' Susan said, sobbing. 'A travel brochure. It was open at the page. It was just as if she'd fallen asleep.'

'I can't believe it,' I said.

She blinked up at me through her tears.

'Why didn't you tell me she had heart disease?' she demanded brokenly.

'Heart disease?'

'Dr Klein told me. He said he'd been treating her with digitalis for years. He supposed you must have been continuing the treatment. . . .'

So that was it.

'I . . . I did, of course. But there was nothing to be done.'

'Nothing?'

'She was quite ill.'

'Then why did you let her go ahead with her plans for the trip? Why didn't you tell me?'

'I wanted to keep her happy,' I lied. 'And there seemed no point in distressing you.'

Tears rolled down her cheeks.

'There's so much I would have said to her if I'd known. Now it's too late.'

'She knew you loved her,' I said. 'She talked about you all the time.'

'She was so looking forward to this trip,' Susan said. 'It was going to be so lovely.'

'She died happy,' I said. 'Think of it like that.'

'Oh God,' Susan said. 'Oh dear God.'

I led her over to the settee.

'Has Sir George been told?'

'I rang him yesterday.'

'Will he be . . . arranging things?'

'No. Daddy's doing that. He came up last night. The funeral is the day after tomorrow. She's being cremated.'

'I'd like to send some flowers.'

She brushed away her tears.

'But you'll come to the funeral?'

'Shouldn't it just be the family?'

'Aunt Grace thought of you as family. You know that.'

'Then I'll come,' I said.

'There won't be many there,' she said. 'Just Daddy and us and perhaps one or two other relatives.'

I put my hand on her shoulder.

'I'll leave you now,' I said. 'I expect you'd prefer to be on your own.'

'Daddy should be back soon,' she said. 'Do you want to stay and have something to eat with us?'

I remembered my fantasy of the night before; the candle-lit table for two; the wine. Now this.

'No,' I said. 'Not tonight.'

She stifled a sob as she walked with me to the door.

'I wish I'd known,' she said. 'I wish you'd told me.'

'I did what I thought best,' I said unhappily.

She started to cry again.

50

I started drinking in the Resolution and had three straight vodkas in quick succession. They warmed my stomach, but not my heart. If I hadn't come to England, I thought, if I'd stayed in India where I belonged, Grace Ammanford would still be alive. She'd have stayed on with Dr Klein and he'd have kept her going with drugs and instead of weeping Susan would now be going over her summer clothes for the trip. It was all my fault and nothing would ever change that. Nothing.

The enormity of what I had done, coupled with my

exhaustion from the night before, made me feel quite faint. I leaned my head against the bar.

'You pissed, or something?'

I straightened up slowly. The publican, a small, ferocious-looking man, was eyeing me suspiciously.

'No. I just felt ill for a moment.'

'You're pissed,' he insisted. 'Finish your drink and clear out.'

'There's nothing wrong with me,' I said. 'I just felt faint suddenly.'

He leaned over the bar.

'If you're looking for trouble, sonny, you've come to just the right place.'

I looked beyond him at the framed photographs decorating the back of the bar. They were all of boxers, signed Jack and Tiger and Pug. There was even a picture of the publican himself, in the ring, holding his arms high above his head.

'I'm not looking for trouble,' I said. 'Believe me, I'm just telling you there's nothing wrong with me.'

His eyes went grey as slate.

'Are you calling me a liar?' he said.

I was sick of this. I finished my drink.

'Something wrong, Bert?'

A large man in a grey sports-coat and cavalry-twill trousers sauntered over, holding a pint of beer in his hand.

'Yes,' the landlord said. 'This little bastard's had a skinful. I'm just telling him to clear out.'

The large man looked me up and down.

'Well,' he said, putting his beer on the counter, 'you heard the man. Clear out.'

'I'm going,' I said, starting towards the door.

'Just a minute.' He put a hand on my arm. 'I've been watching you. What's your game?'

'I don't know what you mean?'

'You know what I mean all right,' he said. 'What were you doing in here? Looking for girls, was that it?'

'Of course not.'

'No "of course" about it,' he said. 'I know you black bastards. Always trying to get your hands on white girls.'

'That's not true. . . .'

'It's all you think about, isn't it?'

I tried to pull away. But he held my arm tightly.

'Will you please let me go?'

'I asked you a question,' the large man said, increasing the pressure on my arm.

'I wasn't looking for girls. I came in here for a quiet drink.'

'Why don't you go drinking with your own kind, then?'

'I live near here,' I said.

'Christ,' he said, turning to the publican. 'Don't tell me they're moving in round here now?'

'They're everywhere,' the publican said. 'You can't turn a corner without seeing them. And everywhere they squat they open an Indian restaurant.'

'Don't talk to me about Indian restaurants,' the large man said. 'I went to one once. Filthy holes. You know what they serve in them, don't you? Dog food.'

'They do not serve dog food,' I said desperately.

'Oh yes they do,' the large man said. 'I read about it in one of the papers. A health inspector looked in without warning and there were all these opened tins, ready for the pot. Makes you sick. Foisting dog food on to the public. And all drowned in curry so they don't notice. There ought to be a law. . . .'

'They should all be sent home,' the publican said.

'You're right,' the large man said.

'Look at all those diseases they bring in,' the publican added. 'Leprosy, cholera —'

'We do not bring in diseases,' I said. 'There's a health check.'

'Health check,' the publican sneered. 'Most of you buggers come in at night on a boat. Everyone knows that.'

'They can't get work in their own stinking country so they come to ours,' the large man said. 'God knows how many have got in. They tell me they've got them living ten to a room in some places.'

'And breeding,' the publican said. 'Breeding like rats.'

'This used to be a good country once,' the large man said.

'That it did,' the publican said. 'Till they let the wogs in.'

'You seem to have forgotten that the British were once in India,' I said heatedly.

'And what were we doing there?' the large man demanded. 'We were civilizing you, weren't we? Helping you down from the trees. It was a bloody wilderness until we got there, from all accounts.' He turned to the publican. 'Talk about primitive. They used to burn the widow along with the dead husband. Did you know that? Flung her on the funeral pyre too.'

'Suttee was banned over a hundred and fifty years ago,' I said. 'Anyway, you used to burn witches. . . .'

'Witches were wicked,' the large man said. 'There's no comparison.'

I tried to pull away again. He held me tightly.

'Nobody's saying the British didn't bring some benefits to India,' I said.

'Some benefits?' he echoed. 'We taught you everything you know. We built half your bloody country for you.'

'It's nothing to be proud of,' I said. 'You should see some of it.'

With his free hand he prodded me hard in the chest. He had knuckles like rivets.

'Oh,' he said. 'And I suppose your mud huts were better?'

At that moment another customer came into the pub.

'Evening, Bert,' he said. 'Evening, Jim.'

The large man relaxed his hold for a moment and turned to acknowledge the greeting.

Seizing my chance, I yanked my arm free and raced for the door. But I was not fast enough. The large man was there before me.

'Oh no you don't,' he said menacingly. 'Not without an apology.'

'All right,' I said. 'I'm sorry. I won't come here again.'

I pushed open the swing doors. As I did so he shot out a foot and I half-tripped. Flinging out my hands to save myself, I found myself clutching at a woman who had just walked in through the outer doors. The large man, who had stepped behind me, presumably to smash his fist into my neck, moved back quickly.

'I'm sorry,' I said to the startled woman.

'Really,' she said crossly. 'You ought to be more careful.'

She brushed the front of her coat, presumably to dislodge any Indian filth I might have deposited there, and pushed past me.

I turned, tense with fury. The large man was holding open one of the inner doors for the woman to pass. I kicked out with all my strength. I felt the toe of my shoe connect with his crotch and he let out a howl of pain and rage and bent over, releasing the door so that it swung back in the woman's face.

'Jeeeeeeeeeeeesus,' he shrieked.

'Oh God,' the woman moaned, clutching her nose.

I didn't wait. I turned and ran. All the way to Marylebone High Street and into the Old Bell. Well, I thought, I wrecked that bastard's love life for a week or two. There was a lot to be said for Gandhi's teaching of Satyagraha, or non-violent action, but there was also considerable satisfaction to be got from kicking a bully in the balls.

I had some more vodkas. Keep drinking, I thought. That's the answer. Drown it all out; angry publicans,

266

blackmailing girls, dead friends. Drown them out and forget them. Get drunk and stay drunk.

Around ten o'clock I moved on to the Prince of Wales. There were some sausages on the bar, and I was feeling hungry, so I ordered a couple with my next drink. They tasted dreadful, and I could not finish the second one. As I pushed the plate away I saw a pimply-faced youth behind the bar smiling furtively in my direction.

'Something wrong?' the publican said sharply, nodding towards the uneaten remains of my second sausage.

'No,' I said. 'I've just had enough.'

Further along the bar, the pimply-faced youth was snickering as he polished a glass.

'They're good sausages,' the publican said firmly. 'I have them myself. I know.'

'Yes, they are good,' I said.

'You won't find better sausages anywhere,' he said.

'I'm sure you're right.'

'It isn't easy to find good sausages,' he said. 'There's an awful lot of rubbish on the market.'

'I've noticed that,' I said.

'Get sausages, do you, where you come from?'

'No,' I said.

'Ah,' he said. 'That's it then. Unless you're used to sausages, you can't tell the good from the bad.'

'I suppose that's true,' I said, finishing my drink.

The publican moved off along the bar and said something to the pimply-faced youth, who burst out laughing.

I reeled home along Devonshire Street, feeling considerably the worse for wear. On one of the houses to the right I noticed a blue plaque: 'Sir Arthur Pinero, 1855–1934, playwright, lived here. 1909–1934.' Well, I thought, whoever he was he didn't get to Devonshire Street until he was fifty-four. I'd done better than that. Perhaps they'd put up a plaque to me one day? How would it read? 'Ram Das, imposter, trainee rapist and slayer of Lady Ammanford, lived here.' It would certainly make a talking point.

When I staggered into the house, the telephone in the hall was ringing. It was Susan.

'I've been so worried about you,' she said. 'Are you all right?'

'No,' I said thickly. 'I'm not.'

'Daddy would like to see you,' she said. 'Could you possibly come round?'

'Tonight?' I said.

'Yes. Now.'

'I can't,' I said. 'I've had too much to drink.'

'It doesn't matter,' she said. 'This is very important.'

'But I feel terrible. . . .'

'Please,' she said.

51

Colonel Partridge turned out to be nice, as far as I could see. Which, by that time, was not very far. He was a tall, military-looking man with grey hair and a small moustache and he wore expensive-looking country tweeds.

'I've heard such a lot about you,' he said. 'I just wish we could have met under happier circumstances.'

I sank into a chair. I was beginning to feel quite ill.

'I'm sorry, sir,' I said. 'I'm afraid I've had rather a lot to drink.'

He didn't look contemptuous. Not even disgusted. He just looked anxious.

'Don't apologize,' he said. 'It's quite understandable.'

He turned to Susan, who was looking at me anxiously.

'What about making a little coffee, Suse? I think we'd all enjoy a cup.' Not: give this drunken wog something to sober him up; nothing like that. Just: 'I think we'd all enjoy a cup.' He was a nice man, Susan's daddy.

When Susan had disappeared along the hall he came and sat down close to me.

'They gave Grace a nice obit in *The Times* this morning. I expect you saw it?'

I shook my head, which made me feel worse.

'They said some damn nice things about her war work. She was with the American Red Cross, as you probably know.'

I slumped towards the floor.

He leaned forward, this nice man, Susan's daddy, registering nothing but concern for the unspeakable guttersnipe who had just killed his sister.

'Are you all right?' he asked.

'I'm ... I'm, all right,' I groaned.

'Coffee won't be long,' he said. 'Susan makes a good cup of coffee.'

I slid lower.

'What I want to talk to you about is this,' he said. 'I am executor of my sister's estate, and I've been going over her will and papers with the solicitor this afternoon. Her estate, as you may have guessed, is considerable.'

I tried hard to focus on him, but he kept floating away.

'She has left, as far as I can estimate at the moment, almost two million pounds.'

I stopped sliding towards the floor.

'Of course I knew she was immensely wealthy,' he said. 'We were both left the same amount when my father died. And she invested more wisely than I.'

I struggled to rise.

'Anyway, doctor, to come to the point. The money has been left, evenly divided, between three parties. Myself, Susan and ...' he paused ... 'you.'

He seemed to have four eyes. I wished he would sit

still, and stop floating about.

'It means, when everything is taken into account and death duties have been paid, you will probably receive around four hundred thousand pounds.'

I uttered a strangled croak.

'I have discussed this at length with my daughter, since we are the immediate family, and it is our decision not to oppose this bequest. It is most unusual, as you know, for a sum of this size to be left by a patient to her doctor. It will — inevitably — create speculation. That need not concern you. Grace, I understand, was devoted to you and you did much to make her last months happy ones. For that I am grateful.'

'What about' — groan — 'him?'

'Who?'

Croak. 'One leg?'

'The divorce came through two days ago,' Colonel Partridge said. 'George has no claim at all on Grace's estate.'

My head fell forward.

'Let me help you back into the chair?'

'No.' Shudder. 'Really.'

'Then I'll just see how Susan is getting on.'

He retreated to the kitchen. I heard the sound of voices, but they were blurred, as if coming through cotton-wool. I struggled to get back into the chair, but it was no use. When the coffee arrived I was still heaped up against it like a sack of potatoes.

'Here,' Susan said, handing me a cup of blackness. 'This will make you feel better.'

'Ugh.'

'Daddy's told you?'

'Mmm.'

I sipped the coffee. It tasted of ink.

'She told me she was going to leave you something,' Susan said. 'She was so pleased you were coming on the trip. She said if you were prepared to abandon your practice for six months just to make sure she was all right, then she wanted to do something for you.'

The floor began spinning.

'She loved you very much,' Susan said.

Then I passed out.

52

We were not following the coffin. We were to meet it at Brigwell Park Crematorium. Which seemed as good a place as any to meet a coffin.

'Aunt Grace liked it,' Susan said. 'She went there last year for a friend's funeral. Apparently the gardens are lovely.'

We drove out in a hired car: Susan, myself, her father and a distant cousin named Daisy who had always sent Lady Ammanford bed-socks for Xmas and had come down from Harrogate.

Sir George was not coming. The man who had spent so much time at other people's funerals had apparently decided that this one simply did not merit serious attention. The fact that it was his late wife who was being disposed of did not come into it. It was not a first-class funeral — there were not enough mourners, cars, or photographers — and to be seen at such an unfashionable event was clearly unthinkable.

'I'm not sorry,' Colonel Partridge said. 'It might have been embarrassing.'

Outside the chapel, among the flower-beds, Simons and the maid Josie were standing, side by side.

They both looked tired, as if they had been at it all night. Which, given that the bell was now stilled and their mistress departed for the Connaught Square of the Sky, they quite probably had.

'Not much of a day,' Simons said, to nobody in particular. He managed to say it without a sneer, for which I was grateful.

271

We stood around awkwardly, saying nothing, for what seemed a long time. Then, just before noon, the hearse trundled up.

When she saw the purple-draped coffin, Susan let out a small sob.

'It's ... so small,' she said.

Her father took her by the arm.

'Steady, girl,' he said.

As the hearse rolled to a stop, the undertaker jumped out and came forward to meet us. He was a sombre, grey-faced man.

'Good morning, Colonel Partridge,' he said. He nodded to each of us in turn.

'My men will be taking the departed into the chapel in just one minute. If you will all please follow her in, we can proceed.'

'Thank you,' Colonel Partridge said, stiffly.

We trouped into the chapel behind the coffin and were greeted by the pale young minister who was going to conduct the service.

'Is this all there is of you?' he said, glumly.

'Yes. It's just family,' Colonel Partridge said.

'I understood there would be more,' the minister said, rather like an actor contemplating a bad matinée audience. 'There are lots of flowers.'

'She had many friends,' Colonel Partridge said.

'Did she?' the minister said, without much enthusiasm.

He marched up to the tiny rostrum while we arranged ourselves in two pews. At the touch of a button the piped music petered out and he began a short service welcoming Grace Ammanford to The Great Upstairs.

Then the music began again and we stood to attention as the wooden platform bearing the coffin began sinking out of sight.

Susan, her eyes closed, gripped my hand tightly.

I closed my eyes too. This was not something I

wanted to see.

When I opened them again the coffin was still there. Halfway down, the platform had stuck.

'Damn,' the minister said, audibly.

He jabbed angrily at the 'Down' button. The platform stayed stuck.

Susan opened her eyes.

'What's happened?' she asked nervously.

'There seems to have been some mishap,' her father said.

'I'm terribly sorry,' the minister said, stepping out of character for a moment. 'I was assured that the lift had been fixed. Apparently not.'

He jabbed at the button again. Still nothing happened.

He tried the 'Up' button. This worked. The platform rose majestically until it was back in its original position.

'Now let's see,' the minister said, pressing the 'Down' button again.

Once more the platform descended. At the same spot as before, it jammed.

'I can get her up all right,' the minister said, helplessly. 'I just can't get her down.'

There was an uneasy silence.

'What do you want us to do?' Colonel Partridge said in a strained voice. 'We can't just leave her there.'

'Perhaps if you'd go out and take a look at the flowers I can get the mechanic in,' the minister said. 'Or we could carry her down. It's most regrettable.'

Colonel Partridge turned to the rest of us.

'Shall we go into the garden?' he said. 'That might be the best idea.'

We shuffled out. As I reached the door I saw an immense, red-faced man in a dirty boiler-suit emerging from somewhere behind the rostrum.

'Bloody hell,' he said to the minister. 'I fixed the sodding thing only yesterday.'

He glared at me angrily as I followed the others out.

'This is all very distressing,' Colonel Partridge said. 'I hope they won't take long.'

The undertaker, who had been waiting outside, reading a newspaper, hurried forward.

'I trust everything went satisfactorily?'

'The platform stuck,' Colonel Partridge said flatly.

The undertaker's face registered disbelief.

'Oh not again,' he said. 'Really, this is the limit.' He disappeared into the chapel.

'Perhaps we ought to look at the flowers?' Susan said.

We went round to the side of the chapel where mounds of flowers and wreaths were grouped under a card reading: 'Tributes to Grace Ammanford'. There must have been two or three hundred pounds worth of blooms there. My own tribute, a rather unimpressive bunch of assorteds which had looked fine at the florists, was completely dwarfed by the giant wreaths and crosses which lay piled up on either side.

'People have been very kind,' Susan said.

'Indeed,' her father said.

'I don't see mine here,' Cousin Daisy said.

'What were they?' Susan asked.

'I had some roses done in the shape of a pair of bedsocks,' Cousin Daisy said. 'She always liked my bedsocks.'

'That was very thoughtful,' Susan said.

'I can't see them anywhere,' Cousin Daisy said.

'I'm sure they're here somewhere,' Colonel Partridge said. 'It's hard to see when there are so many.'

There was a sound of hammering from inside the chapel.

'Oh dear,' Susan said, looking alarmed.

I heard the sound of machinery whirring.

'I think they've fixed it,' I said.

'I do hope so,' Susan said. 'I hate to think of poor Aunt Grace stuck there.'

The whirring stopped.

274

A string of blasphemies came from the chapel.

'Perhaps we should allow them to carry her down,' Colonel Partridge said, uncertainly.

'Who's going to do it?' Cousin Daisy said. 'The undertaker's men have gone.'

'Perhaps we could manage it?' I said.

'I really don't think that's such a good idea,' he said. 'It might be upsetting, you know ... downstairs.'

The undertaker came hurrying up.

'I can't tell you how sorry I am about this,' he said. 'You understand, I hope, that it is not my fault.'

'We realize that,' Colonel Partridge said.

'I've told them that if this happens again that's the last load they'll get out of Dunnit and Bleach,' the undertaker said. 'It's the second time this week.'

'Oh dear,' Susan said faintly.

'The trouble is,' the undertaker said, looking at his watch, 'there's another load due any minute now.'

Colonel Partridge flinched.

'Excuse me, Mr ...?'

'Griddle,' the man said. 'Senior director.'

'Well, Mr Griddle, what exactly do you mean; there's another load due any minute now?'

'They usually allow us a full half-hour,' the undertaker said. 'But there's such a rush on this morning they've given us only fifteen minutes each. ...'

He broke off as another hearse came trundling down the gravelled drive, followed by two black saloons.

A man in a top hat got out of the hearse, looking furious.

'Oh God,' Griddle said. 'There's Angry Clarke of Holland Park. I hope there's not going to be any trouble.'

He hurried over.

'What do you suppose we ought to do?' Susan asked.

'There's nothing we can do,' her father said. 'I'm sure they'll have it fixed shortly.'

Crash! Thud!

275

'Daddy,' Susan said. 'I'm beginning to feel quite ill. I think I'll go and sit in the car.'

She walked away slowly.

'Really,' her father said. 'This is simply appalling. I've never ...'

Our attention was suddenly diverted. In the middle of the drive, right in front of the other mourners, the two undertakers were arguing furiously.

'What do you want me to do?' Griddle said angrily. 'Carry the bloody box down myself?'

'I don't give a damn what you do,' the other man raged. 'But get it down or we'll shove it down for you. You should have been out of there five minutes ago.'

Griddle, his face twitching, turned to us.

'Colonel Partridge. What do you want me to do?'

Susan's father turned to the second undertaker.

'I assure you we have no wish to remain here a moment longer than necessary.'

'Then let us through,' the man said. 'You can finish yours later.'

Colonel Partridge turned very pale.

'We have, as you so charmingly put it, already finished ours,' he said. 'It is just a question of un-jamming the platform.'

'That'll take hours,' the man snapped. 'You'll have to carry it down.'

Griddle nodded.

'That might be best, Colonel Partridge. We could use their bearers.'

Susan's father looked at me. I nodded.

'Very well,' he said.

Angry Clarke turned to his men.

'Right, lads. Into the chapel.'

Before they could reach it there was the sound of further hammering, followed by the whirr of machin-ery. Then a grinding sort of crash.

'Good heavens,' Colonel Partridge said.

Leaving the others standing there, we hurried into

276

the chapel. The platform was now three feet lower than before. The top, which sank flush with the floor when fully lowered, was now so far down that it was impossible to reach the coffin.

'This is just terrible,' the minister said, turning to us. 'In all my years I've never seen anything like it.'

'Just wait till you see what's stacked up out there,' Griddle said. He glanced at his watch. 'And there's another one due any minute.'

'Oh my God,' the minister said.

We looked around. A third hearse was rolling slowly down the drive.

'Well there's nothing my men can do,' Angry Clarke said. 'She could be there till Doomsday.'

'Don't you worry,' the red-faced mechanic said, scrabbling round at the back. 'I'll get this bleeder moving if it's the last thing I do.'

Crash! Thud! Wallop!

'How many more this morning?' Griddle asked.

'Another two,' the minister said.

'You'll have them lined up out there like this was the bloody Palladium,' Angry Clarke said.

'Perhaps we could divert them,' the minister said. 'Brampton Grange isn't far away.'

'Not working,' Griddle said. 'Changing the burners.'

'Then we're stuck,' the minister said desperately.

'We're not,' Angry Clarke said, looking down on Grace Ammanford. 'She is.'

Bash! Wham!

'Any luck?' Griddle asked.

'Not a smell,' said the red-faced mechanic. 'Bleeder's tight as a nun's. ...'

'Please,' the minister said faintly.

Angry Clarke snorted.

'This is the last time I'll book this dump for anybody,' he said. 'I've never seen anything so unprofessional.'

''Ere,' the red-faced mechanic said, looking up. 'Just

you watch it, mate. I've 'ad about enough of your smart-alec remarks for one morning. . . .'

'Well, get the bloody thing fixed,' Angry Clarke said. 'And you won't have to hear any more.'

'What the hell do you think I'm doing down here?' snarled the mechanic. 'Trying to get to Australia?'

'Whatever you're doing it isn't having much effect,' Angry Clarke said.

'I'm warning you,' the mechanic said belligerently.

'Don't you threaten me, you plank-faced twat,' snapped Angry Clarke. 'You're being paid to service the lift. Service it.'

'I'll service you in a minute,' the mechanic said, his voice rising.

'Gentlemen, please,' the minister cried. 'This isn't getting us anywhere.'

Crash! Thump!

Griddle looked at his watch.

'Old Harry Moffat's load should be here any minute,' he said. 'He said he was booked for one o'clock.' He looked through the door. 'Yes,' he said. 'Here he comes.'

Another hearse came sweeping down the drive, followed by three cars full of mourners.

'Dear Lord,' the minister said. 'This is simply dreadful.'

Thud! Whunk!

Whirrrrrrr.

Suddenly the platform began moving again. Down.

'I've done it,' the mechanic cried. 'I've fixed the bleeder.'

There was a sigh as the top of the platform sank flush with the floor.

'Lovely,' the mechanic said.

The minister turned to us.

'I am so terribly sorry.'

'What do we do now?' Colonel Partridge asked.

'Nothing,' the minister said. 'That's it.'

278

'There's no more?'

The minister frowned.

'What did you expect? There isn't a roll of drums, or anything.'

'It just seems ... well, a bit sudden.'

'What do you want me to do?' asked the minister. 'Bring her up and do it all over again?'

'Well it's hardly been a dignified funeral,' Colonel Partridge said.

'I realize that. Believe me, I realize that. And I sympathize.' He glanced anxiously at his watch. 'But we're so late now. And there are all those others out there. ...'

'That's hardly our fault,' Colonel Partridge said. 'I would only remind you that we came here to take leave of'...' he paused '... the departed among peaceful and quiet conditions. We did not expect the anvil chorus.'

'I understand your concern,' the minister said. He looked at his watch again. 'But I don't know what you want me to do?'

'Raise the coffin for just a few moments,' Colonel Partridge said. 'Then let us reassemble in here by ourselves for a final farewell.' He looked around. 'Perhaps these people wouldn't mind leaving?'

'Christ Almighty,' Angry Clarke said. 'We're never going to be finished here.'

Suddenly two more undertakers were at the door.

'Well, well' one of them said. 'If it isn't Angry Clarke of Holland Park.'

'Hello, Harry,' Angry Clarke said. 'There's been a proper balls-up here, and no mistake.'

'What's going on then?' the other demanded.

'The stiff got stuck.'

'Stop it,' shrieked the minister. 'I will not have this kind of talk in my chapel. Will you all please leave, except the Ammanford group.'

With ill-grace and much muttering, they filed out. Colonel Partridge and I were left alone.

279

'Shall I get the others?' I asked.

'Just Cousin Daisy,' he said. 'We'll leave Susan where she is. And I don't think we need bother the servants.'

I went out and beckoned to Cousin Daisy. The entire drive was filled with hearses and cars.

'What's happening?' she demanded.

'Colonel Partridge wants to say goodbye to Lady Ammanford properly,' I said. 'They're going to raise her up. ...'

She clutched my arm.

'What?' she said.

'On the platform,' I said.

'Oh thank God,' she said. 'For a moment. ...' She paused 'Shouldn't we just leave her where she is?'

'It won't take long,' I said.

This time the three of us stood in one pew. Once again the piped music swelled out. Slowly the platform rose.

By the time it was half-way up I knew the worst.

There was no coffin on it.

'Oh my God,' Colonel Partridge said.

The minister became hysterical.

'She's gone,' he blubbered.

'You fool,' Colonel Partridge stormed. 'Why didn't you tell them? Why didn't you let them know we were doing it again?'

'There's no way.' the minister said. 'There's no communication. I just hoped they wouldn't have ... you know ... done it so soon. They must have hurried because of the delay.'

Colonel Partridge stared at him.

'Words fail me,' he said.

He turned to us, white-faced.

'Shall we go?' he said.

We went outside. As soon as we were through the door another coffin was brought in, on the trot, followed by a half-running group of mourners. The piped music started again.

In the car Susan said;

'Is she ... is she all right now?'

'Yes darling,' her father said. 'She's all right now.'

She clasped my hand tightly. She was still holding it when we got back to Hallam Street.

53

'It's hard to believe,' Patel said.

'I know,' I said. 'I'm still in a bit of a daze myself.'

He reached across the kitchen table and grasped my hands.

'You're rich,' he said. 'A wealthy man.'

'Four hundred thousand pounds,' I said.

'Four hundred thousand,' he repeated it slowly. 'How does it feel? Tell me how it feels?'

'Odd,' I said. 'As if it were happening to someone else.'

He looked at me intently.

'And she left you all this because she liked you? It's incredible. There was nothing between you?'

'Nothing.'

'You never slept with her, or anything? Swear you never slept with her?'

'Please,' I said. 'She's dead and gone now.'

'Only just,' he said. 'Judging by that shambles of a funeral.'

'She liked me,' I said. 'That's all there was to it.'

'Women do become infatuated with their doctors,' he said. 'It's a well-known fact. There was that chap down in Dorset. Forgotten his name now. Half a dozen old birds left him their money. Everybody thought he'd bumped them off.'

'We doctors are always vulnerable to that sort of

suspicion,' I said.

His eyebrows rose.

'What did you say?'

I looked at him. Then I realized.

'Sorry,' I said. 'I was forgetting. ...'

'No, no,' he said. 'That's good. That's how it should be.'

He got up and went over to the cupboard against the wall.

'Anyway,' he said. 'I'm starting to believe it myself.'

He rummaged around inside the cupboard and produced a buff envelope.

'Take a look at that,' he said, tossing it across the table.

I opened the envelope. Inside was a dark-navy passport, with the words 'Republic of India' stamped on the front.

'Well,' he said. 'Go on. Look at it.'

I leafed through the passport, my hands trembling. And there it was, under the heading 'Profession'. The one word. Doctor.

I stared at it.

'You did it,' I said.

'Nothing to it.'

'Is it — is it — genuine?'

He looked pained.

'Of course it's genuine. Phoney doctors are one thing; phoney passports quite another. I got it from my friend at the High Commission.'

'Then I'll be able to go.'

'Go?' he said. 'Go where?'

'On the trip. Susan wants me to take her. We discussed it last night. Lady Ammanford had arranged everything, you see. And Susan has some modelling to do in Hong Kong.'

Patel slumped into his chair.

'This is a bit of a surprise,' he said. 'I didn't think you'd be going now.'

'There's nothing to keep me here,' I said. 'I'd already told Hilda Furze and the others that I was taking time off. And Susan would go, even if I didn't.'

He faced me across the table.

'You really love her, don't you?'

'Very much.'

'Can anything come of it?'

'I don't know, do I? I hope so.'

'You mean you'd like to marry her?'

'If she'll have me.'

He shook his head.

'Don't you realize what a terrible risk you're taking?'

'In what way?'

'She's bound to find out that you're not a real doctor.'

'I don't see why,' I said. 'Not now.'

He heaved a sigh.

'How can you be such a fool?' he said. 'What if she becomes ill? What if she has a baby?'

'I'll worry about that when the time comes.'

'Mark my words,' he said. 'She'll find out. And she'll hate you. She'll blame you for the death of her aunt.'

'I'm prepared to take that chance,' I said.

He sat in silence for a while, toying with his tea-cup. Then he said:

'Have I ever given you bad advice?'

'Not so far.'

'Then forget her.'

'I can't,' I said.

'If you don't you're doomed,' he said. 'Your only chance is to take the money and run. If you hang around and start playing at husbands, she'll be on to you in a moment. Why, she'll only have to cough and you'll be in trouble. What would you do? Rub her chest with liniment?'

'I've got away with it so far,' I said.

'You know why?' he demanded. 'Because you've been seeing a lot of half-baked women who had nothing really wrong with them. Anyway, we're not talking about you treating someone twice a week for ten minutes; we're talking about you spending the rest of your life with a girl who is very bright indeed. Whose favourite aunt you helped dispose of. Just in time, I might add.'

'That's a dreadful thing to say,' I cried.

'Perhaps. But have you considered what would have happened if she'd been taken ill on the trip? What you would have done?'

'I could always have called in someone else.'

'Why would you have done that? You were her personal physician. That was her excuse for taking you, wasn't it? Anyway, what if you had called in someone else? They'd have found out right away that you didn't know what you were talking about.'

'I got away with it before,' I said.

'I wish you'd stop saying that,' he remarked crossly. 'You got away with it before because none of them died. But this one did. Just think. What if it had happened in some remote place? Tahiti, for instance. You would have had to sign the death certificate, arrange for the body to be flown home, all sorts of things. Do you really think you'd have got away with it?'

'It didn't happen,' I said. 'So we can stop arguing.'

'I'm not arguing,' he said. 'I'm just trying to make you see that luck has been with you so far. But push Ganesa any further and he'll run out on you.'

'Perhaps,' I said. 'Perhaps not.'

'You're not scared?' he demanded incredulously.

'Of course I'm scared,' I said. 'I'm also in love with Susan.'

'But listen,' he said. 'With the kind of money you'll have you'll be able to get any bird you want. Why pick on the one girl in the whole world who can ruin everything?'

'Because she's the one girl in the whole world I really care about.'

He sighed.

'You know who Kali is?'

'Of course. The goddess of death and destruction.'

'You're sending her an open invitation,' he warned.

'Let's just hope she's got a previous engagement,' I said.

I picked up the passport.

'How much do I owe you for this?' I asked.

'Forget it,' he said. 'It's a present.'

I looked at him. I.Q. Patel, the shabby, unkempt man who had changed my entire life. Suddenly I made a decision.

'I've got a present for you,' I said.

'Oh.'

'I'm giving you £50,000.'

He looked at me blankly.

'What for?' he demanded. 'You only owe me a few hundreds.'

'I'm not talking about the debt,' I said. 'It's thanks to you all this has come about. I just want to share my good fortune with you.'

Suddenly he was weeping; tears welling in his dark eyes.

'You're not supposed to cry,' I said. 'You're supposed to be pleased.'

He searched in his trousers' pocket and produced a grubby handkerchief.

'I don't know what to say,' he mumbled, dabbing his eyes.

'Then don't say anything,' I said.

Snuffling, he gathered up the tea things and went over to the sink.

'I wouldn't know what to do with so much money,' he said.

I glanced around the dreary room.

'Well for a start,' I said, 'you could get a nice new frame for Schwartz. Perhaps even another television set. Some of the programmes on the other channels are supposed to be quite good.'

He cleared his throat noisily.

'You're very generous,' he said.

I picked up the passport.

'You've given me the best present I've ever had,' said.

'You'll need papers and things, if you're serious about Susan,' he said. 'I'll get on to that while you're away.'

'Thanks,' I said.

'Have you any idea when you'll be leaving?'

'When the money comes through, I expect. In about two weeks' time.'

'How long will you be away?'

'Several months, at least.'

He glanced up.

'Will you go to India?'

'No,' I said. 'I decided that wasn't a good idea. I told Susan there simply wasn't enough time to see the place properly. We'll fly direct to Bangkok.'

He stacked the cups and saucers carefully on the drip-tray.

'Have you given any thought to what you'll do when you return?'

'Not really,' I said. 'Everything's happened so fast.'

'You'll have to do something,' he said. 'Everyone needs a reason to get up in the morning.'

'I know that,' I said. 'Perhaps I'll start up some sort of business.'

'Do you know anything about business?'

'No,' I said.

'Then keep out of it,' he said.

He stood in front of me.

'There's one thing you could do,' he said.

'What's that?'

'Study to be a real doctor.'

I laughed.

'You're not serious?'

'Of course I'm serious. With your memory you'd sail

through the exams.'

'But what would I tell Susan?'

'You could say you were taking extra studies,' he said. 'Specializing in tropical medicine. Anything.'

I had the strangest feeling. It was as though I had been wearing blinkers for a long, long time. Now they had been removed.

'You really think I could do it?' I asked.

'That idiot Stirrup did it. Do you think he's brighter than you?'

'I hope not.'

'Well, then.'

'It's certainly something to think about,' I said.

His eyes burned into mine.

'Then think about it,' he said.

I glanced at my watch.

'Time I was off,' I said. 'I'm meeting Susan at six.'

'I hope it works out,' he said. 'You'll make a lovely couple.'

'You must meet her when we get back,' I said.

He shook his head.

'No. That would be a mistake.'

'But you're my friend. I want you to meet her.'

He smiled at me, wanly.

'It's because I'm your friend that I'm telling you it would be a mistake. You must move on, my boy; start a whole new life.'

He put his hands on my shoulders. We hugged each other briefly.

'Blessings,' he said.

'Blessings on you.'

I went down the stairs and along the hall. The sign 'No Women' was still there, tilted at an angle. Beneath it was a plastic sack of rubbish. The whole place smelled sour and dank.

Outside in the street I paused for a moment and looked back at 12 Elm Place. Yes, I thought, I must move on. And now the blinkers were off. I knew what I was going to do; what, indeed, I felt destined to do: become a real doctor.

I looked up at the night-sky. It was full of bright stars. Smiling to myself, I set off along the familiar street. I did not look back again.